Tagged
for Death

Tagged
for Death

Sherry Harris

KENSINGTON PUBLISHING CORP.
http://www.kensingtonbooks.com

KENSINGTON BOOKS are published by

Kensington Publishing Corp.
119 West 40th Street
New York, NY 10018

All Kensington Titles, Imprints, and Distributed Lines are
available at special quantity discounts for bulk purchases
for sales promotions, premiums, fund-raising, and educa-
tional or institutional use. Special book excerpts or cus-
tomized printings can also be created to fit specific needs.
For details, write or phone the office of the Kensington
special sales manager: Kensington Publishing Corp.,
119 West 40th Street, New York, NY 10018, attn: Special
Sales Department, Phone: 1-800-221-2647.

Kensington and the K logo Reg. U.S. Pat & TM Off.

ISBN-13: 978-1-61773-017-7
ISBN-10: 1-61773-017-3
First Kensington Mass Market Edition: December 2014

eISBN-13: 978-1-61773-018-4
eISBN-10: 1-61773-018-1
First Kensington Electronic Edition: December 2014

10 9 8 7 6 5 4 3 2 1

Printed in the United States of America

This book is dedicated to Bob Harris.
Thank you for being so stubborn the night we met.
I love you.

ACKNOWLEDGMENTS

My first rule of writing is to go to conferences and meet other authors. If I hadn't attended Malice Domestic, I wouldn't have met Julie Hennrikus, who told me to join the New England Chapter of Sisters in Crime and then became my good friend. Through that one act, I met the amazing, supportive members. One of them, Barbara Ross, thought of me when her agent, John Talbot, was looking for someone to write this series. Barb, your writing inspires me. Thank you to my agent, John Talbot, and to my editor, Gary Goldstein, for believing in me.

Thank you to my readers: Clare Boggs, Edith Maxwell, Logan, Robin Templeton, Elaine Douts, Mary Ann Corrigan, and Maureen Klover. You all helped make this a better book. My mom, Martha Novinger, always catches something I missed, thank you.

To the Wicked Cozy Authors, Jessie Crockett, Julie Hennrikus, Edith Maxwell, Liz Mugavero, and Barbara Ross, I humbly follow in your wake. Thanks for letting me vent, loving me when I'm cranky, making me laugh, and for telling me what comes next.

To Sergeant Patrick J. Towle, of the Bedford Police Department, thank you for taking me on a ride along, for patiently answering my questions, and showing me things in Bedford, Massachusetts, that I never knew existed. As they say, all mistakes in the police work in this book are mine.

To Lieutenant Colonel (Ret.) Kenneth D. Ribler, thanks for your expertise, your friendship, and the awesome meals you cook. Again, all mistakes are mine. I owe you a Frosty Bobs or two.

Thanks also to the Chesapeake Chapter of Sisters in Crime for your friendship and support. Thanks to my DZ sisters, who took this journey with me and shared my joy. And, of course, to Bob and Elizabeth, who made all of this possible.

CHAPTER 1

A gunshot sounded. I jerked the phone away from my ear. This time I hung up first. That had been the pattern—one gunshot and then the caller disconnected. I couldn't decide if I was mad or freaked out, probably both. What did it say about my life that I knew more people who might be willing to do this than any normal person should?

My mother had warned me not to marry military. "Sarah Winston, stay away from those boys at DLI. They're nothing but trouble." DLI, the Defense Language Institute in Monterey, California, sat a few blocks up the hill from my childhood home in Pacific Grove. Since I'd pretty much always done the opposite of whatever my mom suggested, I marched up that hill, met CJ, and married him when I was eighteen.

So the calls could be from CJ Hooker, my ex-husband, the former Fitch Air Force Base Security Forces squadron commander. He'd retired quickly and quietly four months ago after what was called "misconduct" or, as some would say, "conduct unbecoming an officer." His new career as police chief of Ellington, Massachusetts, the small town just outside

the base gates, where we both lived—separately—
offered him plenty of resources. In my angry, hurt
heart, I couldn't imagine he'd do something like that
to me. Of course, then again, I hadn't thought . . .
I shook my head. I didn't need to go down that path
yet again.

I paced across my second-story apartment, trying
to shake off the remaining edges of fear from the gunshot call. It didn't take long with only a living room,
kitchen, bedroom, and bath. The apartment had looked
a lot bigger empty. The slanted ceilings, two dormer
windows, and uneven wooden floors held some
charm. I'd really warmed up to the place the day I
moved in when CJ had accidentally rammed his head
into the low ceiling.

I'd wanted to knock him upside the head since the
day I figured out the sudden increase in patrols outside
our house on base by the voluptuous Tiffany Lopez
had nothing to do with base security and everything to
do with CJ. He'd looked hurt when I laughed as he
rubbed his head. I could tell him a thing or two about
being hurt.

I stared out the front window onto the town
common. It had the requisite white church surrounded
by a large lawn. The steeple reached to the blue April
sky. Trees on the common were starting to bud and
joggers had reappeared. I was adjusting to the noise
of the bells from the Congregational church. Now, if
only I could sleep through the sirens from the fire department, two buildings up the street from me, on
Great Road.

Tiffany, the nineteen-year-old airman, and co-
conspirator in the "misconduct," was another possible
caller. Tiffany had many skills I lacked. She was

an expert marksman, attended culinary school in preparation for being an enlisted aide to a general, and could cook a four-course dinner. While I'd failed for years to get pregnant, Tiffany could even do that better. She was able to get pregnant on the first try. That was CJ's story when he begged me not to leave him, not that I believed it.

I'd heard she wasn't happy. She'd lost a stripe and the opportunity to work with the general. Although he promised to love and support the baby, CJ wasn't planning a future with her.

Then there was the entire Ellington police force. They'd already bonded with "Chuck," as they called CJ. Promised they had his back. I'd been pulled over so many times in the last few months for "speeding," aka "going one mile over the limit," that I'd started going one mile under the speed limit at all times, not easy to do living fifteen miles from Boston. It caused a lot of honking, brakes squealing, and one-finger waves. It had worked until some smart aleck officer decided to pull me over for obstructing traffic. I had so many warnings that I was sure everyone on the EPD knew the exact number of points left on my driver's license before it got revoked. It was like a game of chicken for the Ellington Police Department: who could get the closest without going over.

The gunshot caller could be one of Tiffany's fellow airmen. The security forces squadron was a tight-knit group of people. CJ and I had called them "our kids," since we hadn't been able to have any of our own. Lots of airmen were eighteen- and nineteen-year-olds fresh from boot camp, far from home, carrying big guns, little guns, and some in between. I'd taken cookies (thank you, Stop & Shop) to the squadron, threw parties for them, and even dried some tears. When "Mom" and "Dad" divorced, they all sided with Dad.

Who wouldn't? CJ had controlled their future, their assignments, and their promotions. They still sought him out for advice. Too many of the Southern boys thought I should stand by my man. Too many young girls believed that leaving nasty messages on my Facebook page would get me out of the way so Tiffany and CJ could be together. What they didn't get, no matter how many times I'd said it, was Tiffany could have him. I was done, checked out—*adios, amigo*.

I regretted the one drunken Facebook message I'd sent Tiffany telling her in no polite words to call off her dogs. The next morning, I'd deleted my Facebook page.

Maybe the gunshot caller hoped they'd wake me. I was already up, ready to head out to some garage sales. I looked out the window. Carol Carson stood in front of her store, Paint and Wine, on the other side of the town common waiting for me to pick her up. I called her shop "Paint and Whine" and was very grateful to have a friend like Carol, who always listened to me. I grabbed a light sweater, then headed out to my Suburban.

I was taking Carol to her first garage sale (tag sale, for those in the Northeast). I'd known Carol, and her husband Brad, since our very first assignment. We had just clicked. This was the first time we'd lived at the same place, at the same time, since we'd met nineteen years ago.

They'd moved from base to Ellington six months ago. Carol opened a store, where her ingenious method meant anyone could create a painting. Between the shop, her eight-year-old twin boys, and six-year-old daughter, she didn't have much free time. After hearing me drone on about garage sales, she'd decided to give it a try. Or maybe she couldn't care less about the sale and knew I was lonely.

I drove around the common. Carol hopped in. She looked like what Mattel would dream up if they decided to have a blond artist Barbie. Fortunately, her personality wasn't plastic. We both wore jeans and T-shirts. Carol's high-heeled boots and a leather jacket made me feel underdressed in flats and a sweater. She handed me a steaming cup of coffee, along with an oversized cinnamon roll. The roll smelled way better than the cinnamon-scented air freshener hanging from the rearview mirror.

"Homemade?" I asked before biting into the warm roll.

"Yes, it made me feel less guilty for deserting the family on a Saturday morning. The kids are attached to our routine of pancakes and snuggling up to watch cartoons."

"These are heavenly. I'm glad we finally ended up at the same base at the same time again. Not just because you make the best cinnamon rolls on earth."

"Me too. I don't know what I would have done without you here to help set up the store."

"How's Brad's new job going?" Brad served his twenty years. He'd retired from the air force about six months ago. Since he was only in his early forties, like most military retirees, he started a second career. Brad now worked for the Edith Nourse Rogers Memorial Veterans Hospital in Bedford.

I ate the cinnamon roll as I drove. Carol filled me in on the latest shop news. Usually, I unloaded my news first. Even though the gunshot call was on my mind, it was time to step back. I'd blathered on about myself too often.

We headed out toward Concord, passing the Sleepy Hollow Cemetery—not the one with the Headless Horseman and Ichabod Crane, made famous by Washington Irving. That cemetery was in New York. Concord's Sleepy Hollow has its own claim to fame because of its Authors Ridge, where Louisa May Alcott, Nathaniel Hawthorne, Ralph Waldo Emerson, and Henry David Thoreau were buried. We passed the Colonial Inn, went through two rotaries—rotaries in Massachusetts, roundabouts or traffic circles in other parts of the country. A right turn took us into a neighborhood full of colonial and Victorian homes. When Carol asked what I'd been up to, I filled her in on the latest phone call.

"How many calls is that?" Carol asked.

"I'm not sure. I haven't kept a tally. Enough to be annoying."

"Annoying?"

"Okay, scary." I slowed the Suburban, looking for the garage sale.

"Don't you think it's about time to report the calls to the authorities?"

"You mean CJ?"

"Oh, right. Wow, that's awkward." She took a long drink of her coffee. "Maybe you should, anyway."

"I have no proof. No one's ever been around when a call came in."

"Couldn't CJ check your phone records?"

"No. I don't want him to know anything about my social life." That was the last thing I needed to have happen.

"You have a social life you don't want him knowing about? Are you holding out on me? I want details."

How did I get out of this gracefully? I'd never been one of those "share everything" people, unless it was CJ. That was another thing that had ended with our marriage. "It's more I don't want him to know about my *lack* of a social life."

"Maybe it's time to get out there."

"I'm not ready. If I call CJ about the gunshot calls, he might think it's my way of trying to get his attention."

"Especially after telling him 'no, no, never' for months. I'm still worried about you."

"Thanks. If it gets worse or anything else happens, I promise I'll call."

I parked in front of the first sale. "No matter how excited you are about something you see, act like you don't care. This is all about the fine art of negotiation. Find your inner poker player."

Carol nodded enthusiastically before jumping out of the car.

I followed her. "Take it down a notch."

"Oh, right." Carol tried to get her smile under control. It's what made her business such a success. It might not help her here.

I did a quick scan of the garage sale. It was a mess. The only reason we'd stopped was because it advertised "like new" designer clothing for kids. If it hadn't been for Carol, I would have kept driving. Clothes were heaped on a table and in bags on the ground. The couple of nice pieces of furniture were barely visible from the road. I shook my head.

I poked around a table, pulling out a perfectly good graduation robe, scrubs, and an old cheerleading uniform. I headed over to the woman in charge of the sale. "If you grouped these together with a little sign that said great for costumes, they'd be gone in no time."

"Thanks," the woman said, looking at me like she was anything but thankful.

Ten minutes later, Carol squealed. "Sarah! Get over here. This platter matches your dishes!"

Yeesh, had she heard nothing I'd told her in the car? "Just a minute!" I yelled as I continued to look at a vintage Christmas tablecloth. I finally meandered over. Carol still bounced with enthusiasm.

She shoved the platter at me. "Look, it's Dansk. Only five dollars. It would cost way more at Macy's. Aren't you excited?"

I glanced at the woman running the garage sale. "I don't need it."

Carol looked like a little girl who'd just had her favorite doll snatched from her. I took it over to the woman. "Would you take two for this?"

"Sure," the woman said.

Back in the car, I broke into a big smile. "Great find. The platter would cost at least forty-five dollars at the store."

Carol looked at me oddly. "Oh, right, poker face. I'll do better next time."

"Smiling and being friendly is fine. No bouncing. No squealing. It leaves no room for negotiating."

CHAPTER 2

Thirty minutes later in Lexington, we stopped in front of a large three-story Victorian with a sweeping lawn. A crowd of people milled around an area full of walnut wardrobes, marble-topped dressers, and tables. I could tell at a glance these beautiful antiques were out of my price range. With that many people interested, the chance to get a good deal was nil. I zeroed in on a parlor table I spotted off to one side, almost hidden behind a rack of clothes.

I dragged Carol over with me. It was in two pieces. The top leaned up against the base. The four barley-twist legs each ended in a large clawed foot holding a glass ball. The undershelf held the four legs together, barely. The oak top was serpentine with a serpentine apron. The wood of the two pieces matched—a sign that it was all original. I turned the tabletop over to examine its underside. The legs hadn't broken off. I could easily fix it with carpenter's glue. It would look perfect by my great-grandmother's rocking chair, if I could get it for a good price.

In an antique store in pristine condition, this piece would sell for around eight hundred dollars. The table was priced at two hundred. I wasn't willing to pay that much for something I had to fix. As much as I wanted it, I had to walk away if I couldn't get a better deal.

I found a gray-haired woman roaming around; she had a partially open fanny pack full of ones around her waist. I presumed she was the seller. If not, with that many single bills, she might be heading to the Chippendales Male Revue I'd heard an ad for on the radio.

"Excuse me. I wanted to ask about the *broken* table over there." I put a slight emphasis on the word broken. "Is that your best price?"

The lady looked over to where I pointed. "It's worth the asking price, even broken. What did you have in mind?"

Here was the tricky part. If I went too low, she'd say no and it was hard to negotiate after that. If I went too high, I wouldn't get the best possible price. "Fifty?" I asked, knowing it was a dangerously low price. Several people were lined up behind me, holding items they wanted to buy. This was good. She was out here alone and wouldn't want to lose paying customers bargaining with me.

She shook her head. "One-fifty."

"Split the difference? One hundred?"

She shook her head again. As I turned to go, she said, "Oh, all right."

Carol, who'd watched the whole process, squealed. This time I joined her. I handed over the money to the seller. "Are you running this by yourself?"

She gave me a look. "My daughter's baby is sick. My husband's out golfing. My cell phone's in the house. Haven't had a minute to go get it."

I handed her my phone so she could call a couple

of friends. With this big of a sale, things could go missing.

Although I'd spent what I'd allotted for myself that day, we hit more sales. Two hours later, after traipsing through Lincoln and Bedford, I dropped Carol in front of her shop. She'd found some barely worn jeans for the boys and a couple of dresses that were as good as new for her daughter. Carol scored a fifty-cent un-opened copy of *Top Gun* for her husband, plus a box of paperbacks for herself. Sometimes she remembered the poker face, but Carol did just as well by charming whoever it was that she talked to. One lady even gave her some free clothes and promised to bring a group of women to her shop for a night of painting.

I hauled the two pieces of the table up to my apart-ment, placing them near the window. Since I'd moved to a smaller place, my new policy was something in, something out. I'd take the small table that had been by the window to the thrift shop for consignment. I scrounged around under the kitchen sink, found the carpenter's glue, some clamps, and bungee cords. After smearing glue on the underside of the table, I set the two pieces together. I used clamps, where I could, bungeed the rest, and then stacked a bunch of hard-back books on top to weigh it down. After the glue dried, it would look as good as new. Or in this case, as good as old.

I made a sandwich, flopped on the couch, and as-sessed my life. Or my former life as a military wife, that is. My literature degree had kept discussions in-teresting in the Spouses' Club reading group. I made killer Cosmos for my friends when we played Bunco, a dice game. Some of the women claimed my Cosmos loosened their wrists just enough to change their luck when rolling the dice during the game. Cooking wasn't my strong suit (thank heaven for potlucks and Costco), but my parties were always fun. I'd edited the Spouses' newsletter, volunteered at the Airman's Attic, Red Cross blood drives, and the base thrift shop.

None of those skills lent themselves to a career now that I needed one. The frequent military moves killed any chance of a long-term career. My responsibilities as the commander's wife at Fitch hadn't left a lot of extra time for a job, anyway.

When I'd finally called my mom about the divorce, she immediately told me to come home. "You are a West Coast girl, Sarah. It's time to come back." Just what I wanted to do—go home with my tail between my legs—return as the big loser who couldn't keep her man and had no job skills. It wasn't entirely true, but some days I pictured myself walking around with a big glowing *D*-for-"divorced" on my forehead. Hmmm, maybe it was my mom making the gunshot calls.

As soon as we'd hung up, I'd looked up apartment listings in Ellington. A few days later, I'd moved off base. I'd let CJ help one last time. While a moving company took care of most of it, some things I preferred moving myself, even if that meant needing CJ. I vowed to myself it was the last time I would ask him for anything. Ever.

I could sit here wallowing in self-pity, or as my mom always said, "Go do something good for the world." Occasionally she was right. I'd spent way too much of the last few months wallowing.

* * *

I headed back out in the Suburban. My passion for garage sales started in second grade when my best friend's family had a sale. I'd run home and searched my room for things I could sell. After grabbing a jar of marbles and a few comic books, I hurried back. They sold right away. I was hooked. My mother sniffed when I told her and said, "We donate what we don't want." To her dismay, I developed a lifelong relationship with other people's castoffs.

I drove over to Lexington. Garage sales were winding down. It was a great time to get a good deal, but I'd also ask people if they wanted to donate their leftovers to the Minuteman Thrift Shop on Fitch. The thrift shop made money by accepting consignments and donations. Part of the profits went to scholarships for military dependents—the spouses and children of active duty troops and retirees. We also donated to other worthy causes.

Massachusetts was one of the most patriotic places I'd lived. They supported the troops. New Englanders were also practical. I took their extra stuff off their hands with very little effort on their part. Sometimes I would buy something to consign myself. Occasionally I even paid full price. It was all about knowing what was worth what. Some of that came from experience; the rest came from my gut.

It was almost three by the time I pulled up in front of the Victorian house in Lexington. I headed here first because it was, by far, the largest sale I'd seen that day.

"Thanks for letting me use your phone this morning," the woman said when she saw me. "A couple of friends came over. I don't know what I would have done without them. Look at this place." The yard looked like wild animals had descended upon it. Only the bare bones were left.

I explained I was collecting things for the base thrift shop.

"Here, take these two crocks. I somehow forgot to set them out. I'm sick of looking at them."

They were nice ivory-colored crocks with blue print—the kind that were popular with collectors and could be pricy. She helped me stuff the remaining clothes into black plastic garbage bags I'd brought with me.

By four-thirty, the Suburban was stuffed to the gills with black plastic garbage bags full of clothes, toys, the two old crocks, and an assortment of dishes. My cinnamon air freshener did its job, keeping the car smelling good instead of like the dusty, musty odors coming from the bags. I'd filled my Suburban without going back to all the sales we'd hit this morning. Tired, hungry, and heading toward grumpy, I parked in front of my building and decided I'd unload everything in the morning.

On Sunday morning I woke, not to a gunshot phone call, but to my landlady, Stella Wild, singing the "Hallelujah Chorus" from Handel's *Messiah*. Her apartment was directly below mine. The sun shone through the windows. Car doors slammed. People greeted each other out on the common as they headed to the eight-thirty service at church.

I poured a bowl of cereal, trying to figure out why cereal either tasted like cardboard or sugar. At least this cardboard kind had been on sale. Once everyone was safely ensconced in church, I started the process of hauling everything from the Suburban to my apartment. My next-door neighbor Tyler walked by, nodding in response to my cheery hello.

"What's up?" he asked. As usual, his clothes looked a little frayed, a little dirty. His brown hair hung around his face in need of a good shampoo.

The greeting was progress. Tyler wasn't one of those "hey, can I give you a hand with that" kind of neighbors. He was a quiet guy, thus the perfect neighbor.

Tyler pivoted and came back to me. "Let me help you with those." He took the two bags out of my hands, taking the porch steps two at a time.

"Thanks," I called after him. I really needed to work on not judging people. He lifted one of the bags in response before disappearing inside. I followed him up, carrying a couple more bags.

"Thanks," I called again. By the time I hauled all the bags up, the living-room floor of my normally neat apartment looked like a sea of black plastic. It groaned a little under the weight, or maybe it was me. The mess already drove me crazy.

I'd been tempted to leave it all in the Suburban to sort at the thrift shop on Tuesday. If I sorted it out now, I'd be a step ahead when I showed up to volunteer. Sorting was the lowest job on the thrift shop totem pole, but I didn't mind it. You never knew when some-one would tuck Waterford crystal in between layers of old clothes. I got to see all the good stuff first.

Stella now sang "For unto Us a Child Is Born." She hit all the notes singing a cappella. I hummed along as I worked. Stella should be a professional singer.

Two hours later, I stood and stretched my back. Three bags left. Piles were neatly sorted: baby clothes, boys', girls', men's, women's. One bag of useless stuff was headed to the garbage. Another was filled with clothing that wasn't good enough to sell. I'd take it to a clothing recycler, where it would get shredded and reused.

People were out on the common again, heading into the eleven o'clock service. I opened the next bag, pulling out some Beanie Babies in surprisingly good shape. Stella sang something operatic I didn't recognize. At least it wasn't Dylan, my mom's favorite.

I lifted out a pile of T-shirts, tossing them toward the recycler bag. They were all too stained to resell. Considering how stained they were, they didn't smell too bad. Someone must have sprayed them with a heavy dose of Febreze, a trick sellers used to cover up odors.

With the Febreze items removed, a funky odor emanated from the bag. I pulled out a set of horribly stained, ripped, and reeking BDUs—battle dress uniform or camouflage. I didn't even want to guess what had happened to them. Why did people put stuff like this in their donation bags? I flung them toward the trash bag. I reached back in, pulling out a white dress shirt, also stained rusty brown. As it sailed toward the trash bag, I glimpsed a monogrammed French cuff. What was that?

Retrieving it, I stared. *CJH*. Charles James Hooker. This was the shirt I'd given CJ for his birthday last year. The stain looked and smelled exactly like what it was—dried blood. I took a better look at the blood-stained BDUs. It was a maternity top and the sewn-on name tag read, *Lopez*.

CHAPTER 3

My stomach churned. I reached back into the bag with shaky hands, tearing through the rest of the clothes. Although shabby, the other items weren't stained the rust color of the BDUs and CJ's shirt. Nothing else in the bag gave me any indication where it came from or how these two items got in there. I tracked down my cell phone on the nightstand by the side of my bed. I sat on the edge, dialed CJ's cell phone, and chanted, "Pick up, pick up, pick up" while it rang. No luck. I left a terse message: "Call me."

All that blood. It wasn't good. I conjured up scenarios that would put that much blood on two different shirts. A mishap with a kitchen knife? A car accident? Deer hunting? Breaking a large mirror? CJ didn't hunt. Tiffany was a whiz with a knife. I would have heard from the base gossips in a heartbeat if anything else had happened. I desperately wanted to come up with some alternative to the one I kept seeing over and over in my mind—a gunshot wound and blood splatter. One of them dead, and one of them a killer.

* * *

By midafternoon I was half crazed. I'd left dozens of messages for CJ. Then I obsessively checked my phone to see if it was on, had a signal, and that it wasn't set to silent. I paced. I checked for voicemail. I put the piles of clothes I'd sorted back in trash bags, marking them with appropriate tags so they wouldn't have to be resorted at the thrift shop.

It was probably my fault CJ hadn't called back. A couple of weeks ago, he'd called to ask me out to dinner. I'd tried to make my feelings clear. "Leave. Me. Alone!" I'd shouted. I wasn't a shouter; my family didn't shout. We discussed, debated, or went to our rooms. We didn't ever raise our voices. CJ's quiet, hurt uttering of "I will," before he hung up, had stuck with me. It made me feel like an evil wench.

How did the two shirts end up in a black plastic bag and in my possession? I thought through every place I'd stopped yesterday, all the plastic bags that had been shoved in the back of my Suburban. Thought about the people who had done the shoving. I didn't recognize any of them. Tyler had carried up two bags for me. He didn't have time to haul the bags up, plant the shirts, and get back to his apartment before I came up.

It wasn't possible someone hoped I'd show back up at their garage sale so they could plant the bag in my car. Maybe someone broke into my Suburban last night or this morning, adding in the extra bag. I'd left the back open while I carted things upstairs today. After grabbing my cell phone, I ran out to the Suburban. None of the locks looked damaged beyond a scratch or two, but this baby had been around a long time. I probably caused the scratches. I went back in and knocked on Stella's door.

She flung it open, humming a little ditty, something

from *The Pirates of Penzance*. We were both about five-six. Stella looked Mediterranean, with her darker skin, deep green eyes, and lovely black hair. I must look washed-out standing next to her, with my pale skin, blue eyes, and hair somewhere between light brown and dark blond. I was never sure what to call it on my driver's license. Her eyes opened a little wider in surprise as she looked me over. It dawned on me I was a mess. No shower, sorting through dirty bags, and dressed like a hobo—sweats, a T-shirt, no bra.

"Did you, by chance, see or hear anyone around my car last night or this morning?" I skipped the chitchat. Stella hadn't been overly friendly since I moved in. Due to the wallowing, I hadn't gone out of my way to be friendly, either.

Stella thought for a minute. I liked that. Instead of a quick no, she took my question seriously. She didn't ask why I wanted to know.

Stella shook her head. "Nothing or no one out of the ordinary. Lots of people park along here for church on Sunday morning. Sorry."

I hopped into the Suburban and drove to CJ's house. CJ lived in what New Englanders called a "two-family." I called it a "duplex." His carport was empty. Maybe that was better. At least I didn't find him cuddled up with Tiffany or some other woman. Since I was out, I drove around the Stop & Shop parking lot, looking for CJ's car. No luck. I continued my search, passing a couple of restaurants and a popular park. No CJ.

That left driving by the police station—I'd really wanted to avoid it—but after his house, it was the most likely place he'd be. I was just going to drive by, nothing illegal about that. He had a reserved parking spot. It should be easy to see if he was there or not. The police station sat across from the Ellington Library. Not too far from the high school, it looked out over a public park.

I gripped the wheel a bit tighter as I turned right, after signaling, onto the small lane in front of the library. I took the first left. The police station was down a bit on the left. No speed limit was posted. This could be tricky. I settled on twenty-five, although I slowed even more as I passed the station. I didn't see CJ's car. I pulled into the lot for the other town offices to turn around. I'd go by a second time just to make sure.

I slowed and looked down the long driveway of the police station. The space with the sign stating it was reserved for the chief sat empty. A cop came out the front door and took a long look at me. I sped away. By "sped," I meant got the car back up to twenty-five. Really, what could they charge me with? Stalking a public official, public nuisance, loitering? All of the above. Once I was back on Great Road, I took the first right, weaving through town, just in case the officer decided to follow me.

Back in my apartment, I finally dialed the nonemergency number for the Ellington Police Department. I chose my words carefully. I had no idea if nonemergency calls were recorded. A woman with a pleasant, calm voice answered.

"I need to speak to Chief Hooker," I said.

"Who's calling?"

"This is Sarah Winston." I'd changed back to my

maiden name after the divorce. Happy to no longer be a Hooker—and free of the jokes that went with the name.

"He's not available. I'll connect you to his voice mail."

She transferred me. I left the same message I'd left on his cell phone. "Call me." An hour later, I tried the nonemergency number again. I asked as politely as I could with a shaky voice for the chief.

"He's not available. I'll—"

"Wait. When will he be available? Is he okay? I have to talk to him. It's an emergency."

"If you are having an emergency, I suggest you hang up and dial 911." *Click.*

Okay, then, that's what I'd do. Maybe something had happened to CJ. Maybe it explained the blood and why he hadn't returned my calls all day.

"911. Where's your emergency?"

Either this was the same woman who answered the nonemergency line or she had a voice twin. Surprise kept me from speaking for a moment.

"Ma'am? Where is your emergency?" The voice sounded a little more urgent this time.

Calling 911 was a mistake; but if I hung up, a squad car would show up to check on me. I gave her my address, even though it had probably popped up on her screen. When I'd moved to Ellington, I'd signed up for the town's free emergency bulletins service.

"What is your emergency?"

Again I had to choose my words carefully. It wasn't like I wanted the news I'd found CJ's bloody shirt along with Lopez's going out over the airways to every cop in Ellington. Maybe every cop in Middlesex County, for all I knew.

"I need to speak to Chief Hooker. It's personal."

"Are you thinking of harming yourself?"

"No. I really just need to . . ." I burst into tears. "I just really need to speak to CJ, Chuck, Chief Hooker."

"I have a car on the way. Just stay with me on the line. Until we can get you help."

I hung up. The police station was about a mile down Great Road. A car would be here any minute. Hopefully, with CJ in it. I ran to the window, looking out just as a police car roared up to the building. An officer jumped out. No CJ. I threw open the window.

"Where's Chief Hooker?" I yelled.

The guy started around the side of the car. "Don't worry. I'll come up. We can talk until he can get here." From the way he spoke, I was sure CJ wasn't on his way. I couldn't have this guy coming up and finding the bloody clothes.

"Don't come up. Only Chief Hooker."

"Ma'am, just keep calm." He spoke into the mike attached to his left shoulder. "I need a crisis counselor at 111 Oak Street."

People were starting to gather on the common. My cell phone rang. It wasn't CJ. I ignored it. Another squad car screeched to a halt in front of the apartment. An officer climbed out. I yelled as calmly as I could when one is forced to yell: "No one comes up but Chief Hooker." An ambulance arrived. I saw a few firemen run over from the firehouse. Stella was escorted out of the building and over to the town common. This had gotten way out of hand. I slammed the window down.

A few minutes later, CJ's red Chevy Sonic pulled

up. Thank heaven. I swiped at some tears; then I raised the window.

He looked up, along with the small crowd standing on the sidewalk.

"Come up here. Alone. Please." I saw a lot of heads shake. People pulled on CJ, trying to dissuade him from coming up. "CJ, for God's sake. You know I'm not going to hurt you or myself. You. Know. Me."

CJ shook off the guy holding his right arm. "Okay, Sarah. I'll come alone."

A murmur of disapproval rippled from the crowd. I lowered the window, letting out a long whoosh of air. Footsteps pounded up the stairs. A few seconds later, there was a brisk rap on the door.

"I'm here. Just me," CJ said.

I hesitated. Once upon a time, I would have believed anything he said. This time I'd have to trust him again. I opened the door, yanked him in, and slammed the door shut. I hugged him, breathing in his fresh, soapy smell until I thought about Tiffany.

I stepped back. "Why didn't you call me?" I asked.

"I was in Portsmouth. For a funeral. The state trooper who was killed last week. What's going on?" CJ looked worn-out. Thinner than the last time I'd seen him a month ago. His already-high cheekbones were more pronounced. He looked warily at the slanted ceiling as he moved into the room. His six-two build kept him in the center of the space this time.

"Is your mike and cell turned off? No one can hear this?" I asked.

"No one." He crossed his heart, gave me a half smile.

I kneeled down, moving the panel that gave me

access to the eaves behind the low wall. I'd hidden the bloody shirts when I realized CJ might not be alone. I held them up for CJ to see. He paled.

He made a call on his cell phone. "It's okay. Everyone can leave. Just a misunderstanding about my whereabouts. You know women. You show up ten minutes late and they panic." He mouthed "sorry" as he listened. For once, I didn't care what he said. I wanted everyone to clear out so CJ could explain what was going on.

He closed his phone. I walked over to the window. The police shooed away the people gathered on the common. The firemen headed back up the street while the squad cars left. I hoped all the folks had enjoyed their Sunday-afternoon show.

CJ came up behind me. "What the hell did you do, Sarah?"

CHAPTER 4

I whipped around and shoved him hard in the chest. He stumbled back a couple of steps. I wanted to do it again, but someone might be out in the hall "just in case," not to mention he was armed and I still didn't even have a bra on.

"*Me?* This is about you and Tiffany."

I walked over to my couch. I would have stomped if Stella hadn't lived below. I plopped down. He sat on the wooden trunk that served as my coffee table and extra storage. Our knees almost touched. His pale blue eyes were serious. The words tumbled out of me: the sales, the bags, finding, realizing. I trembled.

"How did this happen, Chuck?"

Our knees were almost touching. He leaned forward, cupping my face in his hand for a moment. He brushed his thumb across my cheek. Had he ever done that to me before? Was it a gesture he used on Tiffany? I jerked back.

He dropped his hand. "You've never called me *Chuck*. Not once. You hate Chuck."

I let that lie there between us. How had we gotten

to this point? Oh yeah, I remembered. *Not. My. Damn. Fault.*

"Let's focus on the bloody shirts," I said. "Maybe I should have just tossed them in the Dumpster."

"No, I'll take them. I'll call Tiffany. See what she has to say."

"When is the last time you talked to her?" I tried to ask this with a steady voice, but I failed miserably. Part of me wanted to know, but part of me hoped he'd say it was none of my business.

"Last week. She called me about a doctor's appointment."

"You answer her calls." I hated the whiny voice that came out of me. I stood up. "Sorry."

"Yeah, me too. For a lot of things."

"How did the clothes end up this way?"

CJ shook his head. "No idea."

"I almost cut the cuffs off the shirt."

CJ attempted a grin. It turned out nothing like the boyish grin I'd fallen in love with when I was eighteen. "Do you have the original bag the shirts were in? I'll take it all, until I figure out what's going on."

"You'll call me when you know, right?"

"I promise," CJ said. There it was again—the chasm between us—the broken promises.

A few minutes later, I walked back to the window. I watched CJ stuff the bag of clothes in the small space that served as the trunk for his hatchback Sonic. Maybe I should have confronted Tiffany. Letting CJ handle it was easier than facing her myself.

I looked across the town common at DiNapoli's Roast Beef and Pizza and realized I was starving. It was two doors down from Carol's store. After a quick shower, I threw on clean jeans and V-necked shirt. I finished my look with a quick swipe of mascara on my long lashes. I walked to DiNapoli's, a place I discovered soon after moving to Fitch two years ago. Roast Beef and Pizza places were a New England thing. I'd never heard of them at any of our other assignments. Some places added clams: Roast Beef, Pizza, and Clams. Part of New England's quirky charm.

Rosalie DiNapoli rushed out from behind the long counter, where I normally placed my order. She pulled me to a seat at an old wooden table in the long, narrow space to the right, which provided seating. She went back to the open kitchen. Open, due to necessity. It allowed for multitasking. Any employee could ring up customers, wrap orders, answer the phone, or pitch in to chop vegetables—whatever task needed handling in the moment. The cook, Rosalie's husband, Angelo, could deliver food to tables and keep an eye on things. It was my belief knowing what was going on was more important to Angelo than the multitasking aspect of having an open kitchen.

The kitchen had been like this for years and wasn't, as Angelo would tell anyone who'd listen, a desire to imitate high-end restaurants with their showy kitchens and star chefs. (Angelo, however, had a deep-seated belief that he was a star chef, and all who came after were imitators and frauds.)

Rosalie brought me a large basket of fresh, toasted garlic bread topped with gooey fresh mozzarella, which dripped off the sides. She pointed to the bread. "On the house." She looked over at her husband, Angelo; her normally warm eyes were fierce. "It's on the house, Angelo. Sarah's had a bad day."

He raised his arms in surrender. Angelo's name meant "messenger of God" in Italian. He took his role seriously. I'd seen him chase speeders down the road. Rumor had it he'd threatened the town manager more than once. I'd also heard he lectured his priest on a weekly basis. To him, the town codes were guidelines.

"Are you okay?" Rosalie asked, with brown eyes round in her lovely, lined face. Rosalie was a class act. A lady. I'd asked her once if she was from here. To her, "here" meant Ellington; to me, the Boston metropolitan area. "Oh no. Angelo and I grew up in Cambridge. Our parents were very upset when we moved all the way out here." ("Out here" was sixteen miles, a distance any military family would consider living next door to their families.)

"We needed a little space," Rosalie had said. That I understood completely.

"What happened?" she asked, this time pulling out a chair to sit across from me.

I took a big bite of the cheese bread. I could say it was a police exercise, but this was a small town. The dispatcher probably lived next door to someone, who knew someone, who would lunch here tomorrow.

"It was a huge misunderstanding. I was trying to find CJ. I'm so embarrassed."

Rosalie patted my hand. "You want the minestrone? It is better than usual today. I don't know what Angelo did." She dropped her voice. "He doesn't know, either."

Angelo set the soup down in front of me. "This will help." He sat down across from me.

I could tell he had something on his mind. I slurped in a big spoonful. "This is delicious. What did you put in it?" I thought I'd tease him a little.

Angelo glanced over at Rosalie. "She thinks I don't know what I did, but I do."

I laughed.

"I know you think you got it bad right now. Let me tell you a story. When I was growing up, we were so poor we had to eat lobster every Saturday night."

I stopped eating. "Poor" and "lobster" didn't go together in my world.

"Every Saturday, the trains brought the lobsters down from Maine. I had to ride my bike from Cambridge to Boston. After they unloaded, I'd pick up what they'd dropped and take it home for Mama to fix for dinner."

I waited for the punch line. This had to be one of Angelo's jokes. Before he got to it, a group of people came in, calling him over.

When I finished my soup, Rosalie brought me a cannoli. "If Lou told you he knows what he put in the minestrone, he's lying."

"What about the lobster story?" I asked.

"That's true."

At nine o'clock, someone knocked on my door. For the first time in months, I hoped it was CJ with news. It was Stella. She held a bottle of red wine. She lifted it. "I have scotch downstairs, if you'd prefer that."

I guessed she was coming in, whether I wanted her to or not. "The wine is fine," I said, stepping back to let her in.

Stella looked over the place with a critical eye. "You aren't a hoarder, are you?"

I looked at the black bags. "No. They're going to the base thrift shop. I needed to sort them."

"If they weren't here, I'd say the place looked better than it has in ages." She picked her way through them and settled on the couch.

I grabbed a corkscrew and two glasses. I wondered what she wanted, if she was going to ask me to leave. This day had been a fiasco. I sat on the opposite end of the couch. "Is this your way of kicking me out?"

Stella looked surprised. "Of course not. Who hasn't had trouble with the police?"

I couldn't think of anyone I knew who had trouble with the police.

"I wouldn't mind an explanation, though." Stella took a drink, watching me over her glass.

"It was a police exercise."

Stella shook her head.

"A misunderstanding."

This time she raised an eyebrow. "That was one hell of a misunderstanding. I thought, mistakenly perhaps, that you and I were going to be friends." She waited me out.

Good Lord, I'd be terrible in an interrogation. "I just can't tell you. Or anyone."

Stella sipped her wine.

"CJ, Chief Hooker, is my ex-husband."

"The whole town knows that by now. I knew because my aunt is the town manager. She said you'd be trouble."

"I guess I proved her right."

Stella smiled and lifted her glass. "Here's to trouble. I never liked my aunt that well, anyway."

After an hour of chatting, I had a pleasant buzz. "What do you do?"

"I teach voice at Berklee College of Music in

Boston. I also give private lessons here. I hope they won't bother you."

"Not at all. I wondered about all the music coming from your place." We hit an awkward pause in our conversation. I didn't know Stella well enough to sit in silence. "Do you know the DiNapolis?"

"Angelo regularly threatens my aunt, the town manager. He loves my other one. He harasses the selectmen. He thinks his priest should go to him for confession."

She left a few minutes later, singing as she went down the steps. I still didn't know anything about her trouble with the police.

I slept until nine on Monday morning. A lot of the night had involved tossing and turning. I'd even gotten up for a couple of bouts of pacing. My body had been ready for sleep. My mind screamed, *No!* CJ finally called me at ten.

"Sarah, when was the last time you saw the French-cuffed shirt?" He kept his voice low. Voices rumbled in the distance. A couple of car doors slammed. It sounded like he was outside.

"Yesterday, when I gave it to you. Did someone take it out of your car?"

"No. Before then. Did you move it with you to the apartment?"

In the haste of our move—his from being escorted off base because of his "misconduct" and mine to get away from Tiffany—the packers had mixed up a lot of our clothes. I had his favorite sweater. He had my cocktail dresses. We'd long since traded our clothes back, even though we still both had unopened boxes tucked away. Mine were under the eaves, and his were . . . who knows where?

"I gave you everything I had of yours."

"You didn't keep the shirt as a token remembrance? Like when you took my rugby shirt when we were dating?"

I'd loved his rugby shirt. It had dropped to midthigh, was soft, and smelled like CJ. I'd slept in it most nights. It drove my mother crazy. "Trust me. A remembrance was not on my mind four months ago. Burning it maybe, sleeping in something of yours? No way. It had to be at your house. Unless Tiffany took it."

"When did you last see Tiffany?"

"I don't know. Probably the day I moved off base. She sat in the patrol car a few houses down from ours. It kind of creeped me out."

"Have you talked to her since then?"

"No. Why would I?"

"No phone calls?"

"No phone calls." I hoped he didn't pick up on the hesitation in my voice.

"No contact since you left base?"

"A Facebook message . . . one night after a few glasses of wine. . . . It was stupid. Why are you asking me all this?" I heard a dog bark through the phone.

"What did you say in the message?"

"I told her to call off her buddies. They were leaving all kinds of nasty messages on my Facebook page. I told her she was welcome to you, that I was done."

CJ paused before he spoke again. "Could it have been perceived as a threat?"

"Of course not. If anything, Tiffany and her friends were threatening me. What's this have to do with what

I found yesterday?" I didn't want to mention bloody shirts if he was out with other people. "Where are you?"

"At Fitch. Outside the enlisted troops' dormitory. Blood's smeared on the floor of her dorm room. Tiffany's missing."

CHAPTER 5

Late afternoon our kids started to show up. In a crisis, if Dad was busy, Mom wasn't so bad. They were upset about the blood in Tiffany's room and in an uproar that she was missing. The first group included Tiffany's best friend, Jessica, who'd been particularly hateful to me; James, not Jim; and a couple of other guys. Jessica fell into my arms, her blue eyes overflowing with tears. She apologized.

"I shouldn't have said those things. It was stupid."

I patted her back. "It's okay," I said. "You're forgiven." I brushed a piece of long blond hair out of her face. James, who always introduced himself as "James, not Jim"—naturally, everyone called him "Not Jim"—pulled me in for a hug. James is a great hugger. I always called him James, which he appreciated. He was older than the rest, more mature. He was the one who showed up to mow my lawn or shovel snow when CJ was deployed. He lingered after parties to help me clean up. It was never anything more. No misconduct.

I wanted to send them all home, to be by myself. But if Tiffany didn't show up soon, CJ was going to be in a mess way worse than the misconduct charge. Four months ago, I'd wished all sorts of trouble on CJ: body parts falling off, pox, hair loss, but nothing of this magnitude. I decided to keep the kids here, listen to their chatter. Maybe I could find out something helpful.

"Wow, this place is a dump. Your home on base was a lot bigger." Jessica clapped her hands over her mouth. "Sorry."

The living room was still filled with the trash bags full of stuff set to go to the thrift shop tomorrow. I laughed. "You're right. This is all headed to the thrift shop. I need to stick it back in the Suburban."

Everyone grabbed a couple of bags and loaded them into the car. I did a quick count of how many bags were in the back of the Burb. In the morning, I'd recount them. No one else was going to sneak a bag into this old girl again.

"This looks much better," Jessica said when we returned to my apartment. "Where's all of your stuff? That collection of glass hearts, that bronze statue, all your paintings. I loved your painting of the ocean. Why didn't you hang it up?"

"I don't have room for everything. Some of it's at CJ's house. Some of it's in boxes under the eaves." I pointed toward the slanted wall.

"Well, it's cute . . . cozy," Jessica said.

It was cozy. A worn Oriental rug, purchased at a flea market in Ohio, covered the painted-white wooden floors. My grandmother's rocker sat next to the window looking over the common. An indestructible plant I'd inherited when a friend PCSed—had a permanent change of station—which to civilians was simply a move. The couch, with down cushions, I'd bought at a garage sale in Monterey. My mom had made off-white slipcovers for it. Assorted paintings covered the walls—one from the Fitch Thrift Shop, another a steal at a Concord antique store. There was a noticeable lack of photographs. I'd sent most of them with the stuff to CJ's house.

I gave a couple of the guys some money to buy snacks for all of us at Stop & Shop.

"How could she do this to us?" Jessica wailed. "I'm scared. What if some mad ax murderer's running around on base?"

"This isn't about you. It's about Tiffany," James said in a patient tone. "There's no ax murderer. Besides, you know how to use a gun."

"I only get to carry it on duty. What will happen after work?" Jessica asked.

"Stay with other people and you'll be fine," I said. I almost added "the dorms are safe," but maybe not—given the blood in Tiffany's room.

"Tiffany could just be AWOL for some reason," I said. Absent without leave was a serious charge. "She'll turn back up. When's the last time any of you talked to her?"

"The day before she took leave," Jessica said. "She didn't say anything about going on a trip."

"When was that?"

"Last Wednesday. She had a shift Monday morning. They checked her room when she didn't show up."

"Anything new been on her mind?" I asked.

"No. She mentioned her boyfriend back home— that he wanted to take care of her and the baby. Sorry, Sarah, about mentioning the, uh, baby." Then Jessica squealed, "OMG! Maybe they eloped. Wouldn't that be romantic?"

"It doesn't explain the blood in her room," James said.

"Maybe she cut herself shaving. I do it all the time," Jessica answered.

I almost started to say, "No way. It was too much blood." I remembered that none of them knew about the bloody shirts. I looked at James, leaning against the wall. His dark brown hair was longer than a lot of military guys wore theirs, just barely within regulations. He watched me closely with his light brown eyes.

"Have you talked to her lately, James?" I asked.

He crossed his arms across his chest. "No. Barely knew her. I drove Jessica over because she wanted to see you."

The guys returned with the snacks. The rest of the afternoon passed with kids coming and going. James and Jessica stayed. Jessica was now convinced Tiffany had eloped. She was mad because she hadn't been asked to be a bridesmaid. James moved around filling drinks, picking up trash, and refilling the chip bowl. Jessica spent a lot of time on her phone.

"Where was Tiffany from?" I asked.

Jessica looked up. "West Virginia. I think she was a coal miner's daughter. The military was her way out. I don't think her parents or boyfriend liked it at all. Her mom wanted Tiffany to take care of her younger brothers and sisters. She told me her mom drank a lot. Do you think her boyfriend . . . ooh, I mean, husband will move here?" Jessica bounced a little when she said "husband."

Emotions roiled between worries about Tiffany and joy when Jessica convinced someone that Tiffany had eloped. I yawned. I slipped into the kitchen to check my phone, hoping CJ had tried to reach me. Nothing. Normally I wasn't as attached to my phone as these kids were to theirs. Since yesterday, though, I'd kept it near at hand.

James came into my tiny kitchen. "Are you okay, Sarah? Do you want us to leave?"

James had enlisted when he was twenty-seven, the high end of the air force's age limit, and had already served three years. I'm not sure how he survived working with all these young kids.

"I'm fine." My voice wasn't convincing.

"Since the new commander hasn't arrived and Acting Commander Walker just returned from her deployment, everyone still relies on you and Colonel . . . Chief Hooker."

"It's okay. I miss all of you. Most of you." This group wasn't the only one who turned to CJ. He had people from past assignments still calling him for advice.

"You don't think Tiffany's off on her honeymoon?" He grinned.

I smiled back at him. "No. And you don't, either."

"You think it's something more serious. Not a shaving cut."

"I don't know what to think." Boy howdy, was that true. "I hope she's okay. Just went off for a few days to think. Lost track of time."

James nodded. "You've been checking your phone more than you usually do."

"I'm hoping for news. Will you call me if you hear anything?"

"Will do," he said. I started to leave. James put a hand out to stop me. "If you know something about

Tiffany's disappearance, report it now. Protecting Chief Hooker won't help the situation."

"Nothing to protect." I stepped past him back into the living room.

Jessica and one of the other girls had their heads together whispering. They broke apart when I walked back in. With raised eyebrows, Jessica looked at the other girl.

"Go on," the friend said.

Jessica put on what must be her version of a cop face. It looked more like a pout to me.

"When Tiffany got back from culinary school, she went after Colonel Hooker. She said she wanted to bag him. She had it bad. Tiffany volunteered for all sorts of things that would keep her near him." Jessica paused, looking at me like she wanted to say more.

She took my stunned silence as permission to continue.

"After her shifts, she'd change into these microscopic shorts and a sports bra. She'd prance around the office. If Tiffany saw him heading to the shooting range, she went. If he headed to the gym, she did, too. Tiffany was relentless. She kept going to Colonel Hooker for career counseling, even though she was set with the aide job at the general's house."

I didn't want to hear this, but I was trapped. James was right behind me—someone was in the bathroom; someone else sat on the floor by the door to my bedroom.

"He always left the door open when she was in his office. When none of that worked, she started watching you. Once, she even bought the same color of lip gloss after she saw you at the BX. It was getting creepy. I told her to back off."

How could I have been so obtuse? Not to have seen what was going on with Tiffany. Especially not to have noticed any change in CJ or what he was hiding. Our marriage had veered off course at some point. I didn't know when.

"Enough." It was James. "Time to go."

They left reluctantly. Jessica hugged me, chatting about Tiffany's wedding pictures, which she couldn't wait to see. I thanked James for herding them out. I closed the door, for once, grateful to be alone.

I woke with my phone next to me on the pillow Tuesday morning. No word from CJ. Light played around the edges of the ugly white window shade. I quickly showered, dressed, and swallowed some more of the tasteless cereal before heading down to my Suburban. I did a quick trash bag count—the same number as I put in yesterday. I drove toward base on winding, narrow back roads that led to the Patterson gate and the Fitch Visitors Center.

I hoped Laura Nicklas remembered to sponsor me on base. Prior to my divorce, my dependent's ID meant sailing through any of the base security gates. The ID was one more thing taken from me during our divorce. Now I had to make sure one of my base friends sponsored me. They had to go to the visitors' center, leave their name, my name, where I was going, and how long I'd be on base. I had to head to the center, show my license, registration, and proof of insurance, get a pass, and display it in my car.

A line of people waited to get checked in at the visitors center. Luckily, it's staffed by security forces. No one wanted this job because it was often a punishment for some indiscretion, underage drinking, missing curfew, fighting, or breaking any number of other rules. One of "our kids" noticed me and waved me over. Even though he knew me, I still had to show my license, registration, and proof of insurance. He wrote out a pass, which I stuck on the dashboard of the Suburban.

I drove past the back side of the base chapel, took a left on Grant, followed by a right onto Travis at the stoplight. I passed the movie theater (it played two movies a week—sometimes three, if they threw in a matinee), gas station, and library; then I took a left at the next light onto Wright Street. An electronic sign flashed messages about retirements, promotions, and other base activities. I wound my way back to the thrift shop.

It was tucked back in an old building not really good enough for offices, not bad enough to condemn, although most of us working would argue with that. The building backed to a field and woods. The trees were full of turkey vultures. They looked creepy hunched over on the almost-bare tree branches. Some had been nesting in the woods for a while. It looked like they invited all their friends for a party. It probably meant some idiot had dumped food in the Dumpster on the side of the thrift shop—the one that was clearly marked, FOR THRIFT SHOP USE ONLY and NO FOOD WASTE.

We only used it for things that were too bad for us to use or donate, or things that were dropped off that we couldn't resell, like car seats. After parking, I headed over toward the Dumpster, listening to the vultures call to each other. I spotted a KFC bucket with bones scattered around it. That explained the vulture party.

I gingerly picked up the edge of the bucket, using it as a scoop to gather the waste. Why did I show up first today? This was above and beyond what any volunteer should have to do. The vultures had done an excellent job of picking the bones clean and scattering them across the dirt.

The vultures, hunched in the trees, watched me. I yelled at them, waving my arms around. "Go away!" They ignored me. I saw a bigger bone and then another. These bones were way too big to be a chicken. I went around the corner of the Dumpster. A skull with gaping empty eye sockets stared up at me.

CHAPTER 6

The upper left side of the skull looked like it had been crushed. *No, no, no.* I took a step back. And another. I clutched the KFC bucket like it was holding me up instead of the other way around. A couple of vultures circled overhead. Their cries were like a reprimand. *Get out. Get out.* The skeletal remains didn't look complete. Some of the bones had been dragged across the field toward the tree line. Most were picked clean.

I stared at the bones in the KFC bucket. I chucked the bucket away from me. A soul-wrenching ripple of horror shook through me. On the edge of the bone field, I spotted a piece of paper or something. I crept toward it. Stared down. It was a plastic rectangle. A military ID—CJ's active-duty military ID. This was old—no longer valid—once he retired he was issued a new one. The retiree cards looked different than active-duty cards. This one should have been destroyed.

A car pulled up somewhere behind me. I wanted to throw myself over the ID as if it were a grenade that I could keep from exploding. Eventually I'd have to get up. There was no way to hide the ID. I wondered why I thought I should. I glanced over my shoulder. Laura had arrived, thank heaven. She stepped out of her car, slender and athletic, with close-cropped, dark hair. She'd been mistaken for Halle Berry more than once.

"Stay there. Call security!" I shouted.

"What's going on?" Laura yelled. "Are we going to be able to open today? What happened? Did someone break in? We need to open. People plan on it."

"No." I hurried over to her. "I found bones." I choked out the words. This was not the time to fall apart. I waved my hand back at the Dumpster. "A skull and other bones."

Laura's big brown eyes widened. She called 911, sounding amazingly calm while she talked to them. After she hung up, she said, "I'm calling Mark." Having a colonel for a husband, especially the wing commander, came in handy when the thrift shop needed something.

The first security forces cars showed up, followed shortly by Laura's husband. They shuffled us back, near the edge of the parking lot, where we'd be out of the way. We watched the activity in silence. A protocol was in place for emergencies. It started the minute Laura dialed 911 and played out around us.

An agent from the OSI, Office of Special Investigations—the air force equivalent of NCIS—showed up. After he consulted with a few people, it looked like he took over. The base OSI office only consisted of a few agents. As far as I knew, they'd never dealt with a murder on Fitch. If that's what it was.

While the base security forces were in charge of protecting the base and law enforcement, the OSI was in charge of serious offenses. They investigated terrorism, fraud, illegal drug rings, and distribution, as well as violent crimes and computer hacking. They wore suits and were called special agents, instead of by their military rank. I knew that they worked closely with the security forces. Some were scruffy undercover types. A few really believed they were special and smarter.

I recognized Special Agent Bristow. We'd sat at the same table at a base function about a year ago. His wife had died the year before and the sadness was still etched around his eyes.

One of the agents pulled Laura away. I could see her talking, waving her hands around, pointing toward me, then the Dumpster.

"I'm not leaving you here," Laura called over to me. "I'll stay even if that guy"—she pointed to Agent Bristow—"won't let me talk to you." It's what I loved about Laura; she was feisty and got things done. The Minuteman Thrift Shop had blossomed under her leadership. I was happy to have a friend close by. It kept me from focusing too much on the bone field.

However, ten minutes later, I overheard Mark, Laura's husband, tell Laura to go home. Laura shouted her apologies. "Mark's making me leave."

Agent Bristow turned to me. Small coffee stains dotted the front of his shirt. "Mrs. Hooker, you were the first one here?"

I nodded yes to his question without bothering to correct my name.

"Did you see anyone else around?"

"No. It was just me, until Laura Nicklas pulled up."

He quizzed me about what time I'd arrived, my movements, what I'd seen. He didn't seem happy with my lack of information. "Okay." He turned to one of the other OSI agents. "Let her sit in my car for now."

More police cars had arrived, including CJ and

three other Ellington police cars. Base jurisdiction was a funny thing. Technically, parts of the base, housing and schools, were in the town of Lincoln, while other parts were in Bedford and Ellington. Base security forces, as well as the Lincoln police, responded to domestic issues in the housing areas. This section was in Ellington's part of the base. CJ would have been contacted because no one knew if the remains were military, dependent, or civilian.

CJ didn't come near me. People moved carefully around, putting numbered evidence markers down. Others took pictures. I wondered if it was Tiffany out there. I hoped not. As much as I disliked her, I didn't want her life to end this way, head bashed in and her body violated by buzzards and coyotes. I ran a hand over my stomach. If Tiffany was dead, the baby was, too. I wrapped my arms around myself, rocking and shaking.

An hour later, Agent Bristow popped his head into the car. "We're taking you to Ellington to ask you some questions, if that's okay with you?"

Even though he asked, I knew I had no choice. I wasn't surprised we were heading back to Ellington. The base had MOAs—memorandums of agreement with the surrounding cities. They must have decided the EPD was best suited to investigate this murder. They could have taken me to the OSI office. I guess the Ellington Police Station could accommodate the crowd more easily.

"Of course. I'd like to ride with CJ." I really wanted a few minutes alone with CJ first.

"Best I can do is a ride with me." Agent Bristow smiled as if to reassure me this was routine. "Chief Hooker has a bit of a conflict of interest."

If they knew about the bloody shirts, it would be more than a conflict of interest. It would look bad if one of us mentioned them and the other didn't. Which was exactly why I wanted to talk to CJ.

"What about my car?" I asked.

"I can have someone take it to the station and leave the keys at the desk," Agent Bristow said.

"Thanks."

A medical examiner had joined the scene and the security forces maintained a perimeter around the crime scene. One of them tracked who came and went. Since this was a remote part of the base, they didn't have to worry about crowd control. As Bristow walked around the car to the driver's side, an Ellington police officer trotted over. He had thick, dark hair and powerful shoulders. I didn't recognize him. He wasn't one of the officers who delighted in pulling me over. His name tag said, *Pellner.*

"I can escort Miss Winston back to town," he said. When he spoke, I noticed a dimple on his left cheek. Somehow his dimple looked menacing.

Even though every part of me wanted to cling to Agent Bristow and scream "No," I stood my ground and met Pellner's dark eyes. It looked like he was itching to slap some cuffs on me and toss me in the backseat of the squad car.

"Thanks. She's coming with me," Agent Bristow said. Pellner watched as Bristow opened the front passenger door of his car for me. I couldn't help tossing a little wave to Pellner as we passed. It probably meant another ticket loomed in my future.

* * *

Bristow settled me in an interview room. It looked a lot like the one on base: a two-way mirror and a scarred, bolted-down table. I sat in one of the two uncomfortable chairs. He left, came back with a Coke for me, and left again. I took a couple of sips. The acid didn't sit well in my already-upset stomach.

Before long, Bristow returned, alone, which surprised me, since it was a joint investigation. Although, for all I knew, the entire Ellington Police Department could be amassed behind the mirror, probably hoping I'd confess to something, anything, that would let them lock me up.

"When was the last time you were at the thrift shop?" Bristow asked. The lighting in here made the lines around his eyes look even worse, like life had worn him down. His white shirt wasn't crisp and had press marks from a poor iron job. The sleeve of his suit was on the verge of fraying. It looked like fending for himself didn't sit well for him. His vulnerability made me want to trust him.

"Last Thursday. I locked up around two-thirty. We're only open every other Saturday. It's hard to find enough people to keep the place open. A lot of spouses prefer to stick to less messy jobs, like writing stories for the newsletter or organizing the monthly spouses' club meetings. Not that we don't need people to do those things, too. I've done them myself at other assignments. Some spouses volunteer for jobs they think will help get their husbands promoted. The thrift shop isn't it." I look a breath, realizing I'd started to babble.

"Did you notice anything unusual at that time?"

"No. Laura Nicklas and I hauled some junk to the Dumpster when we left. We would have noticed a body. Do you think it is Tiffany Lopez?"

"It's too soon to tell."

"How long will it take to find out?"

"I'm not sure. Her DNA will be on file. They take a sample from all military personnel for identification purposes."

I looked down at my hands. The knuckles were white from clasping them together. "What about her baby?"

"We will have to wait for all the reports to come back. When is the last time you saw Airman Lopez?" he asked.

My eyes widened. I wasn't expecting Agent Bristow to ask about my relationship with Tiffany. Although, I guess, I should have known he'd get around to it. "The day I moved off base. She was parked down the street." I gulped down some of the Coke. I'd thought my only concern was helping CJ.

"No other contact since then?"

I explained to him, as I had to CJ, about the whole Facebook incident. It was embarrassing, like I was some teenage girl. "That's it. I've avoided her."

"Why'd you stay here after your divorce? Doesn't seem like there's a lot to hold you here. No family or job."

What could I say? Somehow the day I'd talked to my mom, I reverted back to my defiant eighteen-year-old self. That didn't make me sound very stable. Would he understand my fondness for this area—its history, the quirky accents and pronunciations, the food? I liked it here. "What does that have to do with anything?"

"Do you have any information about Airman Lopez's whereabouts?"

I thought about the bloody shirts. That didn't tell me anything about Tiffany's whereabouts. I calmly looked Bristow in the eye. "No." Then I asked, "If the EPD is running the investigation, why are you asking me questions?"

"I'm not confident any of them would remain neutral. The chief agreed. Thanks for your cooperation, Miss Winston. If you think of anything, let us know." He handed me his card as he opened the door for me.

That was it. I don't know what I expected. Something a lot more complicated than that innocuous interview. I pictured hours in a too-cold room and warnings not to leave town. I should be relieved. Instead, the process in the interview room left me uneasy. I walked toward the lobby, expecting to see CJ waiting for me. He wasn't around. After picking up my car keys at the front desk, I trotted down the steps. Pellner came around the side of the building as I hit the sidewalk.

"Sarah," he called.

His familiarity pissed me off. I wanted to breeze by him like he didn't exist.

"Yes?"

He walked toward me, got close, in my personal bubble. "Don't make trouble for Chuck. We've got his back." He leaned down, with his lips almost touching my ear. "I know about Lowell."

I jerked back, horrified. That was a night I'd rather forget. I hurried across the street, spotting my Suburban in the municipal lot. Pellner's laugh followed me to the car.

CHAPTER 7

As I turned out of the lot, Pellner flagged me down. *What now?* I wanted to speed off, but I stopped and rolled my window down. He ripped a ticket off his pad, thrusting it at me. "Jaywalking is a ticketable offense in Ellington."

I snatched the ticket out of his hand. "You know, Officer Pellner, I just had the worst day of my life." I shook the ticket at him. "If you think a jaywalking ticket is going to upset me, you are dumber than you look."

Now I'd put my foot in it. I wondered what kind of ticket you got for insulting a police officer.

He took a step back. It almost looked like he smiled. He gave me a small salute as I pulled away. I wrapped my hands around the steering wheel to keep from giving him a different one back. That's probably what he hoped for. Instead, I tossed the ticket in the passenger seat and drove off at a sedate pace.

After parking the Suburban at my apartment, I headed over to DiNapoli's. My stomach rumbled, this time from hunger instead of nerves. I'd keep it light—a salad would do. I crossed the town common.

I wondered if walking across the grass was a ticketable offense, too. The church bell struck three as I waited at the light to cross Great Road. No cars were coming. With my luck, if I tried crossing, some police officer would be lurking to give me another ticket.

By the time I entered DiNapoli's, Rosalie was waiting for me. She hustled me over to a table. "Lou, hurry up with those mozzarella sticks for Sarah. She's probably half starved after being questioned by the police."

Rosalie already knew I'd been questioned. Many people who moved to small towns were surprised by the speed with which news traveled. I was not. The wives' network on any base was a well-oiled machine. Not always accurate, but fast. Sometimes our husbands came to us for information. I'm pretty sure the NSA's business model was based on the efficiency and ability of military wives to gather and disburse news.

"How about a Greek salad?" I asked.

"No. You need something that will stick to you. Lou's making his special ziti for you." Rosalie left for a minute. She returned with the mozzarella sticks, garlic bread, and a glass of red wine in one of their plastic water cups. I knew for a fact they didn't have a liquor license.

"I don't want you to get in trouble." I gestured toward the wine.

"You let me worry about trouble!" Angelo yelled over to me. "The selectmen are a bunch of idiots."

I took a sip, letting the warmth slide through me before digging into the cheese sticks and bread. The DiNapolis left me alone until they served the ziti.

"You need a lawyer, kid?" Angelo asked me as he

set three heaping plates on the table. Rosalie went to the front door and flipped the sign to CLOSED.

I dug into the ziti with its big chunks of Italian sausage, tomato, and cheese. It gave me time to think about what I wanted to say.

"Angelo's cousin is an attorney," Rosalie said as she sat at her place, pouring us all more wine. "He got Mike 'the Big Cheese' Titone off from multiple racketeering charges."

"Mike's got a cheese shop in the North End. They accused him of slicing up more than cheese," Angelo said. "According to my cousin, the case had more holes than Swiss." Angelo laughed at his joke.

"I don't think I need one, but thank you. It means a lot to me."

"You should never talk to the police without a lawyer," Angelo said. "Especially when the chief is your ex-husband."

Someone rattled the door. Angelo deftly swept up our empty wine cups while Rosalie opened the door. They sent me home with enough leftovers to feed the whole security squadron.

At home I repackaged the leftovers into smaller portions. I stuck most of them in the freezer. I put the Greek salad, which Rosalie had included, in the fridge for later. That is, if I ever needed to eat again. Carol called as I finished.

"I'm so glad you called. My day was awful." Probably not as bad as Tiffany's, though. I told her what had happened: the finding, calling, being interviewed.

Carol murmured sympathetically while I talked. "CJ was nowhere. Not during the interview. Not after."

"Did you want him to be?"

I sat at my small kitchen table, tracing my finger around the bright flowers printed on the vintage table-cloth. "He should have been. No. Maybe I did want him there. Not for why you think. I don't want him back."

"Of course you don't."

I took a deep breath. "I'm sorry. You called me. What did you want?"

"It can wait. This sounds more important."

"No. I've been preoccupied with myself. With my problems for months. Tell me what you called about."

"I need your help. My house is overflowing with stuff that we don't have room for. I want to have a garage sale. I need you to organize it for me. Please?"

It was a common problem for military families. At one assignment, you had a giant base house; at the next, a tiny apartment. Carol had moved from Eglin Circle, where the biggest base houses were, to a much smaller place in Ellington. This area was very expensive, even though Ellington was the poor stepchild of Lexington, Concord, and Lincoln—even Bedford, for that matter.

Carol and Brad had bought a 1950s Cape with three bedrooms, two baths, and a single-car garage. A far cry from the spacious colonel's quarters they'd had on base. She'd filled every inch of it.

"Of course. When do you want to do it?"

"Is next Saturday too much to hope for? Besides all the things crammed in the house, the garage is stuffed. Brad is threatening to set it all out on the curb."

"It's not like I have anything else to do. I'll come over tomorrow to start pricing. I can list it on Craigslist and the Wicked Local site. We'll need to make some signs to put up near your house."

"You're a doll. If you need anything or want to talk later about what happened today, call me, even if it's in the middle of the night. Love you."

If Carol was having a garage sale, maybe I should get rid of some things, too. In the living room, I accessed the crawl space to the attic. I dragged out two boxes, pulling them over to the couch. I opened the first one. Right on top was one of our wedding albums. Not the photographer's album with all the formal shots, but the one filled with pictures that friends had taken. I started flipping through it.

Geez, we were young. I was nineteen and CJ twenty-one. We gazed at each other with googly eyes and sappy smiles. CJ in his mess dress, the air force equivalent of a tux; me in a simple white gown. Our mothers stood in the background with forced smiles or actual frowns if they didn't know they were in the pictures. I bet CJ's mom was giving him an earful now about making the mistake of marrying me. At least our dads were happy. Us toasting, cutting the cake, dancing like fools. Even pictures of us doing the sprinkler.

Someone knocked on the door. I slapped the album closed.

"Are you okay?" CJ asked when I answered the door.

"I don't know."

"Can I come in?"

I shrugged. I headed for the couch, where I tried to shove the wedding album out of sight. CJ took it from me and looked through it.

"Hard to believe we went from that to this."

"There's a simple explanation."

CJ set the album down.

"Did you tell Special Agent Bristow about the shirts?" I asked.

CJ shifted on the sofa. "No. I take it you didn't, either?"

"You didn't watch when Bristow interviewed me?"

"I wasn't allowed to. I asked to be in the room with you."

"Why didn't they let you?"

"You're my wife. You found the remains. Bristow didn't think I could remain impartial. He was right."

I didn't remind CJ I was his *ex*-wife. "I didn't tell Bristow about the shirts. I wanted to talk to you first."

"We're digging a big hole for ourselves. This could all blow up in our faces."

"You mean *you're* digging a big hole for *yourself*. It could blow up in *your* face." Even as I said it, I knew I could be in trouble, too. I was no lawyer, but even I could build a case against myself: the wronged woman, the bloody shirts in my car, enough access to the base to have hunted Tiffany down when I was supposed to be working at the thrift shop. "I know we shouldn't hide this, but as despicable as you've been, I know you wouldn't kill anyone."

"Thanks? When he was done with you, Bristow grilled me, too. Especially about my ID."

"How do you think it ended up in the field? Aren't they supposed to be destroyed when you get a new one?"

"Yes. Remember, I lost that one in December?"

"Do you think Tiffany took it?" I asked.

"She must have. It will take a while before the results on the DNA tests come back. Maybe it isn't

Tiffany. She might turn up. Then the shirts won't matter."

"If it is Tiffany, it means the baby is dead, too." Tears welled up in my eyes. I sucked in a deep breath.

CJ ran a hand over his head. "I can't even sort out how I feel about that yet. I'm not even sure it was mine."

It's the first time I'd heard him say that. Up to this point, it was always about supporting the baby. "You could have done a DNA test after the baby was born."

"I know. What I did was wrong. Even if it wasn't mine, that kid was going to need someone. Tiffany couldn't support a baby on her own."

I didn't know whether to toss him out or hug him.

"I saw you with Pellner outside the station. What did he want?" CJ asked.

My stomach full of ziti seemed to solidify. I'd put the whole Lowell thing out of my mind. "Some BS about watching myself and the force having your back. Then he gave me a ticket for jaywalking." I had to admit to myself I was more than a little jealous. I wish some group had my back. CJ had always created a loyal following at all of our assignments.

"I'll talk to him."

That was the last thing I wanted. "Don't worry about it. You're lucky they feel that way about you. It's one of your greatest strengths."

"Did you just give me a compliment?"

"Don't let it go to your head. Do you want some ziti from DiNapoli's to take with you?"

"I'm leaving?"

"Yes, CJ. I have stuff to do." (I had nothing to do.)

"I'd love some ziti. The only way I can get food from there is if someone picks it up for me. With the looks Angelo and Rosalie give me, someone spitting in my food is the least of my worries."

I tried not to smile. I guess someone had my back, after all.

I tried to sleep: Images of vultures, bones, Tiffany, and the baby kaleidoscoped through my head. Those thoughts shifted to Agent Bristow, CJ, and Pellner. Pellner mentioned Lowell. I'd only made one trip to Lowell since I'd left CJ. How did Pellner know anything about it?

It had been on a Friday night. I had called every friend I could think of. None of them were up for a girls' night out. They all had plans with their husbands. I couldn't distract myself cleaning. I'd scrubbed the apartment spotless in the wee hours when I couldn't sleep.

I finally realized I didn't have to sit home. I could go out on my own. After a quick shower, I took extra care with my hair and makeup. I pulled on a black sleeveless dress that clung to my curves. I rooted around in my closet until I found my red peep-toed stilettos. I put them on and admired myself in the full-length mirror, which I'd hung on the back of the bedroom door. My lack of appetite had made my stomach flatter. The shoes made my muscled calves stand out. My cheeks were flushed. My eyes looked a little dangerous. At least I hoped they looked dangerous and not crazed.

I climbed carefully into the Suburban, heading up the 128 toward Lowell. Lowell was an old mill town, not known for its nightlife, although it was a college town. It was far enough from Ellington that I wouldn't run into anyone I knew and close enough to make it back after a drink.

I drove down Lowell's main drag, which looked a little seedier at night than I expected from my visits during the day. Since I was here, I wasn't turning back, not until I had at least one drink out on my own. A little bit of my self-pity seeped away as I'd driven up here. I was an independent woman seeking a night of fun. I didn't need anyone else to provide it for me.

I spotted a bar with a parking spot that wasn't too far away. After parking, I stopped in front of the door of the bar. Walking into someplace new, full of strangers, alone, didn't sound as appealing as it had earlier. A group of people came up behind me. I attached myself to the back of their crowd and went in with them.

A long bar lined the right wall. There was a band set up by a dance floor to the left. A few tables were scattered in the middle, with pool tables in the back. Not biker, not college, not upscale, but popular—the place was packed. I went with the group I'd followed into the bar. A guy at the front of the group announced to the bartender that the first round was on him. He was celebrating something. I didn't catch what. When I finally made it to the front of the bar, the celebrating guy still stood there waiting to pay.

"What do you want?" the bartender asked me.

"A gin and tonic, extra lime," I said. I glanced at the celebrating guy. He leaned one elbow on the bar as he waited. We were inches apart. "I'm not with his group."

The celebrator gave me the once-over and lifted his chin at the bartender. "Add her to my tab."

I looked at the guy, who was about my height, with my stilettos. "Not necessary." I could buy my own drinks. The bartender had moved off to make my drink.

"What is someone like you doing alone in a place like this?" he asked.

I turned to face him. His white dress shirt, open at the collar, strained across his muscular chest and forearms. He was handsome enough that I bet a lot of women responded to his cheesy line.

"Really? That's the best you can do?" I asked him. "That's your opening line?"

"You got something better?"

"Of course," I said. The bartender came back and handed me my drink. I held out a ten to pay him, but he waved me off.

"Seth said it was on his tab."

Seth handed over his credit card. "So let's hear it."

"What?" I took a sip of my drink.

"Your line. You said you had something better. I want to hear it." He grinned, which highlighted his sturdy jaw.

A smile played around my lips. I was out of practice with tossing out lines. I'm not sure I ever had any. CJ and I were very young when we met. "What are you doing for Patriots' Day?"

The band started up. Seth leaned in close. Spicy aftershave wafted off his warm skin. I breathed it in, thinking every man in America should be mandated to wear this stuff.

"That's your line? You think that's better?" His breath brushed my ear.

"Okay, maybe nice shoes."

I'll give him credit. He tried to look down at my

shoes, but we were too close together for him to see anything below my waist.

"You shouldn't make assumptions that I'm alone. My friends might be in the back." I waved a hand toward the pool tables.

Seth glanced over his shoulder. A bunch of pierced, tattooed guys played pool. "You're going with *those guys* are your friends?"

"They could be."

"Not the way you're dressed. I know for a fact you were alone outside the bar. Looked like some wild creature getting ready to bolt from a predator. Then you attached yourself to the nearest herd. My herd."

I would have answered, but his buddies came, pulling Seth over to a table at the other side of the bar.

I found a bar stool, smiling to myself as I sipped my gin and tonic. I was glad I'd come. Maybe I could handle being single. Maybe I could even enjoy it.

I mostly kept my back to the room, chatted with the bartender on the rare occasions when he wasn't busy, and fended off a few drunks. I nursed another drink before switching to tonics without the gin. All in all a pleasant evening but if I drank anymore I wouldn't be in any shape to drive home.

I left a good tip and slipped off my bar stool. I was almost at the door when someone grabbed my hand. Seth.

A noise outside my apartment jolted me back to the present. I pushed all thoughts of Seth aside when Tyler's door slammed. The faint sounds of music came on next door. I rolled on my side. Tried to forget about bones and police interviews, about what CJ and I knew that no one else did. Our sin of omission or obstruction of justice, depending on how you looked at it. Someone else knew about the bloody shirts. Figuring out who was the problem.

CHAPTER 8

I pulled into Carol's driveway after she'd had a chance to get the kids off to school. Her house sat on a cul-de-sac adjoining conservancy land on the outer edges of Ellington, not far from the Concord River. Two other houses shared the large cul-de-sac. The area was full of wildlife. No one would ever guess the 95 and the 495 were only a short trip away. New Englanders harassed me for using my California way of adding "the" before any numbered freeway.

Carol lifted her garage door. "Ta-da," she said, throwing her arms out.

Boxes, furniture, and household goods were stuffed in almost every possible space. I placed my hand over my heart, staggering back a few steps. "It's the worst mess I've ever seen."

"If it's too much, we can put the sale off for a couple of weeks."

"I'm joking. I've seen far worse." For once I was grateful to stare down such a huge, disorganized pile of stuff. It kept me from thinking about the images of bones that had haunted me for most of the night. One small path cut down the center.

"Brad said the lawn mower is hidden in the back somewhere. I think the warmer weather reminded him of that. That explains why he's been moaning about all of this stuff. He's threatening to haul it all off if he can't get to the mower."

I dug into the first box, glad I'd dressed in layers, since the morning was still cool. Carol and I worked well together. Carol slapped sticky notes on any furniture, sports equipment, or boxes that could be sold. I followed behind her pricing and sorting. I envisioned different ways to display all of this. I wanted to get her the best price possible.

"How are you doing?" Carol asked.

"Not bad. There's a lot to do here. I can have it ready by Saturday."

"That's not what I was asking and you know it."

I sighed. "CJ said maybe the bones aren't Tiffany's. That maybe she'll show up."

"When did he tell you that?"

"Last night. He came over." I watched Carol's face. "It's not what you think. He wanted to know how my interview went."

"That's pathetic. How did he think it went? You were being interviewed about a murder. Why does he think she'll show up? Does he know something you don't?"

"No. It was more of a hope. He was trying to make me feel better."

Carol muttered something, then looked at her sparkly, large-faced watch. "It's eleven-thirty. I've got to get to the store. I'll sort some more tonight and you can come back whenever. You still have the key and garage code, don't you?"

"It's eleven-thirty? I'm supposed to be at the thrift shop."

"Will they be open today, after what happened yesterday?"

"I guess so. Nothing happened in the thrift shop. It was all behind it."

"Are you sure you want to go back over there?" Carol asked.

Pictures of the bones flashed through my head. I closed my eyes for a moment. Carol put her arm around me.

"I'll be fine. I'd rather get it over with now than have going back hanging over my head," I said.

Crime scene tape still blocked off the parking lot on the side of the building. If I were Catholic, I would have crossed myself. I was tempted to, anyway. I parked the Suburban near the old, rusted lift on the outside of the thrift shop. We used it to haul things from street level up the four feet to the floor level of the thrift shop. It was great for heavy loads or big items like couches. Since the lift was at street level, I loaded the bags from the back of the Suburban onto it before going inside.

Laura rushed over to me the minute I walked in the front door of the shop. "Are you okay?" she asked as we walked through the thrift shop. A half wall divided the main room into a smaller room with clothing and sporting goods. Beyond it was a storeroom. "It was creepy coming back here today." She glanced over her shoulder as if she expected a monster to be there.

"I wonder who it was out there. Do you think it was Tiffany?"

"I hope not." For more reasons than I could say out loud. "It's awful no matter who it is."

We rolled up the heavy steel, garage-like door. I hit the button to raise the lift. The noises it made as it rose suited the special-effects department of any haunted house. It sounded worse than usual. The base or the spouses' club budgets didn't have the money to fix the lift when it finally did break. I hauled the bags from the lift to the storeroom used for sorting while Laura rang up some customers.

I put on a blue bibbed apron with a name tag that said, *Barb.* Using other people's aprons had started as a joke; but with the whole CJ/Tiffany scandal, I appreciated the anonymity. I helped a few customers, plugging in a TV to make sure it worked for one. During lulls I slipped back to the storeroom to empty the bags I'd brought in.

Laura hollered to me to meet her in the office after some other volunteers arrived. She closed the office door. "They think out by the Dumpster is a secondary crime scene. That the murder was committed somewhere else and then the body dumped."

That made sense, considering the lack of blood around the bones. "We had that heavy rain for a couple of hours on Saturday night."

"Mark said there'd still be evidence, even with the rain," Laura said.

"What about the blood in Tiffany's room?" I asked.

"I heard it wasn't nearly enough to be the murder scene."

Lots of things could explain that. Blankets or using

something to stanch the flow, something like shirts. I kept that thought to myself.

"They're bringing in some cadaver dogs to see if they can find anything else around base," Laura said.

Fitch had K-9 units, but no cadaver dogs. The base K-9 units were either drug sniffers or bomb sniffers. They did regular patrols around the base, including the housing areas. They also performed random searches of cars entering base. I knew teens on base who bragged they'd had pot in the car that the dogs didn't catch. What they didn't realize was how fortunate they had been that the bomb dogs, instead of the drug dogs, had been on duty that day. CJ had done trials with the dogs. They could sniff out as little as a seed of marijuana.

Lots of people complained when they saw the K-9 units at the gates. They were there randomly. Anyone's car could be searched from a teenage dependent to the two-star general to a contractor who worked on base. The K-9 units helped keep the base safe, while giving the dogs practice for deployments.

"I think the dogs come tomorrow," Laura said.

"I wonder why they didn't just toss the body in the Dumpster?"

"I asked about that, too. The theory is the body was left by the Dumpster in hopes animals would drag off the remains."

"Then why leave it by the Dumpster instead of taking it another ten feet into the woods?" I knew better than to ask Laura where she'd heard all of this. Some of it probably came from Mark, although he could be tight-lipped with her at times. Laura always made friends with his secretaries and executive officers, or execs as the name was shortened to. Plus she knew almost everyone on base and managed to charm most of them.

"Between the vultures and the coyotes on base, bones could be scattered all over the place," Laura said.

I shuddered at the thought. After 9/11, the perimeter of the base had been fenced in for security reasons. The surrounding towns had protested. Many people used the base roads to cut through from point A to point B. Coyotes had been trapped inside the fencing and still roamed around the base.

Laura scooted back in her chair. "Go home. I called in a couple of people. We can keep the place open without you." She turned back at the office door. "Let me know if you hear any news."

At dinnertime I looked out my window at DiNapoli's. A family walked out as I watched. A little girl skipped ahead. Her dad hurried behind her, grabbing her hand before she ran into the street. I had a freezer full of ziti I could eat. I should stay home. A walk would be good for me, however—especially one that ended with me at the counter of DiNapoli's.

Thirty minutes later, after a brisk walk, I stood at the counter ordering a medium bianco with garlic and fresh tomatoes to go. I carried the hot pizza box across the common. Lights glowed from Tyler's and Stella's windows, and in the houses around mine. Even Tyler had company. I saw shadows of more than one person through his thin curtains.

I knocked on Stella's door. When she answered, I held up the pizza box. "Want to come up for pizza?"

"Mmmm, I smell garlic. I'll grab a bottle of wine and be up in a minute."

Thirty minutes later, we looked at the empty pizza box. We'd also polished off half the bottle of Chianti that Stella brought.

"Did they figure out whose body that was on base?" Stella asked.

"Not that I've heard. Did you know I found the body?" I looked at Stella.

"I ran into Scott Pellner at the Stop and Shop. He told me. Seemed happy about you finding it. Almost like he hoped you had something to do with it."

"How do you know him?"

"We dated in high school. He thought I was going to be 'Mrs. Scott Pellner.' That tells you something about his personality. I didn't even get to be 'Stella Pellner.'"

"What happened?"

"First of all, I wasn't about to be 'Mrs. Anybody' at that age. The last thing I wanted was to stay home and start popping out babies. I headed off to Europe to become an opera star."

"Scott stayed here?"

"Surprisingly, he enlisted in the air force. Did a four-year stint. He met the girl of his dreams while stationed in Kentucky. As soon as his time was up, they moved back here. She did start popping out kids. They have five."

"It's surprising he's loyal to CJ, an outsider. You'd think he might have been interested in being chief."

"Back in high school, his ambition was all in pursuit of as many varsity letters as he could get on his jacket. Being chief would feel like being the captain of the football team all over again. The status it would give him. It's like he'd always be on the winning team."

"Could he be jealous of CJ? That CJ is the chief, instead of him?"

"The Scott I knew in high school would have been. I don't know him well enough to say anymore," Stella said.

"Who lives in the other apartment down by you? I've never seen them."

"The Callahans. They winter in Florida. Usually, they come back in time for Patriots' Day. A cute little couple that's been married for years. When their kids moved out, they sold their place. It closed faster than they expected, so they rented from me. They talk about buying another place. Never do it, though."

I poured us both more wine. "How long did you stay in Europe?"

"A couple of years. I loved it, but as they say, 'A New Englander's roots run to the middle of the Earth.'" Stella took a sip of her wine. "When I came back, I tried living in the South Shore. Even that was too far from home."

"It's what an hour or two away?" I'm not sure I'd ever understand a New Englander's concept of distance. It took longer to get from Monterey to the California/Oregon border than it did from Ellington to Caribou, Maine.

"Depending on traffic. Here I am, back in Ellington. Even though I missed it when I was gone, I sometimes wonder why I moved back."

* * *

After Stella left, I shut off the lights and turned my grandmother's rocker to look out on the common. By nine-thirty at night, only an occasional car drove down Great Road. People called Bedford "Deadford" because of its lack of nightlife; Ellington wasn't any different. The lights flipped off at DiNapoli's. One person trekked across the town common. A few flakes of snow started to fall. April was one of those months where it could be eighty degrees or we could have a blizzard. I hoped the weather would warm up for Saturday or the garage sale could be a bust.

Putting the bloody shirts in my car had to have been a deliberate act. If anyone else had found them, they'd have tossed them in the trash. Someone was familiar with my routine of going to garage sales and taking stuff to the thrift shop. I hadn't lived in Ellington very long. I didn't know that many people. It must be someone from base.

Even if it was someone connected with Fitch, why put the clothes in my car? That thought didn't take me to a happy place. Someone was trying to set CJ up for Tiffany's murder. Handing me the evidence to put him away might have seemed like a smart move. I'd moved out right after I'd found out about the affair. Hell hath no fury, and all that. Instead of turning the shirts over to the police, I turned them over to CJ. Then I lied about—no, omitted—that bit of information when I talked to Agent Bristow.

I guessed, if any of my speculation was even somewhat close to the mark, whoever had done this didn't expect me to respond this way. What would be their next move when they figured out the shirts hadn't been discovered? Maybe I needed to talk to CJ again. Knowing him, he'd already gone down that path and was way ahead of me. If he had, why hadn't he talked to me about it? Someone, somewhere, might be planning his or her next move and it might involve me. I could sit here speculating all night—or I could do something.

CHAPTER 9

At eleven forty-five at night, I stood outside Tiffany's dorm room with Jessica. She'd sponsored me on the base. Since it was after ten at night, the Fitch Visitors Center at the Patterson gate was closed and I'd had to come through the Offutt gate. I hadn't wanted to involve Jessica, but she'd once bragged about being able to open almost any door with a credit card. It only took a minute for her to prove herself right. We slipped in.

I blinked when Jessica flipped on the light. She'd said this might be hard for me, that it might not be a good idea.

"You don't have to stay. I don't want you to get in trouble," I said. It wasn't like police tape blocked the door anymore, but I didn't think anyone would be too happy to find us looking around in here.

"I'm good," Jessica said.

No blood remained on the linoleum floor, but one area was cleaner than the rest. The room looked like it had been hit with an explosion of pink. Pink comforter, frilly pillows on a twin bed, a jury-rigged pink chandelier, a large pink poof as extra seating, even pink-fringed curtains. A desk, a chair with pink seat cushion, bookshelves, and a small refrigerator covered with pink magnets completed the room.

I went over to the bulletin board hanging over the desk. An official photo of CJ giving Tiffany an Airman of the Quarter Award filled the middle of the board. Another was the squadron volleyball team. Tiffany stood next to CJ in that one. The others were of CJ at various events. Some were clipped from the *Fitch Times,* the base newspaper. One of them had been a picture of CJ and me. He was in his mess dress looking very handsome. My shoulder still showed, a bit of my red sparkly strap. Tiffany had cut out the rest of me.

I moved over to the rickety bookshelf. On top were framed pictures from her ultrasounds. She'd painted the initials *CJ* and *TL* on the top of one of the frames. She'd glued cutout hearts on others that said, *Mrs. Tiffany Hooker* or *CJ plus TL equals love.* I made a little choking noise. Jessica hurried over to me.

"I'm okay. It's not like I didn't know." Seeing the proof had hurt me more than I had expected, but I didn't want to let on in front of Jessica. A round, bare spot stood out on the top of the dusty bookshelf. "Do you know what was there?" I asked.

Jessica shrugged. "She was always redecorating, changing things out from one season to the next."

"I guess it must be pink season then." I looked at the top of the bookshelf again. The photos had been rearranged, too, because clear spots in the dust showed where they used to be.

"A lot of people were in here after you found the bones and Tiffany didn't show up at work. Things got moved around," Jessica said.

I moved back over to the bulletin board. "What about those two pictures?"

"They're people from back home."

One was Tiffany in her uniform with a group of seven people around her. None of them looked happy—except for Tiffany. Her smile could have cut through fog. Perhaps because she knew she was leaving town? Another showed what looked to be a bunch of high-school kids in the back of a black pickup truck. They were all laughing and posing.

"Do you know the name of the town she came from?"

"Stahl, West Virginia. Tiffany said the only thing it had going for it was the coal mines. She wanted out bad."

"What do you know about her boyfriend?" I asked.

"High-school sweethearts. Some jock football player. His grades weren't good enough to get him to college, so he took a job in the mine. Tiffany said he was furious when she left. She didn't want to end up like her mom."

Maybe he was mad enough to kill her.

"Do you know his name? Is he in one of these pictures?"

"She didn't like to talk about home. She talked about guys here. Wouldn't give the enlisted guys the time of day, even though lots of them were interested. Talk about causing drama in the dorm. She liked officers. The higher ranking, the better."

Officers and the enlisted troops weren't supposed to date each other because of chain-of-command issues. The rules about fraternization were spelled out quite clearly in the Uniform Code for Military Justice. Not that it didn't happen, obviously, given my situation.

"Did he ever come here?"

"I don't know."

Footsteps sounded in the hall. We froze. Jessica mimed, *Should I turn off the light?* I shook my head no. Someone rattled the knob, which, fortunately, Jessica had locked when we came in. As the steps headed on down the hall, I let out a huge breath.

"Maybe we should leave," Jessica said.

While tempting, I figured this was my only chance to be in here. "You can go. You have a lot more at stake if we get caught in here. I'll hurry."

"Let me help," Jessica said.

I nodded. I flipped up the pink bed skirt to look under the bed. Plastic bins jammed full of decorations from Halloween to Valentine's Day, and any other holiday I could think of, filled the space. Jessica and I went through them as quickly as possible. I moved to her desk, quickly going through her drawers. Nothing interesting. I guess part of me had been hoping for a journal, something written, that would spell out where she was and that she was alive.

Her computer was gone. Probably Agent Bristow or the Ellington police had it. I did a quick study of her shelves: some schoolbooks, a few romance novels, and some snow globes. The closet had more plastic bins stacked in the bottom, like the ones under her bed. One stopped me. It was crammed full of baby blankets, bibs, and sleepers. A lone teddy bear tucked in a corner. Her clothes hung in a haphazard mix of uniforms, dresses, T-shirts, and jeans. One hot pink ball gown glowed in the sea of neutrals. Nothing here told me anything helpful.

"What do we do next?" Jessica asked.

"I don't know. Hope Tiffany turns up," I said.

"I'll stalk her Facebook page. See if I can find anything out from any of her friends back home," Jessica said.

"Don't worry about it. I was hoping we'd find a note saying, 'I'm at Disney World.' Something everyone else overlooked. It was stupid to come. Thanks," I said. "Let's go."

Jessica turned off the lights and opened the door a crack. We scooted out into the hall, closing the door behind us with a gentle click.

"Are you dating anyone?" I knew Jessica had broken up with someone a few months before.

She grinned. "I'm talking to a couple of guys."

"Anyone I know?" It was easy to meet guys in the security forces field as it still leaned heavily male.

"I don't think you'd know either of them. One of them is from Waltham. A civilian. The other I've been chatting with online."

"Be careful with the online guy."

"I know, I know. My mom gives me the same lecture. It's fine. I think we're going to meet for the first time this weekend. *In a public place.* I won't get in a car with him."

I smiled. We'd taken about two steps when James came bounding up the stairs.

"What are you two doing?" he asked.

We eyed each other. "We went for a walk," I said.

"In the snow? Without coats?"

Oh, crap, it was snowing out? "We were going to go for a walk, saw the snow, and came back for our coats," I said. "Then we realized how late it was. I'd better get going." I hugged Jessica. "Fun night. Let's do it again soon."

I saw James look from us to Tiffany's room, noting

our proximity. He didn't have any proof we'd been in there. "Night, James."

Cuddled under my fluffy blue-and-white comforter, I realized seeing the ultrasound pictures had hurt me more than I even wanted to admit to myself. The last few months had been a disaster. I'd gone from confident air force spouse to the shaky puddle lying here. I had a choice to make: wallow or fight back. I decided to fight back and started going over my options.

Whoever planted the clothes must have also placed CJ's ID with the bones. It sickened me to think I knew someone who was that conniving, that evil. Tomorrow morning I'd try to re-create the route I'd taken going to garage sales on Saturday. Maybe the drive would make me recognize something that would get us out of this mess.

I wondered if the gunshot phone calls played into any of this. After I moved to Ellington, they'd started at random times, on random days, no pattern to them at all. They came from different phone numbers or were blocked calls. Carol wanted me to tell someone. My choices were limited. Notifying the police meant telling CJ. I kept hesitating when it came to telling him. I needed to listen to that little voice.

I could tell Special Agent Bristow, but he wouldn't have jurisdiction over the calls. I wasn't a military dependent; it didn't happen on a military base. I had no proof a military person made the calls. For now, my only option was not to say anything. If it got worse, I'd figure out what to do.

The other thing I'd do was drop by the church to see MaryJo, one of the biggest gossips on base and secretary for the base's Protestant chaplain. She knew more about what was going on than anyone else I could think of. She might know what, if anything, Tiffany was up to. I'd probably feel like I'd been slimed by the time I was done. If that's what it took— I'd do it.

On Thursday morning, sunshine poured into my apartment. I had a plan for the day. I'd be the first to admit since I moved to Ellington, my life hadn't had a lot of purpose. I'd loved being a military spouse, all the volunteering, going to the monthly spouses' meetings, joining a variety of the clubs that were a subset of the spouses' organization. Clubs formed for almost every interest: mahjong, gourmet cooking, bowling, book groups, skiing or surfing, depending on location, lunch bunch, scrapbooking.

Over the years, I watched the club evolve from the Officers Wives Club to the Officers Spouses Clubs (so men could join) to the Spouses Club, which included enlisted spouses, too. When CJ and I were first married, I was a bit intimidated by some of the wives. Some wore their husband's rank—they felt important because of the position or rank of their husband.

I'd heard stories of a fed-up general bringing a female airman to an Officers Wives Club meeting. The general would point to the airman and say, "She has more rank than any of you." Supposedly, that got the snooty wives in line. I'd never seen it happen and suspected it was a military urban legend. Fortunately, the number of great women far outweighed the bad.

I posted ads for Carol's garage sale on Craigslist, the Wicked Local website, and a few other sites. I made flyers to hang near her house on Saturday morning. At eight in the morning, I headed over to Carol's. She had to work and I had the place to myself. I used the key she'd given me to let myself in.

The garage was chilly. Periodically I went inside the house to warm up. Carol had left a plate of brownies out for me. They disappeared at an alarming rate. I forced myself to go back out to the garage. By nine o'clock, I decided to come back when it was warmer.

I drove through Dunkin' Donuts for a large coffee. Then I headed to Concord to start driving my garage sale route. After meandering around Concord, Lincoln, and Lexington, I wondered what the heck I was hoping to accomplish. I recognized some of the places we'd stopped, but were any of them significant to the investigation? I drove through Bedford, even though it was wasting time and gas.

One of the bigger sales had been off Old Billerica Road. I headed over, winding around until I found it. An Ellington patrol car was parked in the drive. Great, just my luck. I slowed, searching for a sign with a family name on it displayed on the front of the house. I hoped for one of those "Winston Family Established, such and such a year" kind of signs. No luck.

The front door opened. An officer kissed his wife good-bye and pried a toddler off his leg. He turned toward me. Pellner stepped out. We made eye contact and his face went from happy to angry in an instant.

CHAPTER 10

I took off. Back at Old Billerica Road, I turned left, heading to Billerica, instead of right into Bedford and then Ellington. I expected flashing lights to show up in my rearview mirror any minute. None did. That worried me. I drove through Billerica. I intended to drop back into Ellington.

Instead, I drove back down Old Billerica Road and turned onto Pellner's street. I could see from a couple of blocks away that the cruiser was gone. I pulled into his driveway. After a couple of deep breaths, I worked up the courage to knock on the door. A pleasant-looking, smallish woman opened the door. The toddler now clung to her leg.

"Hi, I was at your garage sale on Saturday. I'm here about donating your leftovers." All of it true, if somewhat loose on specifics. If she described me or my car to her husband, he'd know me immediately.

"I thought someone was coming tomorrow."

Darn it. She'd called some other organization. I just about lost my nerve. If I took it, they'd arrived tomorrow and the stuff would be gone. "Sorry about the mix-up. I can come back then."

"It's all right. Everything is bagged and ready in the garage. I'll open it for you."

The garage was neat. The floor was free of oil stains. The walls were lined with rows of shelving. A big wooden Ellington police shield hung on the wall. Eight big plastic bags, just like the one I'd found the bloody shirts in, sat on the floor. Not that it surprised me. Stuff showed up at the base thrift shop in those very same bags all the time. Every grocery, hardware, and big-box store carried them.

A handwritten sign taped on one of them said, *For the VFW.* I almost did a happy dance. I could call the VFW to cancel the Pellners' pickup for tomorrow. Officer Pellner wouldn't ever know I'd been by. After I went through the bags, I'd take the stuff over to the VFW. That is, if I didn't find anything important.

I loaded the bags into the back of the Suburban while Mrs. Pellner watched.

"Thanks. The VFW appreciates your support," I said. It wasn't really a lie. The VFW would appreciate the stuff when they got it. I opened the car door.

"Wait. Don't I get a receipt for our taxes?"

Rats. "Hang on," I said as cheerfully as I could. I made a show of digging around in the console. "This is embarrassing. I left them back at the VFW. I'll mail one out to you as soon as I get back." I hopped in the car, waving as I pulled out of her drive.

Thirty minutes later, I knew the Pellner kids dressed well. Some of the clothes had designer labels. All the donated clothes were clean and gently used. The Pellners also donated a half-dozen old Coach purses. I'd found some carefully wrapped Waterford crystal in with the clothes. I was puzzled. If this stuff had been out on Saturday, it would have been snatched up by someone.

After I dropped all this off, I might have to swing back by the VFW thrift shop to buy the red Coach purse. I sorted through a bunch of paperbacks. I'm guessing the thrillers were his, the Regency romances hers, but who knew? Maybe Pellner had a side I didn't know about. I grinned.

After calling the VFW to cancel the Pellners' pickup—I hoped impersonating a police officer's wife wasn't a crime—I took all of their stuff to the VFW drop boxes.

I pulled up in front of the base chapel, a white clapboard church with a tall spire topped by a cross. It wasn't as large or as old as the one on the Ellington town common, but it was typical of New England architecture. The chapel held services for many different faiths: Protestant, Catholic, Jewish, and Islam. MaryJo Speck sat behind her desk when I walked in.

"Sarah! How. Are. You?" Each word dripped with concern, and a slight Southern accent, even though I hadn't heard a word from her since I'd moved off base. She came around the desk, holding out her hands for me to clasp. She wore a lavender twinset, with a gray skirt and sensible-looking black shoes. "Come. In."

"Is Chaplain Black here?" I asked, knowing he wouldn't be. He did hospital rounds on Thursday afternoons. I managed to wrangle my hands away from hers.

"Sarah! He's out this afternoon. Can *I* help you with something?"

MaryJo had worked at the church for years. I'm

fairly certain each chaplain she'd worked for had prayed she'd restrain her loose lips. Each knew trying to do much about it would result in their ship sailing while MaryJo's would remain anchored in port. She lived in Lincoln, a town south of the base, in a gorgeous Colonial with her husband, a retired general. MaryJo was still active in the spouses' club and was generally kowtowed to by the members.

"Maybe, MaryJo. I'm feeling a little overwhelmed with everything. I thought some counseling would be good for me. Perhaps I could make an appointment?"

"Of course. Let me make you some tea. We can have a little chat. It wouldn't be Christian to send you out when you are feeling poorly."

I looked down to hide a smile.

"I'll lock the door. That way no one can interrupt us. Let's go into the chaplain's office. The chairs are much more comfortable."

A few minutes later, I settled into one of the two large, comfy leather chairs across from Chaplain Black's desk. I dropped my purse on the floor, close to the desk. MaryJo bustled in with a tray holding a teapot, cups, and a plate of tiny cupcakes topped with chocolate crosses. She set the tray down on the desk. Instead of sitting next to me, she surprised me by going around to sit in the chaplain's chair. I resisted the urge to comment as she poured us tea. After handing me a cup, she leaned forward, resting her clasped hands on the desk.

"How can I help?"

I had to be careful. MaryJo wasn't stupid; and while she loved gathering information, she could be choosy about sharing.

"It's about Tiffany." I stopped and took a drink of

tea. It tasted delicious. My hand shook a bit as I set it down. "Someone told me Tiffany was searching for a husband from the colonels on base. I'd feel terrible if anyone else was going through the same thing I am." I burst into tears, to my surprise and embarrassment. Not fake, planned tears to gain her sympathy and loosen her lips, but real tears accompanied by a choked-back sob. I would feel bad if someone else was going through this. I just wished I'd refrained from crying in front of MaryJo, of all people.

MaryJo handed me a tissue.

"Well, plenty of military men have succumbed and ended up with a trophy wife. I'm blessed to have kept my Bill grateful to be married to me every day for the past thirty-five years. If more women cooked a decent meal for their men, the divorce rate would plunge."

I dried my tears with the tissue. Had she heard about my lack of cooking skills and the fact Tiffany had been to culinary school? She droned on about the topic. I had to figure out a way to get her back on track.

I interrupted. "You are just an inspiration, MaryJo. You should give a talk on the subject to the Spouses Club." (Forgive me, program chairman and attendees, if she got a burr under her skin to do that.) "If others are having difficulty, you could save them." If this didn't get her back on the topic I wanted her to be on, I'd fake a phone call and scram.

"That is a brilliant idea. I could do a sermon on it, too, while Chaplain Black goes off on his summer vacation. Your compassion for others speaks volumes." She paused, a dreamy look on her face while she probably pictured herself speaking to the masses. Then she gathered herself and directed her attention back to me.

"Between you and me, I know Colonel Brown and his wife are having some troubles."

I guess my suggested speaking topic passed muster. She now rewarded me with information in exchange. This information didn't hearten me. "Not Deena and Ted. I know he's been deployed a lot. It can take a toll."

MaryJo leaned forward in her chair. "They've been in here with the pastor about six times. He recommended a marriage counselor."

"Anyone else?"

MaryJo leaned back. I realized I'd asked too much. I drained my tea. "Thanks, MaryJo. For the tea and listening."

"Sometimes a good cry is just what the doctor ordered."

Or a good lead. MaryJo walked me to the door. "Stop by anytime."

I walked partway down the hall before realizing I'd left my purse in my rush to leave the office. I heard MaryJo's voice as I got back to the office.

"You'll never guess who was just here—" She cut off abruptly when I entered. She reddened as she spoke into the phone. "I have to go."

"Don't hang up on my account. I forgot my purse in the chaplain's office. I'll be out of here in a minute." After grabbing my purse, I waved and left. I wasn't sure if learning the Browns were having marital problems was worth it, knowing before day's end, most of the base would know I'd cried. I hoped that bit of news didn't get back to CJ.

I headed over to the Browns' house. Deena didn't work outside the home, and her kids should still be in school. I might be able to catch her. I hadn't seen her since the day the packers were at our house when I was moving off base. She'd stopped by to see if she could help with anything.

Deena occasionally volunteered at the thrift shop. My excuse for stopping was to see if she'd like to volunteer again. We needed the help. I knocked on her door. No one answered. I walked over to where some of her neighbors sat outside, watching their kids play.

"She's in Boston with friends," one of them said.

I would have to track her down later.

I left base through the Offutt gate, which dumped me out on Hartwell. Took a left on Great Road and headed straight to Bedford Farms Ice Cream. *Ice-cream stands.* I added them to the list of things I loved about living here—all these small operations that made the most amazing ice creams on site. Bedford Farms had even been mentioned in *O* magazine once. While New Englanders had a reputation for being reserved, they could be very vehement about their favorite ice-cream stand. I ordered a kiddie-sized cup of Almond Joy ice cream. The kiddie size was bigger than a softball. The large was about the size of a toddler's head. I sat in my car and ate.

I wished Carol were off work. She might have heard something about the Browns. If I remembered right, Brad and Ted golfed together sometimes. Just because the Browns were getting counseling, it didn't mean Ted had had an affair. Like I told MaryJo, deployments took a toll. Women whose husbands had been in Vietnam or Desert Storm would always say how lucky women today were because they could keep in touch over the Internet. It didn't lessen the loneliness or worry. Sometimes it was even worse, then, when you didn't hear from a loved one. Some women said their husbands called so often, they didn't have anything to tell them, which made them feel even guiltier.

After I finished my ice cream, I went back to work in Carol's garage. I had the place to myself again. Carol must have been home at some point during the day because I found a new pile of stuff to price for the garage sale. It included games, puzzles, and stuffed animals, which hadn't been there earlier. The kids must have decided to get rid of some things.

When Carol brought the kids home, I got them all involved in pricing. It took some work convincing them that their beloved objects weren't worth a hundred dollars apiece. When we talked about how much they could make with a reasonable price, they all disappeared, returning with more stuff from their rooms. When Brad got home, he volunteered to take the kids out to dinner. Carol opened a bottle of wine, brought out sandwiches and a bag of chips, and we went back to work in the garage.

We talked and laughed as we priced. We even danced a little when Carol cranked up some tunes. At some point, Brad and the kids returned home. Brad stuck his head into the garage, saying he'd get the kids to bed.

"Are you sure you don't want to help us?" I asked him.

"I'm good," he said, heading back into the house.

When we were finally exhausted, we went to Carol's family room, dropping into comfy chairs.

"I'll come back tomorrow to finish setting up."

Carol got another glass of wine. "Want one? You only had one glass." She held up the bottle. "You can spend the night here. It'd be fun."

"No thanks. I'd rather sleep in my own bed. I'll just get some water." When I returned with my water, I sat back down and looked around the cozy, messy room. "You're lucky to have Brad, a man who supports you. Adores you. I thought CJ and I had the same thing until Tiffany." Carol and Brad had such a wonderful relationship. Brad teased Carol to no end, but he was always kissing on her.

Carol took a sip of wine. "I am lucky—not that we haven't had some rough spots."

"It never shows."

"After the twins were born, we PCSed right away. Then he was deployed. I wasn't sure we'd make it through all that."

That had been eight years ago. "I remember. You barely had time to talk on the phone."

"Since working through all that, things have been great. Not that we haven't had our share of day-to-day annoyances. We've learned to talk issues out. I hope things will be great for you again soon." Carol gave me a look I couldn't quite interpret. "Why are you running around trying to figure out what happened to Tiffany? Do you still care about CJ?"

Telling Carol about the bloody shirts might make me feel better. We'd known each other almost as long as I'd known CJ. We met one night when we were all at a British pub near the pier in Monterey. I'd been drinking root beer at the time because I was still underage. We'd clicked. Once we both ended up here, we picked up right where we left off. "I owe him."

"You owe him?" Carol looked like she was going to come out of her chair. "After what he did to you?" Carol asked. "I realize you can't just turn feelings off in a

minute. I can't understand why you or anyone would think you owe something to a cheating husband."

"Trust me on this one."

Carol gave me a long, hard look before nodding.

It was after ten when I left. I slipped my coat on. The neighborhood was fine during the day, but I preferred buildings and people as neighbors instead of coyotes, wild turkeys, and deer. The dark night made me shiver.

I turned left off the cul-de-sac onto a narrow, winding road that led to Great Road. The road was lined with towering trees, making a dark night, darker. Low stone walls divided one property from the next. A car flew up behind me, sitting on my tail. It passed on a curve, taking part of my lane. I wrenched the wheel as the passenger side of my car came within an inch of a giant oak. Its bark was scraped bare in one spot from other cars brushing too close. Idiot. The other car's brake lights flashed on. He stopped. I slammed on my brakes. I stopped inches from its bumper, squeezing my steering wheel, thankful I'd managed to stop.

The car sat. Its brake lights remained on. I shifted into reverse. I looked over my shoulder and started to back up. I was undecided if I should try to go around them or head back to Carol's house. Behind me through the trees, I could see red and blue flashing lights toward me. Those lights ought to get the car in front of me moving. I faced forward to put my car back in drive. The car in front of me was gone. I pulled beyond the tree, steering my car as close as I could to a stone wall to get out of the emergency vehicle's way.

The police car didn't go around me; it tucked in behind. What now?

I wasn't surprised when Pellner showed up by my car window, ticket pad in hand. I rolled the window down. I hoped he hadn't figured out I went back to his house this morning. Hopefully, he only knew that I'd been out front.

"I'm sorry, did I do something wrong?"

He snorted. "That's something coming from your mouth. Asking so sweetly if you did something wrong."

"I don't think I was speeding. Maybe your radar picked up the car in front of me."

He frowned. "What car? Do you have a description?"

"No. A car flew up behind me. It passed and jammed on its brakes. I almost hit it."

"How many people were in it?"

"I didn't notice. I was concentrating on *not* hitting it."

Pellner frowned again.

"It was right there." I gestured toward the road in front of me.

He started writing on his ticket pad.

"What's the ticket for?"

"Obscured license plate. I can't read the numbers."

"I think you're wrong. I washed it last week."

"I'll double-check."

"I'll come with you."

He pointed at me. "Stay there."

He went to the back of the car. I watched him in my rearview mirror. He bent over out of sight for a couple of minutes. When he came back to the window, he had a handkerchief and was wiping mud off his hands. He finished writing out the ticket. I reached for it. Pellner grabbed the front of my coat, dragging my upper body through the window. Our faces were almost touching. His coffee breath brushed my cheek. I was inches from his dimple. Yep, still menacing.

"Don't ever go near my family again." Then he stopped and sniffed. "Have you been drinking?"

"I had one glass of wine over a long evening. I'm not drunk."

"I'll write you up for refusing to take a Breathalyzer test."

"I'm not refusing."

Before I could say anything else, he had me out of the car, cuffed, and in the back of his. I sat alone in the back while Pellner leaned against the hood, talking into the mike on his shoulder. I couldn't hear what he said, and maybe I didn't want to.

After a tow truck showed up to impound my car, Pellner took the long way to the station. He'd fly up to a stop sign, slam on the brakes, scan the road, and tear off again. With my hands cuffed behind my back, keeping my balance was impossible on the slippery plastic seat. I bobbed around like a bottle tossed into high seas.

"Pellner, you can stop with the gunshot phone calls. It's not scaring me," I said. "If you don't, I will tell CJ."

Pellner slammed on the brakes again before turning around to look at me. We stared at each other.

"Either you are drunker than I thought or crazy. I have better things to do than call you." He shook his head. "Don't threaten me with your little 'I'll tell.' I've got plenty to tell the chief when it comes to you."

He looked surprised, not guilty. Somehow I believed

him when he said he wasn't making the calls. One suspect down; a gazillion to go. He took off with a jerk. I fell over on my side and stayed down. With the game over, Pellner finally took me to the station.

He dragged me up the stairs—the front stairs. Fortunately, at this time of night, very few people were around to see my perp walk. As he pulled me through the lobby, CJ came out of a door. He was smiling and dressed in his civvies, wearing the brown leather bomber jacket I'd always thought he looked sexy in.

He stopped when he spotted us.

"What's going on?" he asked, glancing at his watch.

Pellner listed my sins: obscured license plate, alcohol on my breath, and my refusal to take a Breathalyzer test. "Chief, I'm sorry. I know she's your wife. Ex-wife. I didn't feel like I should treat her any different than anyone else."

"You did the right thing, Scott." When CJ turned to me, Pellner mouthed the word "Lowell."

My face warmed.

"Sarah, what were you thinking, drinking and driving? Your face is flushed like it gets when you drink."

"I'm not drunk. It's a misunderstanding. I'll take the test." I said it all with my teeth almost grinding. I sounded like one of those very preppy New Englanders who barely opened their mouths to speak. I was furious with Pellner, CJ, and myself. I shouldn't have put myself in this situation, either, by going to Pellner's house this morning or having wine and then driving. Pellner shouldn't have lied, and CJ . . . CJ should have seen through Pellner or trusted me. Although, I guess I should be grateful CJ was here or I probably would have been in a cell for the night.

"I had her vehicle towed here, instead of to the impound lot," Pellner said.

CJ glanced at his watch again. He'd been checking it every few seconds.

"Thanks, Scott. That was really nice of you." CJ looked at me like I should be thanking Pellner, too. That wasn't about to happen. CJ waited while I blew into the Breathalyzer and passed the test.

"Chief, go on and get out of here. I know Lexi is waiting for you," Pellner said. "I'll wrap this up and have her out of here in no time."

CJ looked relieved. He opened his mouth to say something to me. I held up a hand. "Not now." I didn't want to cry in front of him. I didn't want him to know that his having a date hurt me. A date named "Lexi," at that. It sounded like a stripper name.

As he hurried off, Pellner smiled at me. "I set him up with Lexi a couple of weeks ago. He seemed lonely. Needed someone sweet and uncomplicated in his life. They've been spending a lot of time together."

I ignored him. He left. I had to pay for the tow before I could get my car back. The paperwork took a lot longer than it should have. The officer doing it made a lot of trips to the bathroom, took an unusual number of calls, and had other paperwork that was a priority. I sat calmly, knowing any other reaction would just make him happy.

After paying, I headed to my car, hoping I had something in the back of the Suburban to clean the license plate. I didn't want to get another ticket on the way home, but it was clean. CJ must have cleaned it, even though he had a date waiting for him. I didn't know what to think of that.

After the short drive home, I pulled up in front of my apartment. Pellner burst out the front door of my building. He glanced my way as he ran to his car. I'm not sure he even noticed me. He jumped in his squad car. The tires spun before catching and squealed as he raced down the street.

CHAPTER 11

It could have been worse. That's what I told myself as I walked through my apartment. Yes, it was a mess, but nothing was broken or destroyed. Pellner had walked a thin line. Cushions tossed, clothes dumped, shampoo and conditioner splattered around the bathroom, and the kitchen looked like the worst cafeteria food fight in history.

A knock on the door had me yanking it open and almost off the hinges.

Stella looked surprised. "I heard a lot of stomping around. I thought I saw Scott outside. Are you okay?"

She looked over my shoulder at the mess. "Pellner or redecorating?"

"Pellner," I said. "He had his reasons."

"I'll help you clean up."

"I'll get some wine," I said.

Stella didn't ask me what his reasons were, but she volunteered to take the bathroom while I worked on the bedroom. She was an efficient cleaner. We cleaned the kitchen together. Stella hummed 'N Sync's song "Bye Bye Bye."

When we were done, Stella looked at me. "Scott's getting out of hand. You need to report him."

"If something else happens, I will. It's complicated. CJ totally bought Pellner's story at the station. I'm not sure reporting Pellner would do any good. CJ's really loyal to his guys."

Stella headed to the door. "I could talk to my aunt."

"The town manager? No thanks."

"Good Lord, not the town manager. She wouldn't do a thing. She's too worried about her political career to take sides on anything. My aunt who's a cage fighter—she could straighten Scott out."

"A cage fighter?" I asked.

"You know, mixed martial arts. Two women going at it in a cage."

My family didn't have any cage-fighting aunts. It did have a lot of catfighting. I studied Stella's face, looking for any signs she was joking. Her dark eyes looked sincere and her lips weren't turning up. "Thanks, but no."

"She could teach you some moves."

"That, I'll think about." I closed the door, wondering about Stella. Opera-singing music teacher who'd had trouble with the police and an aunt who is a cage fighter.

On Friday morning, I headed to base to track down Deena Brown. She was an exercise fanatic. She'd drop her kids off at school and walk over to the gym. I wanted to catch her on her way there. Laura and I had planned what we called a "Friday Fun Day" at the thrift shop. It was an attempt to make cleaning the back room sound appealing. Laura had probably already sponsored me on base. I'd just show up early, hoping one of our kids was working the desk and would let me on.

I waylaid Deena at the park, just north of the elementary school and across from the gym. Her jet-black hair contrasted with teeth that would make Mr. Clean's T-shirt look beige.

"Sarah, what are you doing here? I heard you stopped by my house yesterday."

I decided I'd be honest with her, instead of trying to pry information out of her in a backhanded way. "I saw MaryJo yesterday."

"I heard. How are you doing?"

"Okay, other than really wishing I wouldn't have cried in front of her."

"Is that why you wanted to talk? Is MaryJo blabbing about me and Ted?"

"It is. She is."

"Let's go sit over there, then." We walked to a bench Deena had pointed to, a little off the beaten path.

"I'm sorry to hear you guys are having problems," I said. "If anyone can understand marital problems, it's me."

"I know." She played with the zipper on her hoodie. "I don't want to end up like you. Alone. It's why we're going to counseling."

That stung, but I pushed the feeling aside. I stared at my hands. This wasn't going to be easy. Maybe I should just go. Then I thought about CJ and it wasn't only about him. It could come out that I had the bloody shirts first. The story of how I found them sounded unbelievable, even to me.

"Just ask me whatever it is you tracked me down to ask. At least I can give you the straight version instead of MaryJo's."

I looked up into Deena's brown eyes. "Did Ted have an affair with Tiffany Lopez?"

Deena stood up, shaking her head. "Just because CJ did doesn't mean everyone did."

I stood, too. "I just heard that Tiffany was going after colonels. I'm sorry. I'll butt out. I didn't mention any of this to MaryJo. I told her it was probably all the deployments. They can wear on families."

Deena glanced off toward the gym. "It was me. I had an affair. It happened during Ted's last deployment. Hate me if you want."

I'm sure my mouth dropped open. I quickly closed it and pasted on what I hoped was a neutral expression.

"It was one of the gate guards," Deena said.

Visions of some of the gate guards slipped through my head like a movie on fast forward. A lot of the gate guards were civilian DOD employees. With deployment rotations at an alarming rate, there weren't enough troops to cover all the gates. Rent-a-cops weren't always in the best shape. I could outrun some of them, but their guns were a great equalizer.

One or two of them were cute, especially the one with his "How you doin'" and his dark, sparkly eyes. Another one looked like Brad Pitt and had a cute Boston accent. Some women called each other when one of those two were at the gate. They would drive off and back on, just for an opportunity to chat with them. Now it was my turn to shake my head. "I'm way beyond judging anyone. I hope you two can work things out. Alone isn't fun."

I headed over to the thrift shop to get a jump start on the Friday Fun Day. Carol and I had organized almost everything for her sale. I could stop over at her house later. Sitting at home held no appeal. It was probably time to think more seriously about getting a job.

I parked at the side of the building. Bits of police tape fluttered from the Dumpster. I hurried past, unlocking the door, darting into the storage room. The narrow room was bursting at the seams. Boxes, bags, and loose items covered the floor. Piles of clothes were mounded on top. Like in Carol's garage, only a tiny pathway was clear from the back door to the hall. Rods lining the walls sagged from the weight of clothes ready to be priced. As I hefted a bag of clothes, I tripped over something. The sound of metal clattering against concrete made me set the bag down to see what I'd done. I'd upended a golf bag. Golf clubs and scorecards sprawled across the floor.

I bit back some curse words and started gathering the clubs. Bits of violet-colored paper mingled with the scorecards. They were notes, heavily perfumed with a violet scent. The one I held had nothing to do with golf and everything to do with Tiffany.

CHAPTER 12

I read a few. Some of the notes were mushy; some were *Fifty Shades of Grey;* all were signed, *Love, Tiffany.* I checked the golf bag. A luggage-like tag attached to the side was marked, *Property of Ted Brown.* Deena's husband. Jessica had said Tiffany wanted to bag a colonel. Maybe, despite what Deena had just told me, CJ wasn't the only one Tiffany had gone after.

I stuffed the notes in my pocket and put the clubs back in the bag. How could Ted let Deena think she was the only one having an affair? If I took the notes to Deena, at least she'd know she wasn't the only cause of their marital problems. I locked the thrift shop, got back in the Suburban, and headed toward Deena's.

Before I took the turn onto Edwards Road into the housing area, I realized I'd rather talk to Ted than Deena. I headed over to his office. Thankfully, Colonel Brown didn't work for one of the green-door programs. They were special-access programs that were top secret. The people who worked them were shut in vaults all day. They weren't allowed to take their cell phones in because the phones could be turned on and used as listening devices.

Colonel Brown was in charge of an SPO—systems program office. He had enough rank and position to have an office instead of one of the many cubicles I'd passed to get here. This wasn't the kind of conversation I wanted anyone to overhear. I checked with his secretary to make sure he was in before I walked into his office. It was large, with an impressive desk and a conference table that seated at least twelve. He had a vanity wall filled with awards, framed certificates, and photos of him posing with generals and troops. I shut the door behind me.

"Sarah, very sorry to hear about you and CJ." I hadn't seen Ted since the divorce. He stood up, tall and lanky, with high cheekbones that were typical, to me, of the upper echelons of the military. "I'm surprised to see you. What can I do for you?"

"Explain these." I tossed the notes on his desk. They fluttered down like purple butterflies. I'd been hoping for a more dramatic result, something with a bit of noise.

He looked from the pile of notes to my face, blushing a little before holding up one of the notes. "And this is?"

"Don't act like you don't know." I slapped my hands onto his desk. "How could you let your wife think she's the only guilty party in your marital problems?"

He sat back down. "I have no idea what you're talking about."

"Read a couple of those notes and then you will."

He started reading. His face flushed, paled, and flushed again before he looked up at me. "I swear, Sarah. I've never seen these before. Does Deena know?"

"No, because I wanted to talk to you before breaking her heart."

"I don't even know Tiffany. The only reason I recognize her name is because of you and CJ."

"You had plenty of opportunities to know her. Our house, the gym, base functions. Apparently, she gets around. Likes colonels."

"Where did you find these?"

"In your golf clubs—the ones you donated to the thrift shop."

Ted's expression smoothed out. "The clubs I loaned CJ? The ones I told him not to bring back? To take to the thrift shop when he was done with them?"

He might as well have slammed my heart with a sledgehammer. "CJ has his own clubs. Why would he need yours?"

"Because some friend came into town last fall and they wanted to play. CJ knew I'd just gotten new clubs and asked if his friend could use my old set."

"It's easier to blame CJ than fess up." Some part of me remembered CJ telling me something about borrowing clubs when a friend had come through town. Maybe he'd taken them back to Ted. It would be easy for Ted to lie to me.

"Get out. I don't know what kind of sick game you're playing. I'm sorry about you and CJ, but that doesn't mean my marriage isn't back on solid ground." Ted grabbed his wastebasket and swept the notes into it. "Keep Deena and me out of it. Don't even think of mentioning this to Deena. She'll believe me. You'll be the laughingstock of the base. Again." Ted got up, went around his desk, and shoved me out the door, closing it firmly behind me.

"Everything okay?" his wide-eyed secretary asked.

I ran a hand over my hair. "Fine. He had an important call he had to take." His secretary and I both eyed the phone on her desk. None of the buttons glowed.

"Someone called his cell," I said.

His secretary nodded. I made my way out of the building. I wasn't sure how I expected Ted to react. I hadn't even thought through that part when I'd shown up. Now I didn't even have the notes.

I drove straight to Bedford Farms Ice Cream. This time I ordered the Green Monster, named for the famed wall at Fenway Park, home of the Red Sox. Mint ice cream with Oreos and fudge swirl. I sat in my car. Anger flared in me as I dug in. I kept thinking that I'd be okay, that I could handle the horror of finding the bones—that even if it wasn't Tiffany, it was somebody.

Then there was CJ's betrayal, his new girlfriend, Lexi. How old was she? Twenty would be my guess. I didn't know anyone my age named Lexi. I dreaded seeing them together. It was inevitable in a small town like Ellington. I savored a large bite of ice cream, letting it melt on my tongue. As the crow flies, CJ and I probably only lived a mile apart. The twisty roads between our two homes gave me the comforting illusion that he lived much farther away.

CJ had borrowed Ted's golf clubs last October. It meant things were going on either between Tiffany and CJ—or Tiffany and Ted—for longer than I'd realized.

The notes didn't specifically refer to Ted. They didn't mention CJ, either. Maybe they hadn't been written to Ted. I hadn't said anything to Deena. On the other hand, I couldn't imagine CJ leaving something like that in Ted's golf bag.

I scooped in some more ice cream. Why was I so eager to shift blame away from CJ? Tiffany's pregnancy was proof enough that he was to blame. Where did that leave me? With another big, fat question mark.

I listed the litany of wrongs I'd endured the past few months as I shoveled in my ice cream. I started with Tiffany and CJ, my life being turned upside down, the persecution by the police, CJ's girlfriend, and finally humiliating myself in front of MaryJo. Ugh, and Ted. The last two I'd brought on myself, but the rest I couldn't control.

I scraped around the cardboard cup to get the last bits of my ice cream. My flare of anger and self-pity had vanished as if the ice cream had cooled not only my mouth, but my soul, too. I stared into the cup, feeling as empty as it was. I jumped out of the car. I dumped the cup in the trash, tossed my hair, and set my shoulders. Time to rebuild my life.

On the way to Carol's house, I posted flyers around town and in her neighborhood. I arrived at Carol's house later than I had planned, but I still had plenty of time to finish setting up. As I dragged things from place to place, I spotted Brad's clubs in a corner of the garage near the lawn mower. Thoughts of the notes I'd found in Ted's golf bag kept me company as I moved around the garage. Brad's clubs stayed in my peripheral vision. *Leave well enough alone,* I told myself.

Do not go through Brad's bag. It's a breach of friend-ship and trust. Two seconds later, I searched his bag. No notes.

Leaving Carol's, I headed back home. At my place, after taking a deep breath, I called CJ. "Can you . . . Would you come over for dinner tonight?" If he said he had a date with Lexi, I was going to crawl into a hole and die. I waited. "CJ?"

"Sure. What's the occasion?" He sounded hesitant.

The occasion was questioning him about the notes in the golf clubs. Questioning him in person sounded like a great idea a moment ago. Now, two seconds later, it seemed like one of the stupidest things I'd ever done. I'd thought I could tell if he was lying to me better if we were face-to-face. However, he'd lied about Tiffany. I'd completely missed that. *Too late now.*

"I just wanted to talk over some things with you. Does seven work?"

By seven o'clock, I flitted around the apartment, moving a pillow, straightening a picture frame. Doing anything I could to keep busy while I waited for CJ. When the anticipated knock on the door came, I opened it reluctantly. CJ's hair was damp. He wore jeans with my favorite blue button-down shirt of his. It was open at the throat, cuffs rolled up. CJ brought his hand out from behind his back, thrusting a bouquet of pink tulips into my arms. He wasn't even in the door when I realized the evening had gone terribly wrong.

"CJ, I didn't . . . I meant . . . Come in." He followed me into the kitchen. I found a vase under the sink, trimmed the stems of the flowers, and arranged them as best I could with my hands shaking. I popped open a bottle of Charles Shaw—"two-buck Chuck"—from Trader Joe's. After pouring the Cabernet Sauvignon and handing CJ a glass, I took a big drink. "I didn't really cook anything. You know me."

Oh, I wished I hadn't said that, because CJ was nodding. Yes, he did know me, probably as well or better than anyone.

From the refrigerator, I pulled the chicken salad I'd thrown together. I'd made it with a rotisserie chicken from Stop & Shop, seedless grapes, walnuts, thyme, and a little mayo. I served it over a bed of lettuce. I set some sautéed asparagus with a squeeze of lime on the table. A nice crusty French bread with butter rounded out the meal.

We sat opposite each other at my small kitchen table. Our knees almost touched. I scooted my chair back until it bumped up against a cupboard. Conversations stopped and started as if this was the world's most awkward blind date. I tried to work up the courage to bring up the notes after realizing CJ clearly hoped this evening was about us.

He reached across the kitchen table, taking my hand. "You're nervous." He smiled.

Oh no! He probably thought I was nervous because I wanted to be with him and didn't know how to say it. I pulled my hand back, jumping up to clear the table. "Go sit in the living room. I'll be out in a minute."

"Let me help."

"No." It came out harsher than I had meant. There wasn't enough air left in this kitchen for us to be in it together another minute. CJ gave me a puzzled look before heading into the living room. I quickly cleaned up. Time to get this over with. I poured myself a glass of wine. CJ sat on the couch. I took my grandma's rocker.

"Just spit it out," CJ said, but he smiled. He had no idea what was about to hit him.

"I worked at the thrift shop today." I filled him in on knocking over the golf clubs, finding the notes. I told him I talked to Ted. "Is what Ted told me true? You had his golf clubs? The notes were for you?"

Watching CJ as I'd talked had been painful. His face had changed from smiling, to grim, to his blank cop face, which I'd always hated.

"Where are the notes? I'd like to read them."

"Ted tossed them in his trash."

"This is why you had me over for dinner? When you called, I thought . . ." CJ cleared his throat. "We couldn't have done this over the phone?" He studied his hands, now clasped in his lap. "You thought you could read me. That's why I'm here." He looked back up at me. "You figured you could tell if I was lying if you watched my face. You didn't figure out Tiffany, though, did you?"

I sat there. CJ was so rarely mean I was stunned. Maybe I didn't know this man at all. I held the smooth, curved arms of the oak rocker.

CJ stood and walked to the door. "I did borrow Ted's clubs. It was when one of my school buddies came through town on business. It was kind of last-minute and you had some spouse function to attend." CJ's voice was even, as if he was reading a report out loud.

"What did you do with the clubs after he left? Tiffany wrote those notes to someone."

CJ yanked the door open, startling Tyler, who was coming up the stairs. "I either left them in our garage or at the office for a few days. I don't really remember. Then I dropped them over at the thrift shop."

I walked over to the door as CJ started down the stairs. He paused. "I never saw Tiffany's notes." He turned and hurried out.

Tyler stopped at his door. "Everything okay?"

"Just peachy." I started to go back in. I had no reason to be rude to Tyler. "Sorry, Tyler. It's been a rough night."

I leaned back against my closed door and fisted my hands. I wanted to throw something across the room. In middle school, I had a friend who regularly tossed stuff around. Makeup out the window, shoes across the room, books onto the floor—whatever was handy. I'd tried it once, tossing my favorite eye shadow down on the counter. It shattered. I ended up being mad at myself for breaking my favorite eye shadow. I'd never thrown anything again. At least I was a fast learner.

I went to the bathroom, where I brushed my teeth and washed my face, both more vigorously than normal. To whom had the notes been written? I should have read the notes more closely or copied them before I'd rushed over to Ted's office. Maybe they contained some hint in them that would have clued me in.

I flipped off the bathroom light and went to bed. I should have known better than to put us through a horrible evening. I thought I was clever. I'd gotten CJ's hopes up and then brutally dashed them. I plucked at the comforter. Why was I beating myself up? I needed a good swift kick. After what CJ had done to me, he didn't deserve my empathy or guilt.

If CJ never saw the notes and really didn't know anything about them, Ted must have been lying. He could have forgotten the notes were in the bag when he loaned them to CJ. Or maybe he planned this so CJ would be found with them. But why? If Tiffany had written the notes to Ted, I'd given him a valuable piece of evidence that he'd thrown away.

The morning of the garage sale, I got up extra early. Bedford had a big Patriots' Day event this morning. Roads in Bedford would either be closed or crowded. The closures would have a ripple effect into Ellington. Patriots' Day events commemorated the days leading up to, and the first day of, the Revolutionary War on April 19, 1775. Bedford held a parade and pole capping every year. Pole capping had been started by colonials in Boston to show their defiance of British rule. Someone would climb to the top of a pole and place a red cap on top. The practice dated back to Roman times.

In the 1770s, the people of the town of Bedford had joined Bostonians by raising their own liberty poles to protest their dissatisfaction with the British government. To commemorate that event, a number of minutemen brigades from throughout New England would meet this morning on Bedford's town common. They'd march with fifes and drums to Wilson Park, playing "Yankee Doodle" and other colonial songs. Four of the men would carry a twenty-five-foot wooden pole to Wilson Park. At the park, after the pole was raised, someone would shinny up it, placing the red cap at the top. Then that person would proclaim "freedom" to the cheering crowd. Bedford's reenactment of that event drew a huge crowd.

As I left the house, Ellington's minuteman troop gathered on the common. They called out to each other and drank steaming cups of coffee as they prepared to head over to Bedford. A drummer tapped a lively marching beat on his drum. The light cast by the rising sun made the whole scene look like a post-card. Attending the Patriots' Day events didn't get old. I cheered myself by thinking about the events next weekend. Some of my favorites were the Paul Revere Capture Ceremony on Battle Road in Lincoln, the Bloody Angle Battle Demonstration, and the Lexington Battle Reenactment. At least I'd be able to attend some of those.

I wended my way to Carol's house. The sun slanted through the oak and maple trees, a perfect day for a garage sale. Planning Carol's sale had offered me a much-needed distraction. Most of the time, sales were a lot of fun. I sang "Oh, What A Beautiful Mornin'" from *Oklahoma!* as I drove. It helped me shake off last night's drama with CJ.

I didn't expect a lot of early birds, people who showed up before the stated starting time, because Carol didn't have any antiques. Listing antiques in a posting brought out all kinds of people, from dealers to collectors, who thought they deserved a preview. It must work for them often enough, because they always tried.

The weather warmed up nicely. Carol handed me a piece of homemade apple coffee cake when I arrived. We dragged some of the tables outside onto the drive-way. I organized like items: kitchen things, knick-knacks, books, and DVDs, clothes separated by kids and adult. Brad helped while the kids ran around put-ting more things out. Some of the stuff stayed in the garage—the sale looked organized and interesting.

That wouldn't last long as people picked things up, carried them around, and then set them back down.

Carol took the money while I did most of the negotiating. Like many people, Carol didn't like haggling. I'd priced everything with bargaining in mind. People wanted to think they were getting a deal. Some people wanted to think they were pulling a fast one on you.

One lady argued over the price of a one-dollar shirt. I told her she could have it for fifty cents. Then she whipped out a hundred-dollar bill. I'd run into people like her before, so Carol was prepared. The woman was none too happy when Carol handed her ninety-nine singles and two quarters. I had a feeling she'd whipped that out more than once and gotten whatever it was she wanted for free.

Jessica sent me a text saying she had news and wanted to talk. The sale ran until three. Carol and I planned to clean up and take the unsold items to the thrift shop. Taking that into consideration, I texted Jessica that I could meet her around four-thirty. I also asked her to sponsor me on base. Carol would be happy not to have to go to base with me after the garage sale.

A woman came up to Carol with an armful of kids' clothes. She didn't ask for a better price, which surprised us both.

"I need to do the same thing at my house," the woman said, gesturing to the sale. "I just don't have time to price everything. I've been to a lot of tag sales, but this one is organized better than any I've seen."

Carol gave me a little shove in the back toward the woman. "This is Sarah Winston. She organized the whole thing. I'm paying her a percentage of the profits."

"What percentage?"

"It depends on how much stuff you have. She'll come by to give you an estimate."

I looked at Carol like she was speaking in tongues.

"I'm Betty Jenkins. Can I have your number?" the woman asked me. "My house has been overtaken by things. My mother died in January. What my brothers and sisters didn't want is in my garage."

"My garage was stuffed, too," Carol said. "My husband was about to blow a gasket. Threatened to set everything out on the curb."

"My husband has been complaining all winter that the cars are sitting out in the weather," the woman said. "If we have any more snow, I'm in trouble." She smiled as she said it. Her husband probably indulged her every whim, lucky woman. As Carol recited my number, the woman typed it into her phone. "Thanks, I'll be in touch."

I looked at Carol after the woman left. "What just happened here?"

Carol gave me an innocent smile. "Weren't you just complaining about not having a job? Now you have one."

Oh, brother. I'd do it this once for Betty Jenkins, but I'd better start looking for a real job before Carol roped me into something else.

At three-thirty, we closed up shop. We sorted and bagged the things that weren't sold. Carol insisted on paying me. She totaled up her earnings and handed me a generous portion.

"I wouldn't have any money if you hadn't done this for me," she said.

I stuffed the wad of money into my purse, smiling. Maybe doing a yard sale for someone else would be okay. I liked having some money in my pocket that I'd earned. Maybe this would be the impetus I needed to get off my duff and find work.

I pulled up to the thrift shop. The area outside the thrift shop looked deserted. No cars sat in the parking lot or on the street. I fired off a quick text to Jessica saying I'd arrived. After finding the bones here, I wasn't anxious to be here by myself. I wanted to unload quickly, talk to Jessica, and get home. It had been a very long day. If I didn't hear from Jessica, I'd stop over at the dorm to see if she was there.

The lift was down. I loaded it with Carol's leftover boxes and bags before unlocking the shop. It was cold and quiet in the shop. My movements echoed as I hurried through the dim room. I hauled open the large steel door and raised the creaking, old lift. I quickly carried everything to the storeroom.

Carol and I had sorted things as we packed. These bags would be easy to deal with later. The storage room was still stuffed to the gills with plastic bags, boxes, and mountains of clothes. The base fire inspector made periodic stops. If he came anytime soon, we'd be in trouble. It looked like the Friday Fun Day I'd skipped hadn't been a big success. Apparently, it was right up there with the "Air Force Fun Runs." The wing commander announced Fun Runs and all military members had to participate. It was part of their mandatory physical training, and usually nothing about them was fun.

As I lowered the steel door, I looked out for signs of Jessica. Nothing. I hustled through the shop, relieved to be outside locking up. It smelled like spring out here, warm earth after the stale, cold air of the thrift shop. I stood on the top step and checked my phone, no word from Jessica. I scanned the area and spotted her. Jessica lay under the lift. I could tell from here that something was horribly wrong.

CHAPTER 13

I ran over to her. Jessica was on her back. A pool of blood spread out from under her head. I pressed shaking fingers on Jessica's neck to check for a pulse. I held them there, silently begging Jessica to be alive. No beat stirred my fingers. I pressed harder, not wanting to give up. Surely, she couldn't be dead.

A car screeched to a halt behind me and two car doors slammed. "Stop. Don't move." I glanced over my shoulder to see James running toward me with a security forces woman not far behind.

"It's Jessica. She's dead." My teeth chattered as I stood.

The woman checked Jessica's pulse. She shook her head at James. "I can't find a pulse," she said.

James pulled me away. I turned into him, buried my face in his shoulders. His arms went around me. "It's okay, Sarah. I'm here."

I gathered myself and stepped out of his embrace.

"You're Sarah Hooker?" the other woman asked, staring openly at me. Obviously, she'd heard the gory details of my life. The woman, more of a girl really, must have arrived at Fitch after I moved off base. I didn't know her.

I shook my head and said, "Sarah Winston."

James led me over to the car and pushed me down on the seat. The front seat, totally against regulations. He instructed his partner to secure the scene. While she strung out police tape, he called in a report.

James's call to the security forces desk would kick in a rigidly followed protocol. They would notify the command post. The command post would notify the wing commander, the center commander, the judge advocate general, medical center, and the fire department. They'd contact the police forces from the towns around the base. And, of course, they'd contact the Fitch OSI.

The process now was different than when I'd found the bones. Even I knew Jessica hadn't been dead for long. It meant a murderer could be loose on base. Maybe ready to kill again.

Minutes after he called in the report, the public-address system crackled on. Every base I'd ever been on had one. It was mostly used to play "Reveille" in the mornings, "The Star-Spangled Banner" in the late afternoon, and "Taps" in the evening. It informed us of weather issues and base exercises. Some people called it the "giant voice." Half the time, when I had lived on base, if I'd been inside, I couldn't understand what the voice was saying. I usually assumed it was an exercise.

"Attention. Attention. Attention. This is the command post. The base commander has ordered all personnel to shelter in place due to a possible threat on the installation. If you are outside, please proceed immediately to the closest facility. All personnel are to remain indoors until the 'shelter in place' order is lifted. I say again . . ." The message repeated.

By "all personnel," they meant every person on base, moms, kids, DoD employees, everyone. The base gates would close, and no one would be allowed on except for law enforcement officials who came to help. No one would leave base—not even if they had an audience with the pope. Every building would lock down. People in the commissary were stuck there until further notice. The order meant go in and lock in. In case you couldn't understand what the giant voice was saying, official notifications would go out via text and e-mail with the same message.

Even though no one knew for sure at this point what had happened to Jessica, all security forces personnel would be called to headquarters. They'd hit the armory, gear up, and fan out across the base, searching building by building. They would follow the perimeter fence around the base.

Parts of the fence went through the woods, which were rumored to be haunted by the soldiers who'd died there during the Revolutionary War. Any teenager on base could tell you stories of mysterious lights. It wasn't just them. More than one adult had seen the same. Even though Fitch was a small base, a murderer had plenty of places to hide. Security forces would go house to house if they had to. Even though you couldn't keep a base locked down forever, it looked like it would be a very long night.

I'd seen all this hundreds of times during exercises, but never for real. People had to be scared. Moms would be gathering kids. A flurry of texts, tweets, and calls would circulate as everyone tried to find out what was going on. Rumors would be flying faster than fighter jets. Nothing like this had ever happened on sleepy, small Fitch. They called it "Fabulous Fitch" for a reason. The worst part was nothing that took place now would help Jessica.

James kneeled down beside me and took my trembling hand. "Did you see anyone?"

I shook my head.

"Hear anything?"

"No. I backed the Suburban up, loaded the lift, raised it, then unloaded it." I glanced over at Jessica under the lift, pale and still. Cold crept through me as if I were sitting on an ice throne instead of the seat of a squad car.

"She must have been under the lift the whole time. If I'd lowered the lift instead of leaving it up, Jessica might have been there until next week when the thrift shop opened again."

Car after car screeched up. The fire department arrived, even though base fire departments don't normally have EMTs and everyone knew it was too late. The security forces arrived, followed by OSI agents. Special Agent Bristow glanced at me before pulling James and his partner over with the growing group of people milling around.

Police cars from all of the small towns surrounding Fitch—Lexington, Concord, Lincoln, Bedford, and Ellington—parked in the lot across the street. Police put on their bulletproof vests. The group listened to instructions shouted through a bullhorn. Police officers paired up with military members. It looked like the building-to-building search was gearing up.

Bristow organized search groups. His agents started

processing the crime scene. James took off with one of the groups. His partner stayed with me by the car. She looked mad that she got stuck babysitting me instead of getting to go on the hunt.

For the most part, she ignored me and paced around the car. Occasionally she'd talked into her mike. At one point, she heard something that made her kick the tire, then hop around because her foot hurt.

"What's going on?" I asked her.

She glared at me and walked away. A few minutes later, shouting erupted from behind the thrift shop. Bristow, followed by James and other searchers, came around the corner of the thrift shop. Bristow carried something in gloved hands. An Art Deco statue, its base crusted with blood. My Art Deco statue, the one CJ had given to me on our honeymoon.

James's partner said, "That's Tiffany's statue."

I stared at the woman. "Tiffany's statue?"

"She told me about it. I know it meant something special to her."

CJ had given Tiffany the statue he bought me on our honeymoon in Santa Cruz. My eyes blurred with tears. That day was ingrained in my head.

We were at a flea market in Santa Cruz, California. The sky was a glorious blue, the sun warm after having burned off the marine layer. We roamed the market, hand in hand. CJ had never been to a flea market before. His mom felt the same way my mom did about secondhand stuff.

I went to the bathroom. When I came back, CJ had a big grin on his face. He held a bronze Art Deco statue of a woman rising from the sea in his hand.

"She reminds me of you," CJ said, handing her to me. I studied the statue. She looked fierce and joyful all at once. I smiled up at CJ and gave him a kiss.

"I love her," I said. "And you. Where did you find her? I want to ask about the statue's history."

CJ pointed to where he'd bought her and then headed off to buy a bag of kettle corn. The statue was about a foot tall, with a serene expression on her face. I could use her as a dumbbell for lifting weights. When I approached the two women, their expressions turned from all smiles to something akin to fear.

"We aren't taking it back," the taller of the two women said. They looked so much alike they had to be sisters.

The other sister took a couple of steps back.

"I don't want to return it. I just wanted some information about it. She looks like an Erté, but I can't make out the signature."

The sisters exchanged looks. The shorter of the two gave a little nod. The taller one shrugged before she spoke. "Our uncle won it in a poker game."

"Supposedly, he cheated," the short one added. "That's why it's cursed."

The taller sister gave her a withering look. "It's not cursed. We just don't take returns."

I looked from one to the other, wondering what was going on. Maybe they were a little crazy. You ran into all kinds at flea markets. Not all of them were stable.

"If it's not cursed, then why did our uncle die the week after he took it home to his wife?"

"That's why some in the family say it's unlucky. But it's not cursed," the taller sister said to me.

I resisted the urge to roll my eyes. They must have sensed my skepticism.

"Their daughter inherited the statue. She couldn't have children," the shorter one said.

"Lots of people can't have children," I said.

"Which is how it came to our mother."

"Let me guess, pox, pestilence, and floods," I said.

The sisters' eyes widened in surprise. "Close enough. Our dad died after a flood. He had a strange rash the doctor couldn't identify. Mom had to move out of the house because of an infestation of rats."

All of that was easily explained by the flood. These two had wild imaginations. "You two look healthy enough."

They nodded in unison. "Although we've been unlucky in love," the taller one said.

"Do you know anything about the signature?" I asked.

"It's an Erté," the taller sister said.

I smiled down at the statue. Erté or not, I would love it forever. I didn't tell CJ anything about the statue's supposed curse, just that it was an Erté, and he'd done well. We had a flat tire on the way back to Monterey. I glanced down at the statue nestled on the backseat. "The two women CJ bought you from would blame you for this—not a nail in the road," I said while CJ changed the tire.

That night on the local news, the lead story was about two sisters involved in a terrible crash on their way home from the Santa Cruz Flea Market. The police surmised that they'd come around a sharp corner and that the load in their pickup shifted, causing them to plunge over an embankment. Neither wore seat belts. Both were thrown from the car and died instantly. It was the two sisters CJ had bought the statue from.

It was an accident, I told myself. They should have worn seat belts. They should have driven more carefully on the hairpin turns.

I watched Special Agent Bristow place her in an evidence bag. Maybe the statue was cursed. She'd stored up all her trouble for years and was raining pain down on me with the wrath of a hundred-year storm.

"Sarah, wasn't that statue in your house?" James asked.

Trust James to notice something like that. "I haven't seen it since the . . . since I moved."

Agent Bristow came over. "Stay with her," he said to James. "No one talks to her."

The giant voice crackled back to life. "Attention. Attention. Attention. This is the command post. The base commander has lifted the 'shelter in place' order. All personnel may resume normal operations. I say again . . ."

I realized whatever the search party found, they'd concluded the ongoing threat to the base at large was over. Jessica's murder had been a single act, although anyone wanting to leave the base would still have his or her car searched.

CJ and Pellner drove up. I wondered why they were late. CJ squatted, as close as the crime scene people let him, to look at Jessica. He stood, heading over toward me. James, on Agent Bristow's orders, stopped him before he got within ten feet of the car. CJ argued with James. At one point in their heated exchange, it looked like CJ was going to punch James. Pellner pulled him back, glaring at me like this was my fault.

Agent Bristow saw the commotion and came over to stand by James. "Take Ms. Winston into the thrift shop to wait." He dropped his voice. "No one talks to her. Not even you."

I unlocked the front door to the thrift shop again. I flipped on lights, but I left the thermostat down. No need to heat the place, because, hopefully, we wouldn't be here for very long.

I headed back to the small office. The room was a bit warmer and had a space heater, which I flipped on. "We can wait in here."

CHAPTER 14

I sat at the desk, shivering. I pulled my knees to my chest, clasping my arms around them. James left, came back with a crazy quilt that was for sale, and tucked it around me. He sat in an old, wooden library chair next to the desk, swiveling back and forth. I couldn't shake the skeletal-remains image out of my head. The skull's head had been crushed in one spot. I wondered if that was how the back of Jessica's head looked, too. The bronze statue could easily have done the damage.

"Tiffany had my statue," I said, breaking the silence.

"How did she end up with it?" James asked. He didn't sound like he was asking as a friend. He sounded like a cop.

I closed my eyes, breathing in through my nose, exhaling through my mouth. "CJ must have given it to her. He bought it for me on our honeymoon." My voice caught on the word "honeymoon." After my divorce, I didn't think anything could humiliate me more. I was wrong.

"Where'd they find it?" I asked.

James quit swiveling. He looked at me with his thickly lashed brown eyes. "We aren't supposed to talk."

"Please. You know as well as I do that statue used to be in my house. I feel connected, responsible, since the statue was mine." When Jessica and I had gone to Tiffany's room, Jessica had promised to track Tiffany through Facebook. I hoped what she'd found didn't have any connection to her death. Or I might not *just feel* responsible but *actually* be *responsible* by involving her in my search of Tiffany's room.

"It was by the fence. Someone had cut a hole in it. Probably got on and off base that way. They must have dropped it when they were fleeing. Maybe you found Jessica sooner than anyone planned."

First I'd found the bloody shirts, then CJ's ID card, and now this. "Or someone left it deliberately. It looks really bad for CJ and me. Like we're involved." I paused. "Like we did it."

"Why you?" James asked.

"It was my statue."

"Tiffany ended up with it."

"I guess you know Jessica and I were in Tiffany's room the night you saw us in the dorm."

"I'd figured that out. You both looked guilty."

"Someone might think I took it the night we were in the room. Jessica can't tell anyone I didn't."

James waited to see if I had more to say. "You have to tell Special Agent Bristow."

"I will." We sat silently for a few minutes. Outside we could hear voices calling to each other.

"James, how come you were at the thrift shop? If you were on a routine patrol, why would you and the other officer come racing up and yell at me to stop? Did you know Jessica was there?"

James leaned back in his chair.

"If you had been on a routine patrol, you would have been driving slowly. You might have rolled the window down and yelled a 'hello' or something. You wouldn't run and yell at me to stop."

I watched James mull my comments over; lines formed around his eyes as he thought.

"You had to have prior knowledge of some sort," I said. "How?"

"Someone called in. Reported a problem at the thrift shop and hung up." He started tapping his foot. "I shouldn't even be telling you this."

"A man or a woman?"

"I don't know. I didn't take the call. Just the dispatch. I was in the closest car. That's all I'm saying. It's all I can say."

It still didn't explain his yelling at me to stop, but I was more concerned about the timing. It was as if someone knew exactly when I would arrive at the thrift shop. Like someone wanted me to be found there.

CHAPTER 15

Agent Bristow drove me to the Ellington police headquarters, again. This time he didn't ask if it was okay. He'd told one of his agents to drive my car to the station. I tried to figure out why Bristow was handing this one off to the EPD. It was, obviously, a military member this time.

I asked. Agent Bristow didn't even acknowledge that I'd spoken. Maybe it was because of the similarity of the two head wounds. I couldn't have been the only one to have noticed that.

CJ's car was already parked in the lot when we arrived. We settled into the same interview room. As Agent Bristow faced me, I noticed his shirt could use a good ironing. He didn't offer me anything to drink or ask if I was okay. I started jiggling my foot as soon as I sat down.

"No one bagged your hands? Have you washed them?"

"Yes, after I used the bathroom at the thrift shop."

He shook his head, mumbling something that included the word "sloppy." Then he said, "Just because everyone around here knows you doesn't mean you didn't do it."

"I didn't. How could I?" I was about to spill that I knew the fence had been cut, but I didn't want to get James in trouble. "The statue wasn't anyplace near me when James pulled up."

Bristow was a lot more on edge than he had been the last time we'd talked. Was I trying to kid myself? It hadn't been a talk, no matter how gentle he'd been. It had been an interrogation. Now I was all set for another one. I might as well just spill what little I knew.

"Jessica texted me earlier today. She asked me to meet her. I was going to base, anyway. I told her to meet me at the thrift shop."

"How did you get on base?"

"Jessica said she'd sponsor me on."

"Why were you coming on base?"

"I was bringing stuff to the thrift shop. A friend had a garage sale today. I brought the things she didn't sell."

"Why did Jessica want to meet you?"

I let out a long breath. I might as well fess up. Protecting Jessica was stupid at this point. If it meant finding her killer, I had to tell the truth. No matter how bad I looked.

"Jessica said she would try to contact some of Tiffany's friends and family back home. She was looking into Tiffany's disappearance. When she texted me this morning, she said she had some information." I handed my phone to Bristow, showing him the text.

"How did you two cook up this plan?" Bristow asked.

This wasn't going to go over well. I looked at the two-way mirror for a moment or two before continuing.

"I was in Tiffany's room three nights ago with Jessica."

"Tiffany Lopez? The missing girl?"

"Yes," I said, shifting in the chair.

Bristow frowned. "How did you get in?"

"Jessica let us in."

"She had a key to the room?"

I shrugged, what did it matter? "She opened the door with a credit card."

"So the two of you broke into a missing woman's room? A woman who is intimately tied to you in a very distressing way."

"Yes." I left it at that. Looking back, I realized it was a very stupid thing to do. If our actions led to Jessica's murder, it was way beyond stupid. I could tell Bristow I'd told Jessica not to try to hunt down any additional information. But it would just look like I was trying to shift blame away from me. I wanted to take full responsibility for what happened. I had to, with CJ hiding the truth about the bloody shirts.

"What are you thinking about? Something that would help the investigation?" Bristow asked.

"No. I was just thinking about that night. If anything happened that could be linked to Jessica's . . . death . . ." I took a deep, shaky breath. "I can't think of a thing."

"Does anyone else know you were in Tiffany's room?"

"Not that I know of. Someone rattled the doorknob. No one saw us going in or out. We saw James, but not until we were in the hall. We were a couple steps from Tiffany's room." Since we'd talked at the thrift shop, James now knew that Jessica and I had been in the room. However, Bristow had told us not to talk. I didn't want to get James in trouble.

"Why go in there?"

"I just wanted to see if I could figure out what happened to Tiffany."

"Again, why?"

I couldn't say because if Tiffany was dead, if those had been her bones behind the Dumpster, there was a very good possibility that CJ would be suspected of murder.

"I . . . I don't have a good reason. I just wanted to help." It sounded piss-poor, even to me.

Bristow leaned back in his chair. "You can go. Don't discuss any of this with anyone."

At home I didn't know what to do with myself. I didn't feel like talking to anyone. Bristow had told me not to, anyway. Calling my mom and trying to pretend nothing had happened held no appeal. I couldn't concentrate on a TV show, let alone sit still to watch one. Rain tapped against my windows. Walking didn't sound good. I roamed my apartment, moving a table this way, a chair that. I wiped away tears.

I looked at my windows. I'd yet to put up curtains, relying on the ugly window shades that came with the place, even though perfectly nice curtain rods were up. It wouldn't chase the thoughts of Jessica's death away, but it would at least keep me busy.

I crawled under the eaves and dug around until I found a box marked as *Curtains*. Almost every military spouse has a box packed to the gills with curtains from different assignments. What worked in one house didn't in the next, but they might in the one after that.

I dragged the box into the living room. The curtains on top, a beautiful blue silk I'd bought at a garage sale, came from our last house. No way I wanted to use those.

I kept digging until I found a set my mom had made for me out of a vintage tropical print I'd bought at the Santa Cruz Flea Market. The beige, pink, and green didn't exactly scream "New England," but they were cheery. Next I found a vintage apple print for the kitchen, also made by my mom. In the bedroom, I hung simple white, which went well with my cobalt-blue-and-white comforter.

As I finished, someone knocked on my door. Maybe company wouldn't be so horrible, after all. I hoped it was Stella with some wine or that scotch she'd mentioned the other day. Maybe I'd even tell her what happened. Although knowing Ellington gossip, she probably already knew. I whipped it open. CJ stood in the hall. I really needed a peephole or a security chain or something. The same push/pull of emotion swept through me as it did every time I saw him. One part of me longed to feel his arms around me; the other part was repulsed because those arms had held Tiffany. I steeled myself.

"How could you?" we both started to say. We paused, stared, and said, "You gave our honeymoon statue to Tiffany." My version came out angry, and CJ's sad.

"Oh, come in. I'd rather not hash this out in the hall."

"What were you thinking snooping around after Tiffany disappeared? You broke into her room," CJ said.

"I was thinking you were up to your eyeballs in it

ever since I found your shirt and Tiffany's. That maybe I could look at things from a different angle and find something out."

"Why do you even care?"

That shut me up. Carol had asked me the same thing the other night. Maybe our marriage had ended with a stroke of a pen. However, my feelings, good and bad, hadn't. I had wanted to hold on to the anger and hurt, but it wore me down. This morning I'd started feeling happy again, a bit like my old self.

CJ took a step toward me. I backed away and sat in my grandmother's rocker.

"Tiffany must have taken the statue at some point," I said. "I didn't give it to her." I couldn't talk about my bundle of feelings right now. Fear and sorrow commingled with my feelings of loss and horror like strands of spaghetti heaped in a bowl. This was no time to try sorting one from another. "She must have taken it from your place."

"She's never been there."

If I had been an eye roller, my eyes would have done a three-sixty. As it was, I just looked at CJ, wishing I could arch an eyebrow to indicate my skepticism.

"I mean it. Other than that one god-awful night, she's never been to my place."

I didn't point out that god-awful night occurred at our place. I had to move beyond that for the moment. Rehashing wouldn't help Jessica. The part of me that had trusted CJ for the past nineteen years—half of my life and half of his—still wanted to. The part of me that didn't trust him at all knew he was a fount of information. I'd better access it while I had the chance.

"Arguing over who gave away our statue—that is now a murder weapon—isn't important when Jessica's dead." The last came out shaky. It was easier to argue with CJ than to think about Jessica's death.

"You're right." CJ settled on the edge of the sofa. "Do you have any idea what Jessica wanted to tell you?"

"No. She sent me a text in the middle of Carol's garage sale. If only I'd taken a moment to talk to her." I paused, playing the alternate ending in my head: Me talking to Jessica. The two of us giving the information to CJ and Special Agent Bristow. The bones identified as someone other than Tiffany. Jessica and I hailed as heroes. A great Hollywood ending. "If I'd done that, Jessica might not be dead."

"You can't second-guess your decisions," CJ said.

That might be the most truthful thing he'd said to me in months. "Jessica told me she was going to look online, make some calls. Maybe there's information on her computer or phone."

"Both are missing. They can track some of her computer records through servers."

I shook my head. "I don't see why someone would kill her. What could she have found out? Unless it's about where Tiffany is and who she's with. Or if the remains are Tiffany's, then who it was that killed her. Why is it taking them so long to figure that out?"

"It's only been a week. There are backlogs and priorities," CJ said. "Did you see anyone when you were driving to the thrift shop? Not a lot of traffic on Wright."

He had a point. A practice area for the base fire department and an FAA access gate to Fitch Field, the joint military and civilian airport, were the only things back there.

"After I pulled onto Wright, I don't remember

seeing anyone. You know how quiet base can be on a Saturday afternoon." Sometimes the place was like a ghost town, especially when the weather was nice. "After what happened with finding Tiffany's . . . the bones, I've been extra alert every time I go to the thrift shop."

I told him what James had said about the call coming into dispatch. "I think someone wanted me to be found there."

"Anyone could have driven by and found Jessica."

"No, they couldn't. The lift was down. It covered her completely."

"How would anyone know you'd go to base or at what time?"

"Through Jessica."

"Bristow has someone trying to track down what she did for the past couple of days. They'll look at her phone records. It will take a while."

"I've thought about who, besides Jessica, would have known when I would be at the thrift shop. I had to get a pass at the visitors' center. Anyone checking in when I did would have known I was on base and heading to the thrift shop. A couple of other people got passes at the same time I did. I didn't pay any attention to them."

"I'll ask someone to see who came in at the same time you did. And who was working when you came through."

"Thanks." We sat pondering for a couple of minutes. "I guess someone could have followed me from town to base and made the call." It was possible; although with the number of times I'd been pulled over, I was usually aware of who was behind me. "I didn't notice anyone, though."

"I'm worried about you."

"Worry about who killed Jessica. That's more important." I tried to shut out the image of Jessica's body. I could hang a thousand sets of curtains and the image of her lying under the lift would still be with me.

"Maybe you should go visit your mom."

"Oh, that would look good. Find two bodies, leave the state."

"You don't have anything keeping you here."

I stared at him. "Get out." Maybe he wanted me out of the way so I wouldn't interfere with his relationship with Lexi. Not that I would. Seeing him with someone would kill me. Even if I didn't want him, I didn't want to see him with someone who did.

"I meant a job. You don't have a job keeping you here."

I walked over and opened the door, infuriated with myself for feeling hurt. "I do have a job." Maybe doing a garage sale for someone wasn't a real job, but it sufficed for now.

"Look, I'm sorry. I didn't know."

"There's a lot you don't know, CJ. Please go."

"I'll call you if I find anything out."

I closed the door a bit more firmly than necessary.

CHAPTER 16

I'd expected to hear from some of our kids last night after CJ left. No one showed up. Not one of them called. Maybe they were with CJ. Going to sleep had been next to impossible. Finding Jessica haunted me, and the guilt over the "would have, should have, and could have." Light poked through my newly hung curtains before I fell asleep.

This morning snow fell lightly, giant flakes drifting slowly down. I wanted to drag my comforter to the couch and watch old movies or read favorite books. I checked my phone. Betty Jenkins had left me a message about her garage sale. Maybe I could run over, look at her stuff, and figure out what to charge her. I needed to do something that would keep me busy enough that I wouldn't have time to think about Jessica. I called her back.

"When did you want to have your sale?" I asked.

"Next weekend would be perfect. Can you work me in?"

That wouldn't be a problem, but I wasn't about to tell her. "I need to see what you want to put in the sale and make sure I have time to price everything. A lot of Patriots' Day events are next weekend."

"Do you think that's a problem?" Betty asked.

"It could go either way. Lots of tourists will be in the area. Who knows if they will want to go to a garage sale?"

Betty lived in a rambling yellow farmhouse off Great Road in Bedford. It looked like each generation had added on another section, putting their stamp on the property. Betty was the complete opposite of her house, neat and small. She looked like the kind of woman who should be out biking or hitting a tennis ball.

Betty led me to an oversized shed next to the house. "What about using this for the sale?" she asked. The space was spacious, but not cavernous.

"It looks perfect," I said. A peach-colored cat jumped on a stool next to me.

We went into her garage. It was stuffed with furniture. Wardrobes, chairs, side tables, dressers, and a couple of old iron beds. Not so long ago, I would have wanted to keep most of it for myself. If this was what she wanted to get rid of, what was in her house must be exceptional.

A few minutes later, I found out, more of the same—a lot more—plus sets of dishes, mostly depression era, and lots and lots of knickknacks.

"This is from the Alcott family," Betty said, pointing to a washstand.

In this area, many people claimed they had things that had once belonged to the Alcott family. The Alcotts had lived in Concord. One of their homes,

Orchard House, is a wonderful, historical museum. If everyone I'd run into who claimed to have something of the Alcotts actually did, they would have needed a much, much bigger house.

"One of my relatives helped at Bronson Alcott's Concord School of Philosophy. In lieu of pay, he gave her this." She must have sensed my skepticism because she opened a drawer, pulling out a letter in a protective sleeve. The letter thanked Chloe Jenkins for her dedication and was signed by Bronson Alcott, Louisa May's father.

"The letter might be worth more than the washstand," I said. "Are you planning to sell them? My friend Kathy Brasheler volunteers at Orchard House. I'm sure they'd want it back."

"Oh no. We couldn't let that go. I just like to show it to people."

"It's a wonderful piece."

We walked through a family room. A locked glass gun case, holding two rifles, stood against one wall. Betty saw me looking at it.

"My husband is part of the Bedford Minuteman Company. He's a descendant of one of the original Bedford minutemen. The smoothbore musket on the left is supposedly original to the family. It was used on the first day of the Revolution. Can you imagine those soldiers lugging those things around? They weigh over ten pounds."

What Betty called a musket looked more like a rifle to me. In my mind, muskets were the things Pilgrims carried around that ended in a round shape, like a trumpet. What a difference from the fast-firing weapons our troops carried.

"It must have taken them a long time to load and fire those," I said.

"An expert can do it in about fifteen to twenty seconds."

"I've read they aren't very accurate."

"You always hear that. More often than not, it was smoke from all of the muskets firing that made it difficult to be accurate—not the musket itself. They're fairly accurate, to about eighty yards."

"What caliber are they?" I asked.

"Seventy-four, but they used a sixty-nine-caliber musket ball. Since the ball is smaller than the barrel, they had to stuff some paper down into it, with the gunpowder and ball. Then they tamped it in with a rod. Do you shoot?" Betty asked.

"I have." Since we had guns in our house, CJ had taught me how to use them.

"I could have my husband take you out sometime. Of course, they use blanks during the Patriots' Day events." She pointed to a glass jar filled with bits of metal. "That's what a blank can do to an aluminum can. My husband keeps it around to make sure our grandkids respect what guns can do.

"The other musket is a replica—the one he uses for official events like the Battle Road Demonstration next Saturday. He's hoping for good weather. The flintlocks don't fire well in rain. He's also hoping it isn't too hot, because marching around, holding a heavy musket in an itchy wool outfit, isn't fun."

I enjoyed the reenactment, but I never thought about the details like worrying if it was raining or not. I spent the next couple of hours moving stuff to the shed. I stopped back over at the house before I left.

"I'll be back tomorrow to move more and start pricing. I'm going to need some help moving some of the bigger things from the garage to the shed."

"I'll get my husband to help with that. Will we be okay for next weekend?"

"Don't you want to go with your husband to the reenactment?"

"He goes to enough events every year that he won't miss me at one. I won't mind having a good excuse for missing one."

Lincoln, Lexington, and Concord all had annual festivities next weekend. Ellington would promote its original Revolutionary War sketch and oil painting by its native son Patrick West. West purportedly made the sketch at the end of the day after the minutemen had chased the Regulars back to Boston. It wasn't as big a draw as the parades and reenactments in the other three towns. Bedford's big event had been yesterday, although their minuteman company would participate in many of the events next weekend, too. "With some well-placed ads and flyers, and all of your antiques, it will go well."

After a huge helping of ziti, I went to bed early. As I started to drift off to sleep, music blared through the wall. My bedroom adjoined Tyler's next door. Tonight, of all nights, Tyler finally decided to have a party, the night I really needed to sleep. It sounded like people were dancing. In the bedroom. Oh, geez, I hoped it was dancing. I grabbed my comforter and took it out to the couch. At least the noise was quieter out here.

Last night CJ told me to leave town. Was it because of Lexi? Thinking of CJ with Lexi made me think of him and Tiffany. I tried to get images of them out of my head. He'd said he didn't love her. It was a one-off. There was only me in his heart. He'd betrayed me and I'd been stupid for trusting him. It made me question what really happened on the long months of his deployments, on all of those TDYs—temporary-duty assignments—business trips in the civilian world. I thought again about the night I'd gone to the bar in Lowell.

Seth had grabbed my hand just as I walked out the door. His hand was warm in mine, soft and strong at the same time. CJ's was always a bit rougher, more calloused.

No, I am not going to think about CJ.

"We haven't even danced yet." Seth linked his fingers through mine, tugging me toward the dance floor. I resisted.

"That's better than your first line," I said.

He grinned.

I shrugged. Why not? It would give me a little more time to get the alcohol out of my system.

"Was that a yes?"

I smiled. I loved to dance, and it had been a long time. "Yes."

Our dance had turned into many. Drinks appeared like magic in my hand. The next morning, Seth drove us from his place back to my car. The morning had been beyond awkward, even though Seth had done his best to smooth over my obvious discomfort. He offered me breakfast, a toothbrush, a comb. He was practiced at the "morning after," unlike me. I turned down all three.

Seth pulled up behind my Suburban, still parked across from the bar. He leaned over the console and gave me one last, incredible, nerve-thrumming kiss.

"Good night?" He stroked a piece of my blond hair back from my face, tucking it behind my ear. He expected a "yes," as he had last night when he asked me to dance.

"It was okay."

Seth leaned back, eyes wide.

"That's your best parting line?" I asked, smiling.

He laughed. "It's a good exit line."

I climbed out of the car, but I turned back and leaned down. "Great night." I closed the door and walked back to my car. Seth stayed until I was in and had it started. Then he roared around me with a toot of his horn.

I smiled as I started my car. This was the new me, an independent woman. I glanced in the rearview mirror. My smile faded. Mascara was smudged under my eyes. My hair was wild. It looked like it had been teased, but not brushed out. I tried to smush it down. As I drove home, I felt doubts bubble up.

I didn't know Seth's last name. I wasn't sure he even knew my first name. He'd called me a generic "babe" all night. And this morning? My stomach started to feel queasy. We hadn't even made a pretense of exchanging numbers or promises to call each other.

I pulled into my parking space and did the "walk of shame"—walking into the house in the same clothes I'd left in last night. I hoped my neighbors didn't notice or care. As I showered, I realized I cared. I sat on my couch, cuddled in a quilt, gazing out over the town common. I'd curled up on the couch and thought about who I wanted to be.

A few days later, Seth called. At some point during the night, I'd either given him my number or he'd taken it off my phone. He called me almost every night for the next week. We chatted, flirted a bit, but I always turned him down when he asked to get together.

The next week, I sat home, reading a magazine. I flipped a page and there was a picture of Seth, in a tux, leaning against a lamppost in the North End. The caption read, *Seth Anderson, Massachusetts's Most Eligible Bachelor.* I read the accompanying article. He was from an old Massachusetts family whose friends included the Kennedys, Krafts, and Kerrys. He'd grown up in swanky Beacon Hill and had the requisite family compound on Nantucket Island.

He'd recently broken up with his Victoria's Secret model girlfriend. I Googled her. The online articles said she'd dumped him; and from what I could tell, it was only a couple of days before I met him in Lowell.

I'm the rebound girl?

If that troubled me, it got even worse. For me, not for Seth. Right after the breakup, Seth was appointed as the new district attorney of Middlesex County, to replace the ailing DA until the next election. The magazine article said he'd vowed to work closely with law enforcement, not only in the bigger cities like Lowell, but also in the small communities of the county. That meant Seth would work closely with CJ.

After that, I quit answering his calls and texts.

All of this was why I had refused when Carol suggested CJ could check my phone records to find out who was making the gunshot calls.

I hated that Pellner somehow knew about my night

in Lowell. Even more, I hated picturing CJ and Seth working together, and Pellner watching them.

The music from Tyler's apartment finally stopped. I grabbed my comforter and pillow and went back to bed.

My phone rang at five on Monday morning. I patted my hand around, searching for my phone, worried it might be another gunshot call. I'd told myself repeatedly that someone—a very cruel someone—was trying to scare me with the calls. Nothing more. Their strategy obviously worked, or I wouldn't be sitting here deciding whether or not to answer the phone. Screw them. They weren't going to dictate my life. The number was blocked. I answered, anyway.

"This is Pellner."

What new torture had he thought up now?

"Chief's been brought in for questioning. For some reason, he's asking for you."

He disconnected before I said a word.

CHAPTER 17

Thirty minutes later, I sat in the lobby of the Ellington Police Station. Cool air circulated in the lobby like icy fingers caressing my skin. I'd rushed out of the house so quickly I'd forgotten a jacket or sweater. It was amazing I'd remembered to shove my feet in a pair of boots. I tucked my jeans into my boots as I waited. I smoothed my hair back from my face. I hadn't taken the time to brush it before leaving.

Police officers buzzed back and forth. Phones rang. It was a lot of activity for this early in the morning. What had happened that made them bring CJ in for questioning? Maybe he'd told them about the bloody shirts. He should have let me know what he was planning before he took any action. Would I be questioned, too?

I couldn't imagine seeing CJ behind bars or handcuffed to a table in an interview room. Although, as recently as a couple of weeks ago, I'd delighted in imagining him in this exact scenario. This week had taught me the hard reality between fantasy and real life.

The officers who walked by threw me scathing looks, which made me cringe. I stood up, straightening my shoulders. I told the officer behind the window, "I want to see CJ. Now."

A door opened on the other side of the lobby. Pellner stood there, looking bigger than usual. "Come with me."

I followed him down a corridor, past CJ's office. We were in the opposite side of the building than the interview rooms or cells. Pellner unlocked a door on the right side of the hall. CJ sat behind a bare-topped desk in a small, unused office. The only other thing in the room was a folding chair. No two-way mirror, no cameras, and no tape recorders.

CJ had stubble on his usually clean-shaven face. Not the sexy, trimmed Hollywood kind, but the "rushed out of the house" kind. He was dressed in jeans and a blue-and-white striped rugby shirt. The shirt was almost identical to the one I'd slept in all those years ago.

"You sure about this, Chief?" Pellner asked.

"Yes. Thanks, Scott."

The door closed behind me. I heard the *snick* of the lock.

"What's this about? Pellner said you'd been brought in for questioning. Why?"

"Someone called a tip into the station around three this morning. Told them about the bloody clothes in the back of my car. Two officers came to my door. I opened my trunk and showed them it was empty." He tipped his chair back on two legs, something I'd always asked him not to do with our antique dining-room chairs. "I had to tell them at that point. The bag was in my basement. I handed it over."

"What a mess. I guess I'm next then."

"No. I didn't tell them you were involved. I won't tell them."

"But—"

"No *buts* about this. I said I found them when I was going through bags and boxes in the basement last night, and that I was bringing them in this morning."

"I can't let you do that."

He dropped his chair back down to all four legs. "Listen to me. If you tell them otherwise, it will look worse for me. Me lying to my own guys. You have to go along with this. It's why I asked to see you."

His words weighed on me like a stack of cement blocks.

"Do they know it's Tiffany?" I asked.

"They measured the bones. Females have rounder chins than males, smaller bones. They know it's a female about her size. Jessica's head wound and the one on the skull are similar. They're fairly certain the same weapon was used for both crimes."

This was bad, very bad. "It's all circumstantial."

"Pellner asked me what the ruckus was at your house the Sunday you found the clothes. He's suspicious. I stuck with my story that I was late and you were worried."

"Someone knows, CJ. Someone must have seen you put the bag in your car."

"None of the evidence proves Tiffany's dead. They haven't gotten the DNA back yet. They can only hold me for six hours. Then they have to let me go or arrest me and have me arraigned."

"If they were at your house at three, that means by nine they'll have made that decision."

"They searched the house before bringing me here. They'll release me soon. In the meantime, I'm stuck in here. It's better than a cell."

"What will happen if you're arraigned?" I asked. "Will they bring you back here?"

"Ellington used to be part of the county jail system. The facility is too old now. We don't have enough cells. People who are arrested and arraigned are sent to either Billerica or Cambridge."

"They can't do that to you. Why aren't the results of the DNA test back? Bristow told me all military personnel had a sample stored somewhere."

"This isn't the highest priority. The embassy bombing last month and helicopter crash in Guam come first. It's not as simple a process. Sixty days is fast. Six months in the civilian world."

"What about Jessica? Did they question you about her death?"

"No. They will soon enough."

"Do you need me to find you a lawyer? Angelo DiNapoli told me he has a cousin who's a defense attorney."

"Thanks. I've got it covered. He should be here soon. The last thing I need is Angelo's Mob cousin defending me."

Angelo's cousin is in the Mob?

Boston had a reputation about the Mob and crime families, but it always seemed more fictional than real. Even with the Whitey Bulger case.

"Sarah, I've been thinking about all this. You have to be careful. The bags were planted in your car. That person knew I transferred them to mine. Someone knew exactly when you'd be on base. So they have access to Fitch. I'm going to ask Pellner to make sure someone's driving by your house more often than usual."

I wanted to protest. The last thing I needed was more police presence in my life. I pictured being harassed for light pollution, noise, and whatever other trumped-up charges the very creative Ellington Police Department could come up with. But I didn't want to burden CJ with anything else when he was going to extreme lengths to protect me.

"It's not necessary. This is Ellington, after all. Everything happened on base."

"It will make me feel better," CJ said.

How can I argue with that?

CJ leaned forward, taking my hand. "You have to promise me that you won't tell the true story about the shirts. You have to take it to your grave. Otherwise, when I get out of here, no one will ever trust me again."

"Okay. I promise." I drew my hand back. CJ's touch still sent a zing up my spine—no matter how much I didn't want that.

"I need you to do something for me. Lexi's at my house. Would you go over—"

"You want me to go to your house to talk to your girlfriend? No."

"Lexi's not my girlfriend."

"I don't care what you call her or what she is. I won't do it."

I saw a spark in his eye for a second that showed me the old CJ, not the world-weary version I'd observed since our divorce.

"Lexi's a dog. I dog-sat for two weeks for an officer on leave. Pellner thought I looked lonely. Said I needed the company."

Pellner had gotten me again.

"The owner's coming to pick her up this morning. Can you meet her at nine? Everyone here is busy trying to help me get out of this mess."

I hoped they were trying to help him. "Sure. What else can I do?"

"Interesting that you're upset at the thought of me having a girlfriend."

"Bloody shirts upset me. Murderers on the loose upset me. What you do with your personal time? I don't care." I stood up, pounding on the door to be let out.

After a shower, I made breakfast, the official state sandwich of Massachusetts, a Fluffernutter. I put equal amounts of Marshmallow Fluff and peanut butter on white bread. Massachusetts is renowned for the Revolutionary War, Plymouth Rock, the Salem Witch Trials of 1692, and its colleges and universities. The state also had many other achievements: Marshmallow Fluff (still made with the original recipe, not only vegan but also kosher), Oliver Chase's lozenge cutter (the first American candy machine), and the Necco candy company (famous for its wafers—thanks to the lozenge cutter—and candy conversation hearts).

The sandwich was gooey, with the right combination

of sweet and salty. It was just what my stressed psyche needed. While I cleaned up the kitchen, I decided to pay a call on Special Agent Bristow. Thus fortified in mind and stomach, I left the house and soon stood in front of Agent Bristow's desk.

He wasn't surprised to see me, since I'd had to get him to sponsor me on base. His office was dark. Books fought for space with files in the cramped room. The blinds were closed and the fluorescent lights were harsh.

"What were you thinking?" I asked. "Having CJ taken in for questioning."

"The Ellington police have the lead on this. CJ's a civilian." Bristow's shirt was missing a button and his tie was rumpled.

"You're giving them information. Cooperating with them."

"Of course I am. Would you expect anything else? What if Tiffany or Jessica was part of your family?"

In a way, they had been. "You're right."

"Why don't you sit?" Bristow pointed to a tattered office chair.

"I'm fine." I was way too antsy—perhaps from my breakfast—to sit down.

"I have to follow the evidence, not my emotions." He gave me a sharp look. "The *evidence* led to CJ."

"Some circumstantial *evidence*." I mimicked his tone. "You have no proof. CJ didn't murder anyone."

"You know this how?" Agent Bristow asked. "I'd like nothing more than to find some kind of evidence and get CJ out of jail. Do you know someone else with means, motive, and access to the murder weapon?"

"Lots of people have the means. A whole base

filled with people. With the fence cut, anyone from the outside, too. You don't know who had access to the murder weapon because apparently it was in Tiffany's possession at some point."

"But it was yours? And CJ's?" Agent Bristow asked.

"Yes."

"When did you last see it?"

Somehow Bristow ended up asking the questions, instead of me. "I'm not sure. It was in our house when we were moving. One of the packers could have taken it. For all we know, that's what happened."

Agent Bristow looked at me. His eyes were sadder than usual. "Do you have any proof at all that CJ didn't do this?"

"No. I can't imagine he did it. I know he didn't do it." I wanted to believe CJ didn't do it. Doubt crept through me again. He'd stood in my apartment, telling me I couldn't read him.

"I wish I could act on your feelings. But I can't."

"Why is CJ being questioned about Tiffany's murder and not Jessica's?" I asked.

"I have no doubt he'll be questioned in connection with Jessica's murder, too. It's just a matter of time."

Now I wished I'd sat down when Agent Bristow had asked me. Instead, I pivoted and left.

I headed over to CJ's apartment. Lexi's owner was supposed to pick her up around nine. I parked in his drive, wishing I hadn't agreed to this. I'd never been in here and didn't have any desire to go in now. I forced myself out of the car. A dog barked frantically. Poor thing probably needed a walk.

I unlocked the side door off the carport with the key Pellner had grudgingly given me. A fluff ball attacked me, licking, jumping, and whirling. I couldn't picture a dog like this living with a rough, tough police officer. Her dark eyes sparkled when she looked up at me. Her tail wagged so hard that it looked like a propeller.

We stood in a little foyer. To the left, three steps led up to the kitchen. In front of me, a steeper set of stairs led to the basement. Lexi rolled over so I could see her tummy. I scratched it until she jumped back up. I grabbed a leash hanging on a hook by the door and took Lexi out. Every time we breathed, vapor hung briefly in the air. I wished I'd grabbed the jacket in my car. We walked down a couple of blocks. The houses looked almost identical, two stories with carports on either side, only a few had cars in the drive. Lexi wanted to keep going, but I turned her around.

I wanted to wait outside, but Lexi's little tongue hung out. "Okay, we'll go in and get you some water."

The kitchen was plain but neat, with yellowed Formica countertops and cheap cupboards. It led to a dining room. The table was covered with papers, books, and CJ's computer. Sliding glass doors opened to a small backyard. Lexi's food and water bowl were in the corner.

Lexi lapped up the water I had put in the bowl. She flopped down, apparently exhausted from our walk. We could wait on the front steps, but curiosity got the better of me. I was here alone. I might as well poke around.

I headed to the basement, stopping at the top of the steps. My grandparents' dark basement had had a shelf full of old, scary-looking coconut heads that my grandpa had brought back from the Philippines. They had leered at me with their creepy shell eyes when I walked down my grandparents' steps. I'd always been afraid that one would come to life and attack me.

I trotted down the rickety wooden steps. The basement wasn't big. Some attempt had been made to finish it. The walls were concrete block and painted. A drop ceiling missed a few panels. A poorly hung fluorescent light flickered and buzzed. Unopened moving boxes lined the walls. Most were labeled, showing that they were books, kitchen, pictures, and so on. I wasn't going to open boxes, because it would be too obvious I'd snooped.

I started digging through everything else. I opened doors of cupboards filled with sports stuff. I pulled out toolboxes, searching them. I spotted CJ's golf clubs. The notes I'd found in the golf bag at the thrift shop really bugged me. Were they meant for CJ or was Ted bluffing? Part of me hoped they were for CJ, because that meant Deena wouldn't have to go through the same heartache I was experiencing. But a tiny, very selfish part of me hoped they were for Ted, and I wasn't the only one who'd been duped.

I went through his new golf club bag as thoroughly as any CSI team. I didn't find another note or anything the least bit suspicious. What was I thinking? If CJ had any other notes, he would have tossed them by now. I went upstairs, chiding myself for being afraid of basements. Lexi and I would wait outside. She wasn't in the dining room. I called for her. My curiosity spent, I really didn't want to go around the rest of CJ's house looking for her. "Come here, girl."

No response. A hall to the left must lead to the bedrooms and bath. I headed into the living room. A big picture window let in a lot of light. A TV, couch, CJ's favorite leather chair, and moving boxes marked as *Books,* which served as end tables, were all that was in the room. No pictures, no drapes, nothing pretty. A temporary home. A depressing home.

Lexi yapped from down the hall. I called again. She didn't come. I walked down the hall to what must be CJ's room. The king-sized bed was unmade; our silk comforter was a rumpled mess. A purple beach towel tacked up over the sole window served as a curtain. Our massive mahogany dresser took up most of the rest of the room. Lexi barked at the foot of the bed. A toy lobster sat on the bed out of her reach. I grabbed it and tossed it down the hall.

Two framed photos stood on the nightstand. One was of me from not long after we met. We had driven down to Big Sur. I stood on a hill, wind blowing my hair, the Pacific Ocean stretching out behind me. I picked up the second one. A stranger had snapped it for us when we'd gone to Maine last year. It had been near sunset. Our faces glowed in the sunlight. This time it was the Atlantic, endless behind us. Both photos had been in albums last time I'd seen them. Sometime since CJ had moved here, he'd taken them to be framed. I couldn't imagine why he'd do that. Until the other night, when I'd found our wedding album, I hadn't looked at a photo of the two of us.

Something creaked behind me. I was slammed onto the bed. My face was buried in the mattress before I had time to scream. A body pinned me down. Harsh breath panted near my ear. The comforter was dragged over my head. My attacker rolled me in it like a cocoon. I could smell CJ's aftershave on the comforter. I gasped for air. Something hard poked through the comforter onto the back of my head.

"Stay or die," a deep voice commanded.

CHAPTER 18

Footsteps pounded away from me down the hall. Lexi barked and growled before a door slammed. I wrestled my way out of the comforter. Thoughts of a bullet to the brain danced madly in my head. I wanted a fighting chance to defend myself if the guy came back. When I freed myself, Lexi ran to me. I picked her up. She lapped my face like she was asking if I was okay.

Holding her tightly, I ran out the front door and barreled into a woman. I jumped back.

"What the hell are you doing to Lexi?"

"A man attacked me." I gestured toward the house as Lexi strained toward the woman speaking. I didn't want to give up her warm, comforting presence. Lexi wiggled again. I handed her over to the woman. "He slammed me on the bed. Wrapped me in a comforter." It sounded crazy. Who would do that?

The woman whipped out a cell phone; and after making a call, she chattered in police code. "Are you hurt? Do you need an ambulance?" she asked.

"No. I'm okay. I don't need an ambulance." I plopped

down on the stoop. "A little scared. I don't know where he came from."

She ended the call. Lexi wiggled in the woman's arms, so she set her down. Lexi leaned against me, her little head on my leg.

"Did you see anyone coming out of the house when you got here?" I asked.

"No."

"Anyone who hurried away?"

"A guy was jogging down the street. A car heading east. No one suspicious."

"I can show you where I was." It surprised me how calm I sounded. I couldn't shake off the feeling of being wrapped up and barely able to breathe.

"We'll wait out here for the other units."

Two cop cars raced up from opposite directions, lights flashing, sirens killed as they parked. Pellner and two other officers ran into the house, coming back out minutes later.

"It's clear," Pellner said. "So, what were you doing here?"

I looked at him, astonished. He knew exactly why I was here. He'd handed me CJ's keys, under protest, when CJ asked him to. "I was here so I could give Lexi to her." I pointed at the woman, who was searching the yard with the other two officers.

"How did you obtain entry into the premises?"

"With CJ's keys—the one's you gave me early this morning." The other officers had split up and disappeared around the side of the house. I wondered if Pellner had asked them to leave us alone.

"Which door did you enter through?"

"I went through the side door."

"And then?"

"I took Lexi for a walk."

"Did you secure the house before you left?" Pellner's tone indicated that this was all my fault, that I'd probably deserved what happened.

"No. We just went a couple of blocks."

"Could you see the house the whole time you were walking the dog?"

"No. But it wasn't out of my sight for long."

"Long enough for someone to enter the home, allegedly, without your knowledge?"

"Yes. For all I know, he could have already been in there." That was a scary thought.

"Are you in the habit of leaving houses unlocked when you leave the premises?"

"No." That wasn't entirely true. Fitch had very little crime. When they went on vacation, people would leave their houses unlocked for a week if someone was caring for their pets. I wouldn't do that, but I didn't always lock up when I ran an errand or took a walk on base. CJ had always lectured me if he found the door unlocked. The whole "even though we're on a base, crimes can happen" speech. Not to mention the doors had old-fashioned mail slots. Anyone with a skinny arm could reach in from the outside and unlock the door. It was great if you locked yourself out. All you had to do was grab the nearest kid, seconds later you were in.

"Sometimes on base, if I could avoid one of CJ's safety lectures."

The other officers came back to the front. "No sign of forced entry."

Pellner nodded. "Knock on some doors. See if anyone saw anything."

I didn't want to be left alone with Pellner.

"Walk me through what happened," Pellner said.

We went in the side door. I showed him where the leash had been, walked him down the street and back, which he timed on his watch. I went through the motions of putting water out and looking for Lexi. I didn't mention searching the basement.

"You didn't hear or see anything suspicious? Notice any unusual cars parked outside?"

"I'm not familiar enough with the neighborhood to know whose cars belong and whose don't."

"Really?"

"This is the first time I've been in here."

"But not the first time you've been by."

Now Pellner was making me angry, which was probably a good thing, because I was rapidly getting over being scared. I studied Pellner for a minute. That might have been his intention all along. Then again I didn't think he was that smart.

"It's a public street. I've driven down it before."

Pellner looked smug as if he'd just elicited a confession for some major crime. We walked into the bedroom. My breath became ragged.

"It's okay. He's long gone," Pellner said.

Wow, Pellner being human. "The closet door wasn't open when I came in the bedroom." I sketched out being hit, wrapped in the comforter.

"He must have been hiding in it. Does anything look different or out of place since you first came in?"

I looked around. The nightstand was empty.

"Two pictures are missing from the nightstand. I noticed them when I came in."

"What kind of pictures?"

I described them. He looked a little annoyed, giving

his head a shake. We hunted around to see if they had been knocked down. They were gone.

"You think someone broke in here and attacked you over a couple of pictures?"

Back to the Pellner I knew and disliked. "I don't know."

We walked back through the house. CJ's computer still sat on the table. We stopped in the kitchen.

"As far as I can tell, nothing else looks out of place."

"What about the basement?" Pellner asked.

"I don't like basements. They're creepy." It was a nonanswer. I hoped Pellner wouldn't realize it.

"Wait here." Pellner trotted down the steps.

I leaned against the kitchen counter until he came back up. "What's in the basement?" I asked.

He shrugged. "A lot of boxes and furniture. Without the chief taking a look, we won't know for sure if anything is missing. He's not available to come, is he?"

It sounded like an accusation. "Pellner—" I was ready to light into him, but the front door creaked open. I moved a step closer to Pellner. He stepped in front of me, pushing me back.

"Pellner?" One of the officers came into the dining room. "We canvassed the neighbors who are home. No one saw anything."

"Okay, you can take off." Pellner turned to me. "Something about all this bugs me. Chief said he found the shirts when he was going through boxes and bags in his basement. There aren't any bags down there. Just boxes."

I shrugged. At least I hoped it came off as a casual shrug rather than an involuntary shudder. "Like I said, I don't like basements."

We walked out to the front lawn. Lexi ran over to me, until her owner said, "Ride." She jumped twice, then bounded to the car.

"Do you have any idea of who would do this or why?" Pellner asked.

"Maybe I was just here at the wrong time." I almost told him it was possible someone was watching CJ and knew the house would be empty. Then I'd have to explain about my role in finding the bloody shirts. CJ had asked me not to do that.

Pellner looked skyward for a minute before looking back at me. "I don't know whether to believe you or if this is some kind of crazy bid for attention from the chief."

"It's not. I've been around law enforcement since the day I met CJ. I wouldn't waste the resources."

Pellner thought for a minute. "Okay. Give me the keys and I'll lock up."

"What about CJ? Will he be released?"

"I don't know. They're waiting for the DNA to come back. They will check the DNA on the bloody clothes. Something is really bugging me about those shirts. CJ's too smart to keep them around his house if he killed Lopez."

"Exactly." Pellner and I agreed on something. "Someone must have planted them." Of course *that someone* had planted them in my Suburban, not in CJ's basement.

"Interesting there's no sign of forced entry. You said CJ was very careful about locking doors. He even yelled at you if you didn't."

"Lectured me. CJ isn't a yeller."

"If someone planted the shirts, there'd be some indication," Pellner said.

I flushed. Pellner might be smarter than I was giving him credit for. Because it really felt like he was the guy who set out bear traps, and I was the innocent bear wandering around in the woods. "I can't explain that."

"Too bad."

We walked out to the carport. I unlocked my car.

I looked at Pellner. "Please don't tell CJ about what happened here today. He's got enough on his mind. I don't want him worrying about me."

Pellner squinted at me before finally nodding. "Okay. I'm not sure if it's because you really don't want him to worry. Or nothing happened here for him to worry about. I won't tell him. I'll make sure no one else does, either."

Trust and betrayal. I thought about both as I drove to Bedford. I needed to price more things for Betty's garage sale on Saturday. Pellner was suspicious about the bloody shirts being found at CJ's house. If I told the truth, I betrayed CJ's trust. I would damage his reputation and might end a career he loved. CJ trusted me, even though he betrayed me. That trust was a heavy burden. It made me angry. What did I owe CJ after what he'd done to me?

I found the hauling, sorting, and pricing comforting. My mind wandered occasionally to Tiffany, Jessica, CJ, or the attack this morning. Pricing old Ball jars and arranging them with other kitchen items kept me from dwelling too much on any one thing. Before the garage sale, I'd pick up some daisies to brighten this dreary space.

I'd also check with Betty to see if she had any

strands of white lights I could string around the shed. I wanted the room to look nice, but I didn't want to waste time overstaging the place. Ever since garage sale shows had started popping up on TV, people overemphasized the importance of staging a garage sale. My philosophy was to have the sale organized and the merchandise clean. Wasting too much time making things pretty was as bad as heaping everything in a pile on the ground. I'd seen both ends of the spectrum and tried to hit the middle.

Carol called me just before noon. "Where are you?" She blurted it out without any of her usual "Hi, how are you?" preambles.

"I'm in Bedford. What's wrong?"

"CJ was just arraigned and charged with Tiffany's murder."

CHAPTER 19

"Where did you hear that?" I hoped it was just the rumor mill kicking in. Someone had heard that CJ was being questioned, didn't understand the process, and leaped to that conclusion. I glanced at my watch. It was just after noon.

"I was in the Dunkin' Donuts. Two cops came in. They were talking about it."

"You must have misunderstood."

"No. I asked them. They looked really embarrassed. One admitted to me that CJ had been arraigned and charged."

I peered through the thick glass in the lobby of the Ellington Police Department, waiting for someone to help me. A woman, one of the dispatchers, came over.

"I want to see CJ."

"You are?"

"His wife. His ex-wife. Sarah Winston. Please just buzz me in."

"He's not here. He's still being processed."

That sounded awful. Picturing CJ in an orange jumpsuit turned my stomach. "Where will they take him?"

"He caught a lucky break today," she said, looking at me as if I was the cause of all his problems. On this one issue, she was right. If I admitted I'd found the bloody shirts—that CJ had taken them from me—they'd have to let him go. But it was only a few hours since I'd promised CJ I wouldn't tell anyone.

"What's his lucky break?" Nothing about this situation sounded lucky to me.

"The Middlesex Jail in Cambridge is old. It's in the process of being shut down. Some idiots tried to steal some of the copper wiring at a nearby construction site. It caused an explosion this morning. They're in the process of evacuating the building. The worst of the lot will be sent to Billerica. The others will be farmed out. We know some of them are coming back here. Hopefully, CJ will be among them. We take care of our own." Her look clearly indicated I wasn't part of "our own."

As I headed back to Betty's, I wondered if Pellner had known about the arraignment when I'd seen him at CJ's house.

My cell phone started ringing repeatedly around two. I ignored most of the calls, choosing to listen to messages, instead. The news of CJ's arrest was out. The calls were divided between people who were worried about me and those who wanted some good gossip. MaryJo left a long message offering me her counsel, help, and her recipe for Yankee pot roast. She didn't offer the chaplain's help, just hers.

I kept my jacket on as I worked. I added a pair of fingerless gloves I had found stuck in the drawer of a garden bench. No one, other than Betty, knew I was here. Hiding was exactly what I needed to do right now. Betty showed up at three with tea sandwiches and scones. I realized I hadn't had lunch and that my Fluffernutter had worn off a long time ago. I devoured them.

"My friends keep asking me if they can come by early, before the sale. I'm not sure what to do," Betty said.

"We could have a preview sale on Friday night. Invite friends and neighbors over from seven to nine."

"How about five to seven? Can you come? I wouldn't know what to say if one of my friends tried to bargain me down on some piece I love."

I pulled out my phone like I was checking my calendar. "I can squeeze it in." That and any other event she might be interested in having me attend in the next year or so.

I drove over to Betty's house Tuesday morning. I'd spent most of the evening on Monday hanging around the Ellington Police Department, trying to see CJ. No one let me. I found out the name of his lawyer. I'd left what had to be an irritating number of messages for him. The jerk didn't call me back.

My phone rang as I entered Bedford. A gunshot sounded. I jerked the wheel of my car, hitting the granite curb. I yanked it back onto the road—lucky, I hadn't popped a tire. Now I was just plain old mad. This time I wasn't going to yell into the phone or hang up. I was going to listen and try to figure out who was doing this. I heard a click. The call disconnected.

I didn't think anyone was really being shot. Whoever was doing this hung up quickly this time. On some of the calls, they waited for my reaction before hanging up. I pulled into Betty's driveway. Not much I could do about it. The best course of action was no reaction. Hopefully, they'd get tired of this game.

I decided I needed a lobster roll for lunch. I drove over to West Concord Seafoods. I moved past their lobster tank and long seafood counter to the order counter. They had a few tables if you wanted to dine in. I decided to take mine with me. They had giant lobster rolls—lobster meat and mayo—no fillers like celery or lettuce. Instead of the traditional New England–style hot dog bun, they served theirs on a soft hamburger roll.

I could see a guy in the back picking meat from a lobster. "Excuse me," I called.

The guy washed his hands and then turned, all frowny from being interrupted.

"Tyler. I didn't know you worked here."

Tyler came out from the back to the register. "I didn't know you ate here. It's amazing what we don't know about each other." He smiled and winked.

It made me realize I hadn't been very neighborly. I was sick and tired of always worrying about me. I needed to invite Tyler, Stella, and the Callahans, who were due back from their winter home in Florida any day, over for a party.

"When the Callahans get back, I'll have a party."

"That would be fun. I'll bring the chowder." Tyler

said it with a wink, using an exaggerated Boston accent and pronouncing it "chowdah."

I placed my order, asking for fries instead of chips. Fat sizzled when Tyler plunged the fries into the oil. I watched him pile the lobster meat high on the bun. Higher than normal, I noted.

He handed me my food, with a nod. "I stuck in some seafood chowder for later."

I put a way-too-generous tip in the jar, which earned me another nod. As I headed to the door, Scott Pellner's wife walked in. I looked around, but I didn't see anyplace to hide.

"You're the lady from the VFW," she said.

I glanced at Tyler, my face warming. Tyler didn't know if I worked for the VFW or not. Still, this is what I got for lying. "I do some volunteer work there." Add that to the list of things I needed to do: volunteer at the VFW so I wasn't a liar. I hoped the blush spreading up my face wasn't too visible. I noticed a trace of a Southern accent. Stella had told me Pellner's wife was from Kentucky.

"Are you from Kentucky?" Changing the subject was the only way to keep from further lies or from a lengthy explanation about who I really was.

"West Virginia. I met my husband in Kentucky. I always think the accent is gone. I try to cover it by saying things like 'This place is wicked awesome.'"

I laughed. "I'm a transplant, too. I know what you mean."

"I forget and throw in a 'y'all' or a 'bless your heart,' which gives me away."

"I remember the first time I went to the Home-Goods in Bedford. One lady told her friend, 'I'll go get a carriage.' I was thinking, 'Cinderella.' She came back with a shopping cart."

"Pocketbooks instead of purses."

"Jimmies on ice cream, not sprinkles," I said. "So, is your husband a police officer?"

Scott's wife gave me an odd look.

"I saw the police shield in the garage when I picked up your stuff."

"Oh, aren't you observant? Yes, he is."

"It must be a tough job, even in a small town like Ellington." If she ever found out who I was, I would be embarrassed.

"He loves it."

"I heard the new chief was an outside hire. That must have angered some people."

"It did." She frowned. "Scott would have made a wonderful chief. What they did wasn't right. That guy has been arrested for murder. They should have stuck with someone local."

Mrs. Pellner confirmed my growing suspicions that the Ellington police weren't all that loyal to CJ. CJ was depending on his troops to rally around and protect him. That might never happen. I was never going to convince him otherwise.

"Nice seeing you again." I waved a good-bye to Pellner's wife and Tyler.

"Hey, Tyler," she said. "I need some advice on what to serve a crowd. Chelsea's singing 'The Star-Spangled Banner' at the Celtics game. We're going to have a big party."

It was hard for me to imagine Scott Pellner at a party.

* * *

My phone rang as I walked out. "They're finally letting us move the thrift shop to a new location. Wait until you see it," Laura said after the "hello" and a few sympathetic comments about CJ. "Can you come help this afternoon? I'll have you work at the new shop, setting up."

I'd planned to go back over to Betty's. I wasn't anxious to go back on base. It had only been two and a half days since I'd found Jessica. If I went now, I could face everyone, listen to all the comments about Jessica and CJ, and get that out of the way. Laura would be there to support me.

"Sure. Sponsor me on?"

An hour later, I stood inside the new thrift shop space. It was at the corner of Travis and Wright Street. Much more centrally located than the old out-of-the-way building. This space had large windows and water you could drink. Everyone always referred to the building as "the old Chinese restaurant." I'm not sure when it had been one, because I'd never met anyone who had eaten there. I'd always heard it had been shut down for unsanitary practices. No one ever mentioned what those unsanitary practices were.

Colonel Nicklas showed up midafternoon with a tray of Italian pastries from Royal Pastry in Lexington for the ten of us who were working. He'd brought enough for three times that number. Only a few of the women working today volunteered regularly. Colonel Nicklas left to take another tray over to the group at the old thrift shop. I couldn't bear working over there. I didn't ever want to see that building again.

Before I finished my cannoli, it started.

One woman looked at me and said, "I'm sorry to hear about CJ."

"Me too, Sarah. It's like your life has become a bad country song. Cheating man, dead girl, prison." The woman didn't sound sorry at all, more like excited.

"Show Jessica some respect. She was a young airman who was murdered," I said.

Laura looked like she was about to say something. I stood up. "CJs not in prison. He's at the jail in Ellington. It's a huge difference. He didn't do it. Anyone who thinks he did is a fool." I dumped my half-eaten pastry in the garbage and walked to the back room. The murmur of voices followed me.

CHAPTER 20

Since I was still on base, I drove to the enlisted dorm. Technically, I was only supposed to go to the thrift shop with my visitor's pass. It wouldn't be the first time I'd added in another errand. Someone might know what Jessica had been up to after Tiffany's murder. A group of kids, some from the security squadron, sat around a large-screen TV in a lounge area. The ones from the security squadron looked weary. I'm sure they'd been putting in long hours.

"Hey, Miss Sarah. What are you doing here?" Shaniqua, the girl who asked, was short, muscular, and had beautiful dark skin, which contrasted with her light green eyes. Her hair was still pulled back in a tight bun. She must have gotten off work recently.

How to answer that question? Especially when all those pairs of eyes now turned away from the TV and were watching me. "I was over at the thrift shop, helping out, and thought I'd stop by. I miss you guys."

A couple of the kids waved hello; others turned back to the TV.

"How are your classes going, Shaniqua?"

"Why don't you come up to my room—we can talk up there without bothering anyone."

I followed Shaniqua to her room, where she turned her stunning eyes on me.

"What do you really want?" Shaniqua asked.

"I've been thinking about Jessica. She told me she was going to look into Tiffany's death. Or disappearance. Whichever it is."

Shaniqua went over and sat on her bed, hugging a pillow. I took the chair at her desk. "I'm not sure talking to you is the best idea. Jessica did . . . and she's dead."

"Is that what people are saying at the squadron?" My stomach clenched. They thought I was a jinx, like my statue. No wonder none of our kids had shown up after Jessica died.

"Some are. I'm more practical. The ones saying it, though, are superstitious types."

"So have you heard anything?" I asked.

"Jessica and I didn't really hang out that much. I overheard her talking to someone on the phone last Friday when we headed into the squadron. She mentioned Tiffany. She told the person, 'thanks,' and that they'd been very helpful."

"Any idea who Jessica was talking to?" I asked.

"No."

"Jessica told me Tiffany ignored the enlisted guys. That it caused problems. Do you know anyone specific who was upset?" I asked.

"With Tiffany's Jennifer Lopez curves and big brown eyes, it was more a matter of who didn't want to date her. I could name a dozen guys who were interested. Other than some testosterone-fueled posturing, no one stands out as a troublemaker."

"What about Jessica? She mentioned dating someone. Or at least talking to a guy. Do you know who?"

"I don't. I know lots of guys who wanted to date her, too."

"Were any of the guys upset with her?"

"No. Jessica was a friendly girl. Cute, if you like that type. I've overheard guys make comments. Nothing out of line."

"Do you think Jessica's dating had anything to do with her death?"

Shaniqua shrugged. "I think anything's possible at this point."

"Have you told Special Agent Bristow?"

"No. It's all conjecture. The only thing I know for a fact is that phone call I told you about. I mentioned it to the acting commander, Major Walker. She didn't seem too interested. That's another thing that worries me. Why isn't she more interested?"

A warm breeze lifted my hair as I crossed the parking lot. Cars were starting to stream up the hill on their way home. As I unlocked my Suburban, a car door slammed nearby. The girl who'd gotten stuck guarding me after I found Jessica locked her car.

"Can I ask you a question?" I called to her.

She glanced around before giving me a wary nod. "I only have a minute. I'm meeting some friends at the gym. I need time to change out of my uniform."

I walked over to her. I didn't want to keep yelling. "The day I found Jessica, you said the statue Agent Bristow had was Tiffany's. Why'd you think that?"

"Because she told me about it, how much she loved it."

"Did you ever see it in her room?"

"No."

Darn. "So she could have made it up that it was hers?"

"I guess so. But she described it to me in detail."

I wished she could place the statue in Tiffany's room. It would have made it less likely that CJ had it. Others would have had access to it, too.

"Did you tell Agent Bristow any of this?"

She took a step back from me. "Of course I did. Do you think I'd withhold information during a murder investigation? Do you think anyone would?" She turned.

I watched her stride into the dorm. Did I think anyone would withhold information? Yeah, I thought I would. CJ would. And, definitely, the murderer would.

I drove over to the security forces headquarters. This was the first time I'd been over here since I'd moved off base. I parked my car across the street in the commissary's parking lot. I called Agent Bristow, filling him in on what Shaniqua told me.

"Why didn't she tell me this herself?"

"I don't know. Probably because she feels comfortable with me."

"Okay, then. Now I'm wondering if I need to reinterview the entire security force. Maybe you could sit in on all the interviews. Hold some hands. Pass out milk and cookies."

His comment would have made me angry, but I heard the weariness in his voice. I'm sure he didn't want my advice or help, but I took the plunge, anyway.

"Have you looked into who Jessica was dating? She had an active social life."

"Do you have anyone specific in mind?"

Did I? "No. Maybe give Acting Commander Walker a call."

"Gee, thanks, I wouldn't have thought of that." Special Agent Bristow paused and sighed. "I'm sorry. That was uncalled for. I appreciate you letting me know about the phone call Jessica made on Friday. We've been looking at her phone records. She made a lot of calls to a lot of people. The girl was on her phone all day and most of the night. I'm not sure when she slept. This information will help us narrow down what's important."

I walked across the parking lot to the security forces headquarters. They'd spared no expense on the lobby. By "no expense," I meant they hadn't spent a dime on it, except for security precautions. It was a big box of a room, with security cameras, linoleum floors, and grimy walls. The only relief was the big, mirrored window to the left as you entered. One of those "they can see me/I can't see you" affairs. Very disconcerting, even for someone like me who'd been in the building hundreds of times. A sturdy metal door was the only relief on the back wall.

"Mrs. Hooker," a voice boomed out behind the mirror. "What are you doing here?"

With the distortion from the speaker, I wasn't sure who was talking. "I wanted to see Fran. Acting Commander Walker," I amended. "Is she available?"

"Sure. Hang on."

The door on the back side of the wall buzzed. I headed up to CJ's old office.

The door was open. Fran sat behind the grand walnut desk, chair tilted back. She smiled as she talked on the phone. She spotted me and motioned me in. I sat in the chair opposite her, waiting for her to finish her conversation. The office was stripped of any personal items. I'd tried to warm it up for CJ with a painting of the rugged California coast, the almost requisite photograph of the Thunderbirds—the air force demonstration team—flying in formation, and a shot of a missile launching from Vandenberg Air Force Base. CJ had added a photograph of me on his desk. All of that stuff was probably in CJ's basement now or in his office in Ellington.

"Do you mind if I close the door?" I asked when she finished her call.

"Go ahead," Fran said.

After closing the door, I sat back down. She leaned forward, resting her arms on the desk.

"I wondered if you'd had any problems with Jessica," I said. "Anything that might help figure out who killed her."

She ran her fingers across the desk like she was playing a piano. "Is this any of your business?"

"How can you ask that? I found the bones and the body. It's CJ sitting in jail."

Fran plucked at a curl in her short hair. "Jessica was always on time, did her job well, and was well liked," Fran said. "CJ could have told you that."

"Was Jessica having any personal problems?"

"Not that I know of."

"Was she dating someone from the squadron?"

"I really don't know what she was up to in her free time."

That surprised me. CJ always knew almost everything that was going on with the troops. If he didn't know something, I did. Different commanders handled things in very different ways. Fran had just returned from a yearlong deployment right before CJ's very sudden retirement. She was getting ready to PCS.

"Nothing was bothering her? Even for just the last week or so before her murder?"

"She was a stellar airman," Fran said.

"Do you know Colonel Brown and his wife, Deena?"

Fran gave a short nod. "Not well. I've run into them in the neighborhood and at base functions."

"Deena told me she'd dated someone from the security squadron. Any idea who?" ("Dated" was the nicest term I could come up with.)

"Where are you going with this stuff, Sarah? Do you have any evidence that Deena Brown's personal life has any bearing on this case?"

"No, but—"

"We are questioning everyone. Everything. I've been told to stand down more than once by Agent Bristow. He thinks we're interfering. No one here wants to see CJ in jail." She pushed her chair back. "I find it curious that you're running around asking questions. Don't think I haven't heard."

"I'm worried about CJ."

"Many women in your position wouldn't feel that way. They'd be happy or thinking about revenge."

If Fran knew some of the things I'd thought about doing to CJ, she might think different. She might be worried about having me sit across the desk from her.

"It makes me wonder what's going on with you," Fran said.

As I left the building, the PA system crackled to life. I froze. What now? "The Star-Spangled Banner" started playing. I let out a sigh of relief. It played every day at four-thirty. I looked around, spotting a flag in front of the security headquarters. Everyone outside stopped, turning to face the nearest flag. If a flag wasn't available, I would have turned toward the sound of the music.

The active-duty personnel came to attention, some in the parking lot, some on the sidewalk and steps leading to the building. I placed my hand over my heart. On the playground across the street, little kids quit playing. They climbed off the equipment, stood in a row. Most of them had their hands over their hearts; some sang along. All traffic stopped, too, pulling to the side of the road until the song ended.

As the last strains faded on the breeze, I headed to my car. I spotted Deena driving toward me. Someone else was in the car with her. She said something and the passenger bent down out of sight. She sped around a corner with a brief wave. I stared at the back of her car and saw the person pop back up. He or she glanced back, but then snapped back around when they saw me watching.

I banged out the door of the station after another fruitless attempt to see CJ. A group of people, all dressed in business suits, headed up the steps as I started down. Seth was in the middle of them. He looked even better in his power suit than he had that night at the bar or the morning after with his hair tousled.

I tried to slip around them. Seth glanced at the group and said, "Give me a minute." They looked at me curiously as they bounded by. I was grateful that I'd at least changed into clean jeans and a clean V-neck before heading over here.

"Babe." Seth took my hands and brushed his lips across my cheek. His aftershave froze me for an instant.

Good God, he still doesn't know my name.

"You quit answering my calls," he said.

"You quit calling." I wiggled my hands out from his.

"I took the hint." He flashed his white teeth in a smile. "A guy can only take so much rejection."

"I'm sure that's a real problem for 'Mr. Most Eligible Bachelor.'"

Seth reddened a bit. "You saw that? I'm embarrassed."

"Congratulations on your promotion, District Attorney."

"That's what I was celebrating the night we met."

"And here I thought you'd been made head of the used-car lot."

"You thought I was a used-car salesman?"

"Your lines were more used-car salesman than DA."

"My lines. What about yours?"

"What are you doing in Ellington?" I asked. I wanted to veer from any further conversation about the night we'd spent together.

"Checking up on the case with the local police chief. I'm sure in a town the size of Ellington, you've heard about it."

I begged my knees not to buckle. I stammered out an "O-oh." Now I was grateful he didn't know my name.

His forehead creased. "What are you doing here? Not in trouble, are you?"

"No. Just a ticket. They're real sticklers about jay-walking in Ellington. Watch yourself. I've got to run."

As I moved past, Seth snagged my hand.

"Sarah," he said.

I guess he did know my name, but not my connection to CJ.

"Answer next time I call, okay?"

I nodded. I turned to watch him run up the steps. Pellner held the door open for Seth, but he watched me.

After dinner Laura called.

"I'm too tired to come back to work," I said before she could ask. After leaving base, I'd tried to see CJ, but I had ended up just sitting in the lobby for a frustrating hour.

"That's not why I called. Do you think that's the only reason I call?" Laura gasped then. "It is the only reason I've called you lately. I'm sorry. This time I called to check on you."

"I'm fine." I filled her in on the rest of my day. "I tried to see CJ. They wouldn't let me."

"Why are you running around asking questions? After what CJ did to you, just let him rot."

This wasn't Laura's normal demeanor. Usually, she was more compassionate, but her brother's wife had run off with another man last year. Her brother was still traumatized. Laura's indignation level was high. I understood because my life had been turned upside down, too.

"I'm not sure why. I know he couldn't have done it. Now he can't get out to defend himself."

"They always say there's a thin line between love and hate. I don't think there's any line. Just a damn blurry mess. How are you staying busy when you aren't helping at the thrift shop?" Laura asked.

"A woman is paying me to organize a garage sale for her."

"Perfect. It's about time, after all the ones you've run as a volunteer."

"It's just a one-off. She has some beautiful things. Under different circumstances, I'd be dragging half of it home. It's Saturday morning. You should come."

"Then I'd be the one in trouble."

We fell silent for a couple of seconds.

"Thanks for calling," I said. "I know how busy you are."

"I'm rooting for you," Laura said.

I settled on the couch with a magazine. I tried to shove all thoughts of Seth out of my head. It didn't work as well as I'd have liked. He was a guy who dated Victoria's Secret models—why would he want to go out with me? I'd agreed to answer the next time he called. I wanted to write it off as being polite, the easiest way out of an awkward situation. However, Seth intrigued me, no doubt about that. I wondered if Pellner heard much of what we'd said, and if he told Seth who I was.

I shook my magazine and refocused on an article about the best flea markets in New England. Thoughts about my meeting at the security headquarters with Fran intruded. Shaniqua had said Fran wasn't interested in Jessica's murder. She certainly didn't know much about Jessica, but she did have the whole deployment/ moving thing going on.

Fran wasn't in charge of the investigation; the Ellington police were. She might be honoring that arrangement and staying out of it. But why would she want to do that when Jessica was on her squadron and had been murdered on her watch? Being an acting commander put you in a strange position—all of the responsibility, with none of the perks. When CJ had been an acting commander at past assignments, he'd been all in.

It was hard to sit here, knowing CJ was locked up. He'd taken a big risk for me. He was the only one who knew I had a stake in this. I'd honor that obligation. Something was off with Deena. I'd seen Deena's name on the list of people working at the thrift shop tomorrow. I'd start with her.

CHAPTER 21

After spending Wednesday morning at Betty's house, I headed over to the thrift shop. I ate a Fluffer-nutter sandwich I'd brought with me as I drove. Laura had once again sponsored me on base. I needed to ask her to get me a thirty-day pass. Then I could get on base without always having to bug someone.

Things were beginning to take shape in the new building. Deena and one of her closest friends worked in the kitchen area. We stocked everything from dishes to old electric fry pans. Heading straight over to them would be too obvious. I sorted things in the backroom. When I found some kitchen items, I'd take them over.

About fifteen minutes later, I came across a set of dishes. *Perfect.* I carried the box over, plunking them down near Deena.

"Here's a set of dishes. They're in good shape. It's a whole set of eight."

Deena looked me over like she was trying to determine if she could take me or not. I was sure she could, but I didn't know why she'd want to.

"Stay away from my husband." Her voice rang

across the room. All other talk stopped. I glanced around. Everyone stared.

"I haven't been *around* your husband." I had been in his office, but her tone indicated to everyone listening that something sordid was going on.

"You always come off as 'Little Miss Helpful.' Wanting to be volunteer of the year." She took a step forward. "It's time people knew what you're willing to volunteer for." Deena looked around the room. "Watch your husbands, ladies. Sarah's single and on the hunt."

"Enough." Laura's voice rang out. "Deena, if you have a problem, take it up in private. Let's get back to work."

That didn't go as planned. I wanted to slink out. Instead, I headed back to the sorting room, trying to look casual. The burn in my cheeks said otherwise. What was that about, anyway? Laura and a couple of my other friends followed me into the sorting room.

"Ignore her," Laura said. "Everyone knows she's having problems." The others agreed, patting me on the back.

"Do you want to go?" Laura asked.

"No. No way I'm leaving now."

"That's my girl. I'll stay back here and work with you."

After a while, Laura was called to the front, leaving me alone.

Deena and her friend came back a few minutes later.

"Why are you even here?" Deena asked. "You aren't a spouse or a dependent anymore. You certainly aren't a veteran. You don't belong here anymore. You can't even get on base without a sponsor."

Each word jabbed my heart. Her friend stood with a hand on her hip, nodding.

"I'm here because I work hard. I like the women here. They're friends. I don't appreciate you implying I'm out to steal someone's husband. That is the last thing I'm interested in." I wanted to add "especially yours," but I held my tongue.

Laura came running back in. "What's with you today, Deena? Sarah does twice as much work as most of you. It looks like you're on your way out. Why don't you just go?"

Deena turned on her heel. She jerked her head at her friend and they left.

"Are you okay?" Laura asked again.

"You don't have to fight my battles for me, Laura. There might be some truth to what she said." Maybe I was clinging to my old life, using the thrift shop as a crutch. Perhaps it was time to move on.

"Whatever you're thinking, ignore it."

I opened my mouth. Laura shook her head at me. "I need you here. Don't desert me. Please?"

The more I thought about it, the more I realized Deena might be right.

"You look upset. Don't let those gossips get to you. You handled them well."

"I didn't stop them."

"No one can. Forget them."

Laura left me alone. I'd come here wondering who it was that Deena had an affair with. Now I wondered a lot more. She could have made the story up about her affair to cover for Ted. If he'd had an affair with Tiffany, he might be who the police should be looking at, not CJ.

The other thing I realized is when she said she'd had an affair with a gate guard, I'd jumped to the conclusion it was one of the civilian DOD employees. Although they did the lion's share of guarding the gates, the security forces rotated through, too. A friend of mine had been furious when one of the active-duty guards had asked her daughter for her number. She'd reamed CJ and the young man up one side and down the other. Before I left base, I'd swing by the dorm and see James. He might have heard something.

At two-thirty, Laura called it a day at the thrift shop. Only a few volunteers were still working. Most of the women had headed home about the time school let out. As we walked to our cars, Laura chatted about a grand opening, getting a cake from the commissary, and hoping someone would contribute drinks.

James wasn't at the dorm. Someone told me he was out on patrol. I left a message on his cell phone. He wasn't supposed to have it on when he was on patrol. I hoped he'd check it when he got a break. I drove over to the parking lot behind the shoppette—the base version of a 7-Eleven. It also had the class six—military parlance for a liquor store. In Massachusetts, they called a liquor store a "package store," or "packy" for short.

The gym—free to active-duty troops, retirees, and dependents—shared the parking lot, as did the bowling alley, with its small café. The base library was a short stroll down a walk past a small gazebo.

I hoped James had broken regulations, listened to my message, and that he would drive through here in the next few minutes. It was part of the routine patrol route. Even if he didn't get my message, he might come by. I could stop by the security forces headquarters and ask them to find him for me. I decided it might be better to leave them out of it, especially after my visit with Fran yesterday. If he didn't show up, I'd drive around looking for him. Fitch was small. My plan, although it sounded impractical, wasn't impossible.

A few minutes later, a patrol car pulled in. James climbed out, putting on his beret. Only the security forces wore berets. Everyone else wore flight caps—a blue cap that folded flat, if they were in their blues—or a BDU cap, more like a baseball cap, if they were in their BDUs.

"James, over here," I called as he turned to go into the shoppette. He looked surprised to see me.

We met in the middle of the parking lot.

"What do you want, ma'am?" James asked.

"What's with the 'ma'am'?"

"Protocol." He stood stiffly, a good two feet from me.

"What is going on?"

His face softened for a moment. "You're getting to be persona non grata around here."

He came closer, lowering his voice. "There's talk of not allowing you on base. If the current acting security forces commander didn't know you so well, and know you were good friends with the wing commander's wife, you wouldn't be allowed on."

Wow! First Deena and now this.

"Agent Bristow warned the security force not to give you any special treatment. Major Walker reiterated that warning."

"Thanks for letting me know. I hope you're okay."

James turned to leave, but then he swung around to face me again. "I need to tell you something."

"What about Agent Bristow? The last thing I want to do is get you in trouble."

He looked around the parking lot. An older man in civilian clothing helped his wife out of the car. They headed into the shoppette. A couple of kids on skateboards rolled by. The only other people out were over by the gym, too far to recognize us.

"We're friends. Don't worry about Bristow. It's just . . . Do you know how CJ got the job in Ellington?"

"He applied, like everyone else. Although knowing the chief from basic didn't hurt him any."

"I've heard rumors around the dorm about corruption in Ellington's police department. A few of the high-school kids talked to the younger troops."

I nodded. After CJ and I married and moved to our first assignment, it had taken me a while to get used to seeing eighteen-year-olds carrying around enormous guns. Some of the troops and high-school kids hung out together.

"I've heard some of the younger airmen talking about high-school kids being harassed, beaten, drugs taken and not turned in. Ellington may look picturesque, but it doesn't mean they don't have problems." James gave a brief nod before hurrying into the shoppette.

The Ellington police had harassed me. If they did it to me, why not others?

After taking my purse, an officer led me to the same office I'd been to on Monday to see CJ. The desk had been removed. All that was in the room was a cot with a scratchy, stained blanket. The officer brought in a wooden chair for me to sit on. One leg was slightly shorter than the others. It rocked every time I moved. The lock clicked into place when he left.

CJ sat on the cot, leaning his back against the wall. He looked like he'd lost ten pounds and his best friend. Which I guess he had, since he had always told me I was his best friend. It hurt my heart to see him this way. I steeled myself against that kind of thinking. It wouldn't help now.

"What's going on with this room?" I asked, waving my hand around. "They can't even get you a pillow?" I noticed a camera had been jury-rigged in a corner near the ceiling.

"I'm lucky to be here and not a cell in Cambridge or Billerica. Even a cell here, for that matter."

"What's with the camera?"

"I'm on suicide watch. Not that it's on my mind," CJ hurried to add. "It's standard procedure whenever a cop is arrested. Someone checks on me every fifteen minutes, even with the camera."

"It's not right. I'll ask them to let me bring you a few things."

"They won't let you. I'm not at camp. Even letting you in here is a breach of protocol."

"How'd you get this job?" I asked.

CJ sat up. "What do you mean? You know how I got it. The chief asked me to apply. He knew I was getting ready to retire." CJ rubbed a hand over his stubbled cheek.

"I'm guessing knowing the chief since boot camp didn't hurt."

"It didn't. We worked closely together while I was the commander at Fitch. We appreciated each other."

"Don't small departments usually promote from within their own ranks?"

"Often, but not always. I got to know a lot of the guys since we moved here. We've gotten along well. The town always hires some fancy outside consultant to run a nationwide search." CJ sounded defensive.

"I know your record is . . . mostly stellar—that you have the experience needed to run a department like this. What if there's more to your being hired?"

CJ started jiggling his leg up and down.

"Come on, CJ. Something else is going on here. I've heard the department's corrupt."

"It's a bunch of hogwash. Rumors," CJ said.

"Like high-school kids getting pulled over. Their drugs taken, but not turned in? Beatings? Illegal body searches?"

"Why are you asking about this?"

Now what was I going to say? I didn't want to add to his worries. But it might be too late for that now. "What if these guys thought you were corruptible after . . . after your affair with Tiffany?"

"They'd find out pretty damn fast I wasn't corruptible."

"I know that. Maybe they didn't. Maybe because of the affair, everyone thought you were loosey-goosey with your morals. Or what if whoever really wanted the job and didn't get it found a way to set you up?"

"I applied for the job before any of the trouble with Tiffany."

It wasn't unusual for a military member to have a job lined up before his or her official retirement. The retiree knew the day months in advance.

"These guys have my back. They're all working

overtime without pay to find out what's really going on."

"Or letting you think they're doing that while they make the case against you."

"Why?"

"Because one of them wanted the job. Your getting the job might interfere with whatever is going on in this town. Who applied from the department?"

"I don't know. The applications are probably over at the town manager's office. I've never seen them. You're way off on this one."

"You must have heard something about who wanted the job."

CJ leaned back. He folded his arms over his chest.

I got up from the tippy chair, heading to the door. Angry that CJ wasn't willing to help himself.

"Why are we divorced?" CJ asked. "You must still care, the way you're pursuing all of this."

I stopped with my hand on the doorknob. "We're divorced because you broke my heart. I'm doing this because of the shirts. Don't read anything else into it."

CJ pushed off the cot. I yelled to the guard to unlock the door, hustling out before he could get near me.

"Sarah!"

CJ sounded beyond frustrated, but I didn't stop until I was down the hall and knew he couldn't follow me. I retrieved my purse. CJ hadn't answered any of my questions. I pulled out my phone and called Stella. "I need your help."

CHAPTER 22

After a quick shower to rinse off the thrift shop dust, I sat in Stella's living room. I held a predinner martini, a big favorite of her family's, according to Stella. Her aunt, the cage fighter, shared the aqua couch with me. Stella sat across from us with her other aunt, the town manager. She'd been serving them cocktails when I just happened, prearranged with Stella, to stop by. Everyone looked happy. Stella said if I wanted any information about the town and its dirty secrets, the best way to get it was lots of alcohol and a gently guided conversation. Any overt questions would cause everyone to clam up.

"So, Sarah, what do you do?" Stella's aunt, the cage fighter, asked.

"I'm sort of between things right now."

Stella had also warned me I was going to have to give up some personal details if I had any hope of getting anything in return. I took a large drink of my martini, having forgotten that Stella had promised to water mine down. It tasted terrible.

"She organizes garage sales for people," Stella said. "She's had a bit of a rough time. Be nice, you two."

Eyebrows shot up. The town manager had a knowing look. After all, she'd warned Stella against renting to me.

"Man troubles. My husband, ex-husband, is CJ Hooker. The now-infamous Ellington police chief," I said, "Madam Town Manager."

Is that how you address a town manager?

She perked up a little. I guess she liked it. Stella rolled her eyes.

"I can't imagine what you must think of him. Me." I took another drink. Yuck, I kept forgetting how nasty this was.

"Honey, you aren't the first woman to be taken in by a man," the cage fighter said.

Good heaven, I'd hate to be on her bad side. It looked like she could crack heads open like they were nuts between those well-muscled thighs.

"I know he wouldn't kill anybody. I'm sure this will all be cleared up."

The town manager looked skeptical. "I've seen his résumé. He was in the air force, had multiple deployments. You think he never killed anyone?"

"He might have. That is entirely different from this."

"You kill once, and it's easier to kill again."

I opened my mouth to respond, but Stella shot me a look that said, *Don't argue with her.*

"Like you know that for a fact," the cage fighter said to her sister.

Stella refilled her aunts' drinks from a cocktail shaker she'd set on the end table beside her. "If the worst happens and you have to hire a new chief, at least you probably have plenty of résumés on hand.

I'm sure one of our local officers would jump at the chance."

Thank you, Stella, for bringing the subject up.

"Not as many as you might think. We were a bit disappointed."

The cage fighter leaned toward the town manager. "Who? Who wanted it?"

The town manager smiled, raising an eyebrow. "One of Stella's old boyfriends, among others."

Stella and I exchanged a look: *Pellner.*

"Why do you always have to be secretive?" The cage-fighting aunt asked.

The remnants of old sibling rivalry almost crackled between them. The older sister had chosen politics, the younger physical strength.

"Because I have to protect Ellington and its good name."

"Then why did you hire an outsider?" the cage fighter asked.

The town manager glanced over at me. "At the time, I thought some fresh blood would be good for the city. Shake things up a bit. I just didn't think he'd shake them up this much."

"I heard there are some problems with corruption in Ellington's police force," I said.

Stella looked heavenward. The cage fighter grinned like *Now you're in for it.* She obviously loved a good fight.

The town manager straightened herself before honing in on me. "Like any town, we have some problems. Don't think the base doesn't contribute to them. You know the OSI just swept up a group of base teens for distributing marijuana. Just because they haven't found the ringleader doesn't mean they won't.

They wouldn't have gotten as far as they did without the help of my police department."

I'd moved off base by the time all of that had happened. While I'd heard about it, I hadn't paid much attention with the divorce.

"CJ always said the military is just a microcosm of the civilian world, good and bad."

"Well, he's right about that," the town manger said.

After leaving Stella's, I ran upstairs to my apartment. I called Laura. "Tell me about the drug bust on base."

One of the many things I liked about Laura was that even though she knew the base gossip, she didn't spread it around like MaryJo did. She wouldn't tell me anything she didn't think she should.

"They snared five high-school kids and one airman from the dorm. One of the kids moved here from Los Angeles Air Force Base. He's supposedly the one who had the connections."

"No adults were involved?"

"No one anyone is willing to talk about. They put a ton of pressure on those kids. All of them were kicked off base. They were told they'd go easy on them if they gave up the bigger fish."

"They wouldn't?"

"They all denied knowing anyone up the food chain. Places to drop and pick up the drugs were pre-arranged. No one saw who made the drops. They were told if they tried to find out, they'd be in big trouble. The kid from LA was as high, pardon my pun, as they ever got. He's a tough cookie. Wouldn't talk. Why are you asking?"

"I just wondered if it had anything to do with Jessica's death or with Tiffany."

"Not that I know of. Other than the usual endless speculation, I haven't heard anything like that."

"Thanks, Laura. I'll let you go." Darn, I was hoping for something more.

By the time I got off the phone with Laura, my stomach rumbled wildly. I headed over to DiNapoli's. The place was unusually quiet for six o'clock at night. A young girl was at the counter instead of Rosalie, which might explain why the place was empty. I ordered a Greek salad with grilled chicken to go, since Rosalie wasn't around. I sat at a table for two to wait. Meat sizzled when Angelo slapped the chicken on the grill. I hadn't realized how much I was counting on Rosalie's warm presence.

Angelo brought over my salad, on a plate, not packed to go. "I'm guessing you came to see Rosalie. She's over in Cambridge at her sister's."

I nodded, a lump in my throat preventing me from speaking. I took a deep breath and a drink of water from the glass Angelo had brought.

"You need some wine?"

I shook my head no.

Angelo pulled out a chair, sitting across from me while I picked at the salad.

"What? You don't like my chicken?"

"No, it's just—"

"I'm teasing you. Everyone loves my chicken." He leaned across the table and patted my hand. "You have a stomach problem? Have you eaten over at Tony's in Billerica? You don't know what you're getting at

Tony's. He cuts corners. Watch his cheese. A lot of it is blue, if you know what I mean."

"I wouldn't cheat on your food with Tony's."

"Good thing or you might end up at Lahey."

I didn't think Tony's food was bad enough to land me in the hospital, but I wouldn't take the chance.

"Your heart is still broken."

I opened my mouth to answer.

"Of course it is."

I nodded.

"If it isn't your stomach and you can't eat my chicken, it must be your head. Does it hurt?"

I almost smiled.

"You look worried, like you're feeling sorry for yourself." He shook a finger at me when I started to deny it. "I'm not asking you to tell me what's going on. My father always said, 'If you mess with the bull, you get the horns.'" Angelo put his fingers up by his head and made a jabbing motion like he was a bull. "Don't sit around feeling sorry for yourself. Be the bull."

CHAPTER 23

I carried my barely touched salad and a large chunk of tiramisu that Angelo insisted I take across the common. James sat on the front porch of my apartment building. So much for Agent Bristow's instructions to stay away from me. He stood when he saw me approach. Dressed in worn jeans and a T-shirt, he looked less serious than he did in his uniform.

"I felt bad about this afternoon and wanted to check on you."

"Come on up." James might open up more in the privacy of my apartment. Angelo had just told me to be the bull. Finding out what James knew might help me find a way out of this for CJ. And for myself.

I divided the tiramisu and asked James to uncork a bottle of Chianti. I set plates of tiramisu on the kitchen table while James poured two glasses of wine.

"You didn't have to feed me."

"Angelo just gave this to me. I don't want it to go to waste." Or waist, if I ate the whole thing myself.

We ate in silence for a bit. From Stella's apartment, we could hear someone singing "The Star-Spangled Banner," over and over. The female voice would stop.

I could hear Stella demonstrating a note with her clear tone. I wondered if she coached the Pellners' daughter.

"Does that drive you nuts?" James asked.

"Not usually." I paused. "Do they have any suspects in Jessica's murder?"

James put his fork down and leaned back in his chair. It looked to me like he was trying to get as far away from me as possible without moving his chair.

"They're looking at CJ. His fingerprints were on the statue."

"Of course they were. It belonged to us. Mine were probably on it too."

"And Tiffany's."

"Any unidentified?"

"No."

"Which means whoever did this could have worn gloves," I said.

"It's a possibility. I don't think anyone is pushing that theory too hard."

"Someone told me Major Walker isn't too interested in Jessica's murder. Did you get that impression?"

James shrugged. "She's leaving next week. The new commander will be here. I think she's moved on mentally."

"She worked for CJ for a year. He got her the deployment that led to her in-residence slot at Air Command and Staff College." Going to ACSC in residence, instead of taking the course online, almost guaranteed she'd pin on lieutenant colonel when the time came. "How could she possibly think he murdered someone?"

"No one would have ever thought of CJ as a

cheater, either. Some people think if he could do that, he could do this."

"If that's the thinking on base, he's screwed," I said.

"It's not everyone. A group of us is still working hard to find the truth. Don't discount everyone because of Major Walker."

"I can't figure out why Tiffany had the statue, that she had it sitting in her room, where someone would have seen it. If she had it in her room, why didn't Jessica know it?"

The round space in the dust on Tiffany's bookshelf?

It was the perfect size for the base of the statue. Someone, at some point, had taken it and then rearranged the pictures to make it look like nothing was missing.

"What?" James asked.

"I think she kept it on her bookshelf. Anyone could have taken it. The murderer." I cleared our plates, putting them into the sink with a growing number of dishes that needed to be washed.

James leaped up to help. He nudged me out of the way and filled the sink with soapy water. "Jessica might have known Tiffany had it and didn't want to hurt your feelings."

"Even I'm starting to think that statue is cursed."

James looked over his shoulder as he started washing the dishes.

"I didn't believe it, either, at first." I filled him in on the statue's history. "So Tiffany took it, and she's dead. Jessica might have taken it from Tiffany. Or maybe Tiffany gave it to her. Either way she ended up dead."

I grabbed a dish towel to start drying.

"Why would Tiffany take it? It could have ruined her career if she stole something from your house."

"I think she'd already done a good job of that by sleeping with CJ."

"I was at the bowling alley the night they, uh . . ."

"Slept together?"

James drained the water out of the sink and wiped it down with a purple sponge. "I know CJ had a few drinks, but he didn't act drunk."

"Are you trying to make me feel better? Because knowing that CJ made the decision to sleep with Tiffany without being drunk isn't helping."

James blew out a breath of air. "I'm an ass. What I was trying to say was Colonel Brown was drunk. Really drunk. He and Tiffany were very flirty. CJ pulled him aside and said something to him. They argued and Colonel Brown left—even though his team wasn't finished bowling yet."

Oh, my God. Ted had denied knowing her the day I went to his office. This proved he did.

"What's wrong, Sarah?"

I didn't want to get into any of this with James. "Tiffany might have flirted with Brown, but she slept with CJ." I put the last plate away. I was hesitant to share what Deena had told me. Although, after the way she'd been treating me, I decided she didn't deserve any kind of loyalty from me. And this was about CJ, not me.

"Have you ever heard any rumors about Colonel Brown's wife?"

"Deena? What kind of rumors?" James took the dish towel from me, folded it, and put it by the sink.

"That she was sleeping with a gate guard, and it's

not a rumor. She told me she did. Anyone talking about that?"

James thought for a moment; then he shook his head. "I haven't heard a word."

"Would you have if it was one of the civilians?"

"Not necessarily. I'll ask around. See if I can find anything out."

"Thanks for stopping by. It means a lot to me. Your friendship."

"If I can do anything . . ."

"I'll let you know."

Not long after James left, Carol called me. "I'm still at the store. Come over. I have everything out to paint and a no-show."

It was only eight, so I walked back across the common to Carol's store. It smelled of paint and the vanilla-scented candles she burned. She put a glass of wine in my hand and plunked me in front of an easel.

"I'm not going to paint. Remember what happened last time?" I'd gone with a group from the Spouses Club last fall, when I still was a spouse.

"Yes, you painted a lovely tree of life."

"Mine looked like a head of moldy broccoli."

Carol popped up a picture of a wineglass holding red wine, which sat on a table covered with a blue tablecloth. "Here this one is easy. My kids can paint this one."

"Thanks. Now if it comes out looking like an alien or algae, I'll really feel good about myself."

Carol set up her own easel. She wasn't painting from a picture, though. She was doing an oil of the

Old North Bridge in Concord. It was a winter scene as the sun set. She'd splashed bright shades of orange, pink, and blue across the sky. The colors reflected in the Concord River and on the snowy banks.

"Is that for me?" I asked. I had one other painting she'd done. It was of the coast in Monterey. I'd been bugging her for another one for years.

"Maybe. Quit watching me work and paint. It will relax you."

"I doubt it." I picked up my brush and started filling in strokes. Carol would occasionally lean over, helping me with a detail or blending a color.

"Have you had any more gunshot calls?" Carol asked.

"Yesterday morning. I was driving to Bedford to work on Betty's garage sale."

Carol put down her paintbrush. "What are you going to do about them?"

"I'm not sure. I can't even figure out who'd care." I waved my brush around, splattering blue paint on the table.

"It sounds like CJ would."

"I can't tell him while he's locked up. He can't do anything."

"I get that. Someone should do something."

"At least you know," I said as I turned back to my painting.

"What about that social life you mentioned the day we went to the garage sales? Anything going on with that?"

My cheeks grew warm, but, fortunately, Carol continued to paint and didn't notice. *Seth*. Where did he fit into my life? He didn't.

"Not a thing," I finally answered.

Carol glanced over at me, but she let it go without comment. My painting started to take shape. It looked like a wineglass. I'd managed to make the tablecloth drape nicely. I imitated Carol's bold splashes of color for the background instead of doing the more bland background in the picture.

Carol's phone rang. She glanced at it, frowned, and said, "I have to take this. Keep working." She moved to the back of the store, mostly listening, occasionally saying, "Uh-huh" or "You're kidding." She glanced over at me more than once before she hung up.

She came back over. She took a slug of wine before refilling my glass. "Your painting looks good."

"Just tell me."

Carol shook her head; then she sighed. "I have some bad news."

"Okay." How much worse could it be than two murders?

"That was Laura. You've been banned from the base."

CHAPTER 24

I dropped my paintbrush. "What? Why?"

"I'm sure it's just temporary. Laura said Deena threw a hissy after she left the thrift shop. She said you'd been harassing her and Ted."

"That's not true."

"Ted backed her up. Did you go to his office?"

"Yes. Once."

"And their house? She said you blocked her way when she was trying to go to the gym."

"All that happened, but it's wildly exaggerated. Why would she do that?"

"I don't know. Laura said Deena's been strange lately. I'm sure it will get straightened out in a few days. I'm sorry."

"It's . . ." I was going to say "okay," but it wasn't. It hurt.

"Laura wanted you to know tonight, instead of having you show up on base. Having someone tell you at the gate or visitors center. She told her husband the whole thing was ridiculous. He'll try to get it straightened out soon."

"I wonder if they have pictures of me posted at all

the gates with a big sign that says, 'Don't let this woman on base.'"

Carol shook her head at me. "Leave your painting here tonight. You can come pick it up tomorrow."

At home I sat on my couch, flipping through TV channels, unable to find anything that interested me. I left it on a singing competition. The judges laughed at some poor contestant who thought he could sing. Public humiliation. I felt for the guy.

I hadn't only lost my husband in the divorce; it looked like I was also losing the life I'd known for the past nineteen years. While a large part of it had ended with CJ, at least I'd been able to continue some of my volunteer work and hang out with my base friends.

Then the same feeling came over me that had at the thrift shop. Life might be telling me it was time to move on. I was used to change. Anyone who either made the military a career or married someone in the military knew what it was like to start over: new towns, friends, doctors, dentists, and, the worst, trying to find a new hairstylist. It was always a huge adjustment. What would moving on be like this time, now that I was alone? I wouldn't live on a base or have an instant support group. Would I move away from Ellington? Even with all that had happened, I didn't want to go. I liked it here.

Agent Bristow called me at ten on Thursday morning. "I need to talk to you."

"I've been banned from base."

"So I heard. I can have you escorted on and off, unless you'd rather meet somewhere else."

Being seen on base with a formal escort was way too humiliating. "Somewhere else sounds good."

"Why not meet me at Ellington's library. In, say, half an hour?"

Thirty minutes later, I walked into the library. I'd dressed for the occasion in a black dress, tights, and boots. It somehow made me feel ready for battle. Bristow wasn't in the entrance. I roamed around, looking for him. I stopped to admire Ellington's famed artworks by Revolutionary War minuteman and artist Patrick West. The minutemen chased the British troops back toward Boston in the painting.

I wished sides were that clearly drawn in my life— that I could tell who was on my team by the clothing worn. A throat cleared behind me. It was Bristow.

We sat at a table near the painting. Bristow leaned forward, placing his forearms on the table. The cuffs from his white shirt peeked out under the frayed edge of his hounds-tooth sports jacket. The stained, mis-buttoned, frayed clothes might be a ploy to gain my sympathy. If so, it worked. We'd both lost people we loved, although in very different ways.

"Did you ever find out who Jessica was talking to the Friday before she was killed?" I asked. I'd better get my question in before Bristow got to whatever topic he called me to discuss.

Bristow hesitated before giving a little nod. "She made a lot of calls to West Virginia that day. We're in the process of following up with the people she called to see if they can shed any light on what Jessica wanted. No one has been very willing to talk. I might need to send someone out there. She made a lot of local calls that day, too. It's time-consuming work."

I was surprised Agent Bristow shared that with me. I'd really expected a "none of your business" answer. His willingness to tell me something, share anything, made me wonder why I was here. I might as well see what else I could find out before he shut me down.

"I've heard rumors that the drug ring is still operating on base," I said. "That even after the arrests, you still haven't found the ringleader."

"Why are you asking me about that investigation?"

"It could be related to Tiffany and Jessica. Have you looked into that?"

"The drug investigation has nothing to do with them."

I wasn't satisfied, but I didn't want to make him angry. "Why did you want to meet with me?"

Bristow cleared his throat. "We have news. The DNA results came back. I wanted to tell you myself. It was a ninety-eight percent match to Tiffany. I'm sorry. The results confirm it's her."

I gritted my teeth. A hot wave of emotion roiled through me. I expected to feel sad, but I felt angry. Tiffany had screwed up my life in so many ways. Not just my life. I forced myself to relax my jaw. Tiffany was dead, not off living on a beach somewhere, or eloping or visiting Disney World. I hadn't wanted her to be dead because of CJ.

It never made sense that she'd leave when she had CJ here to support their child. She might have been mad at him for his refusal to stay with her, but running away only hurt her and the baby.

"What will happen to CJ?"

"The special treatment he's been getting will end. He'll be moved to Billerica on Saturday."

"Do you have any new evidence?" I picked at a loose thread on the hem of my dress.

"No. If you know anything, now is the time to tell me. Withholding information wouldn't help CJ."

I thought about the bloody shirts again, my promise about them to CJ. I was very conscious of Agent Bristow studying me. Little beads of sweat popped out on my forehead. CJ would only be safe for another forty-eight hours. Then he'd be in a jail with the general prison population—men who didn't like cops.

I weighed that against knowing CJ wanted to continue his career in law enforcement. CJ wouldn't have killed Tiffany, no matter how angry he'd been with her. CJ had begged me not to tell anyone about the shirts. I would honor that request for now.

"He'll be charged with Jessica's murder. Possibly in the death of the baby, too. Now's the time to tell me anything you know, if you want to help him."

Three murders. I had to say something. "Of course I want to help him. What makes you think he killed Jessica?"

Bristow came close to rolling his eyes. "CJ knows the base as well as anyone. He'd know the weak points in the perimeter. He knows the patrol routine."

"He'd know better than to leave behind a murder weapon with his fingerprints on it—a murder weapon that would be easily linked to him," I said.

"We figure he dropped it in haste as he was leaving."

"How do you know he fled in haste?" I didn't think Agent Bristow would answer many more questions. I sensed his impatience. He leaned back in his chair, a physical move that proved my theory right. He was almost done with me. Any questions he'd answered were only to get more information from me.

"Doesn't his ID being by Tiffany's remains and the statue at Jessica's look just a little too convenient?" I asked.

"I can see how you'd think that. I think these were both crimes of passion."

"Why would CJ kill Jessica? What would make him that angry with her?"

"I was hoping you could answer those questions. Did they have a relationship outside the office? Something inappropriate?"

Could they have? I shook my head. "No. There's no reason to believe that. If they did, why not suspect me?"

"You've been looked at. Thoroughly."

That made me extremely uncomfortable. I tried hard not to let it show. "Why aren't I sitting in jail? I'm the wronged woman."

"I don't think you're the kind of woman to blame the other woman. You'd aim your anger at CJ. If you were going to kill someone, I'd put my money on CJ's head, not Tiffany's or Jessica's."

I didn't know what to say to that.

"You didn't try to cling to CJ after you found out about the affair. You left. Until Tiffany disappeared, you two had very little contact, even though you live just a few miles apart. Yes, you had opportunity, with everyone and their second cousin willing to sponsor you on base day or night. Unless I've read you completely wrong, your reactions to both finding the bones and Jessica's body were real."

They must have gone through CJ's phone and computer records if they knew how little contact we'd had until recently. Or mine. I hoped they hadn't gone through mine. "Then you must know there wasn't anything going on between Jessica and CJ."

Agent Bristow leaned back in his chair and waited. "You're the one who gave me the information that Jessica dated a lot."

I should have just kept my big mouth shut if he was going to use that against CJ. "Agent Bristow, you are way off on all this."

"Even if they weren't in a relationship, Jessica might have uncovered evidence that proved CJ killed Tiffany."

"CJ didn't kill either Jessica or Tiffany. You have to find out who did."

"You must still really care for him."

I stifled a groan. First Carol, then CJ, and now Bristow. How many more people were going to say that to me? I couldn't explain it was guilt over the bloody shirts that made me act this way.

"Have you looked closely at the Ellington Police Department? I've heard a lot of rumors about corruption. Someone may be setting CJ up."

Bristow looked startled, like he was expecting me to say something else. That worried me. "I'll take it into consideration," he said.

After my conversation with Bristow, I realized no one was interested in the real murderer. The evidence against CJ continued to pile up. I thought about Deena, a lot. Maybe Ted did have an affair with Tiffany. Deena might have flipped out and confronted her. They could have argued. Deena grabbed the nearest thing, my statue, and whacked Tiffany over the head with it.

She could have planted rumors about her affair so no one would suspect her. I couldn't figure out how she would have had access to CJ's ID—unless he'd lost it at the gym. She might have found it and meant to give it back to him. I remembered she'd been at our house, too, on the day I'd moved out. Deena could have taken it then.

If Jessica found out, Deena could have killed her, too. If it wasn't Deena, it could be someone from the dorm. Jessica had said Tiffany ignored the enlisted guys. Maybe one of them couldn't take it. Figuring out how anyone pulled it off wouldn't be easy, since I didn't have access to the base. I only had two days to find out who'd killed Tiffany and Jessica before CJ was moved. I had to take action.

I parked my car in the lot behind Bedford High School, the school that the kids from Fitch attended. Time to put into action the best plan I could come up with. Thankfully, it was chilly. I pulled my hoodie up, hiding as much of my face as possible. I slapped on a giant wraparound pair of sunglasses, which, hopefully, would cover my laugh lines. I wore yoga pants from Victoria's Secret and some UGGs I'd dug out of the back of my closet. Pink lipstick and a ton of gloss completed my look. Kids started pouring out of the school. I walked over to where the school buses were lined up.

Earlier in the day, I'd gone through all my options for getting on base. Until recently I could have called the visitors center, pretended I was someone living on base, and sponsored myself on. Someone had spotted that gap in security procedures. To sponsor someone on, you either had to send an e-mail request from an official government address or show up in person. This was the best plan I could come up with on short notice.

The bus for the base kids opened its doors. I almost turned around, but I heard Angelo's voice in my head, *"Be the bull."* I hoped I had a little more finesse than a bull would. My outfit blended in with what the kids were wearing. I worked my way to the middle of the group. The bus driver took no notice of me as I climbed on the bus. I grabbed a seat near the back of the bus, popped in earbuds, and concentrated on my phone. Glancing out of the corner of my eye, I could see I wasn't the only one doing this.

The bus took off with a jarring bounce. I readjusted my sunglasses and tugged my hood forward, making sure as little of my face showed as possible. The bus headed down Great Road and took a right on Hartwell. The two girls in the seat in front of me chatted away. One looked like your typical blond-cheerleader type. The other was all dark, Goth, spiked-hair gloom. An odd combination for friends. The cheerleader turned around and looked at me.

"Are you new? I don't remember seeing you before."

I nodded, too afraid to speak. The Goth girl glanced over her shoulder at me. This had to be better than climbing over the fence topped with razor wire or trying to cut through it. I was sure they'd increased perimeter patrols since Jessica's murder. They probably added more security cameras. I looked back down at my phone. The girl flounced back around after she realized I wasn't going to say anything else.

"I skipped algebra today. I saw Phil Crawford at the Dunkin' Donuts," the Goth girl said.

"He's so hot. Why'd he have to get kicked off base?" the cheerleader asked.

"Why do all the hot ones have to be idiots and sell drugs," Goth girl said.

I perked up.

"I thought he moved back to LA," the cheerleader said.

"He's living with an aunt in Bedford. He asked for my number."

"Kyle is going to come around any day now," the cheerleader said.

"Kyle Brown? Oh, please."

Kyle Brown was Ted and Deena's son. I edged forward on my seat, kept my head down, fidgeting with my phone.

"You're dreaming if you think he's going to break up with Chelsea," the Goth girl said.

"She's impossible, now that she's singing at the Celtics game," the cheerleader said. "It's not fair. I'm the one that cheered for him all through football and basketball season."

Kyle was dating Scott Pellner's daughter.

"You don't stand a chance."

The cheerleader gestured toward her body. "You don't think he's going to want some of this? Chelsea lives in town. I'm convenient."

The Goth girl laughed. "He was sweating bullets when they arrested Phil and those other kids."

"That's a bunch of bull. Kyle was just trying to act cool."

The bus approached the gate. This was the tricky part. The bus driver would have to stop at the gate to show his ID. Buses were checked randomly to make sure kids had IDs with them. If they found me, I'd never be allowed back on base, no matter how many strings Laura's husband tried to pull.

"Damn," the Goth girl said. "I forgot my ID."

"Just hide under the seat. I'll distract the security guard." The cheerleader tossed her hair.

I eyed the space under the bus seat. I wasn't limber enough to stuff my body under there. Hopefully, it wouldn't come to that. The gate guard motioned the bus through. I let out a sigh of relief. When the bus made its first stop by the youth center, I hopped off.

After walking to the library from there, I grabbed a book and took it to a back corner. I hoped no one I knew came by. Most of my friends were either fixing dinner or getting ready to go out. It was steak night at the club. There used to be a separate officer and enlisted club. At some point, they'd combined into one club. A band was playing tonight. They would raffle prizes. That should keep everyone occupied until the library closed.

The girls on the bus had talked about Kyle Brown and the drug bust. I grabbed a base paper from a pile stacked near the door. The drug bust wasn't mentioned. It was old news by now. Just before eight, I left the library.

I headed up the hill to the new thrift shop. It should be empty this time of night. Even though it was dark, I scooted around the backs of buildings to stay off the main road. I let myself into the thrift shop with the key Laura had given me. I left the lights off, grateful they'd moved the thrift shop. I couldn't sit in the old one, knowing Jessica and Tiffany had been killed right outside. I curled up in the corner of a couch and, amazingly, fell asleep.

At eleven o'clock, I woke and left the thrift shop.

The base had a curfew for anyone under eighteen unaccompanied by an adult. Eleven at night to six in the morning on weekdays, and midnight to six on weekends. If I ran into a patrol, looking like I was sneaking around, they'd stop me and ask for my ID. They wouldn't fall for my "I forgot my ID" routine.

With that in mind, I cut through a baseball field by the swimming pool on my way to the housing area. I turned right on Edwards and then took a left on Luke. I tried not to give into my instinct to scurry. Instead I walked confidently, like I belonged here. Not long ago I did. I jogged a little in case anyone drove by. The steep hill quickly slowed me back to a walk.

One side of the street was lined with old town houses; the other with little brick Cape Cods. The higher the rank, the bigger the house was the usual rule of thumb. Most lights were out. Some of the houses were empty, since a section of new housing had just opened. People were transitioning from old to new.

A dog barked off in the distance as I got to the house CJ and I had lived in. Someone had already moved in. That's the military for you: all hellos and good-byes, packing and unpacking. I broke into a jog again. I passed Eglin Circle, where Laura had lived until the new housing opened up—she'd kill me if she knew what I was up to—and finally slowed to a walk when I could barely draw in a breath. Deena lived in the last house on the left side of Luke. It backed to the woods. A tot lot sat across the street to its side.

I walked by their house. No lights were on. An owl hooted as I headed to the tree line. I circled back to their detached garage. About six months ago, Deena had complained about the amount of stuff Ted kept in the garage. They couldn't park a car in it. Deena wanted to get rid of most of it. Laura had told her to bring it to the thrift shop, just to get her to shut up.

The brick garage sat about ten feet back, to the side of the house. I pressed my ear to the cracked and peeling side door. I didn't hear anything expect the echo of my heartbeat pounding. Paint chips stuck to my cheek as I pulled back. I slowly turned the knob of the wooden door on the side of the Browns' garage, relieved it was unlocked.

People were notoriously bad about locking up on base. Even though CJ regularly reminded them through a safety column in the *Fitch Times* that there was crime on Fitch. Until the two murders, crime was mostly bike thefts and misuse of official government computers. CJ had to assign one of his staff to deal solely with tracking civilian use of porn sites while at work on base.

I eased the door open an inch, relieved it didn't creak or stick. I peered in as I pushed it open. It was packed to the gills. The only open floor space was an area by a workbench littered with tools. The rest looked worse than the sorting room at the thrift shop.

I slipped in and turned on the flashlight feature on my phone. I held it down, even though there was little chance any light would show outside. I started my search with Ted's golf clubs. Nothing. My light flicked out. In the dark, I fumbled with my phone. I managed to get the light back on. It already drained my battery to one bar.

I couldn't search everything without taking hours. With limited light, I prioritized. I worked the perimeter, starting to my right. I pawed through boxes of old electronics. They'd saved stacks of old magazines and college textbooks. I moved to the workbench. I opened a toolbox. I lifted out a set of wrenches and found an old tin box. It was stuffed full of purple notes. I spread them out on the bench.

My hands trembled. All of them were signed by Tiffany. I stuffed them back in the tin box and snapped a couple of pictures. Finding these might help CJ. This time I wasn't leaving the notes behind. I stuffed them in the pocket of my hoodie.

Halfway out of the garage, the sound of a door opening came from the house. No lights came on, at least on the back or side of the house, which was the extent of what I could see. The side door opened inward. I shut the garage door as much as I could without making any noise and ducked behind two garbage cans. I glanced down at my phone. It was only eleven-thirty. I would have sworn I'd been in the garage for hours. I peered between the two garbage cans as the storm door slowly swung out.

CHAPTER 25

Deena stepped out, dressed in dark jogging clothes. She didn't glance back. She surely would have noticed the partially opened garage door and me crouching by the garbage. I tried not to play out, in my head, the ending to that scenario. She crept down the driveway, turned right on Luke, and jogged out of sight. I eased the garage door the rest of the way shut and went after Deena.

I crept down her driveway, knowing at the bottom I'd be exposed. If Deena was around, she'd see me. She'd already jogged almost to Eglin Circle by the time I got to the end of the driveway. I sighed and started after her, sticking to the grass to deaden the sound of my footfalls.

She ran all the way down Luke. My breath started coming in harsh pants. Deena passed a little community center and entered the joint elementary- and middle-school parking lot. She disappeared around the side of the school. When I peeked around the corner, I saw her turn behind the school. A little creek, a branch off the Shawsheen River, and some woods were the only things back there.

I stuck close to the side of the building. As I neared the back, I heard voices. Deena argued with someone. I peeked around the corner of the school. I saw two people and they'd gone from arguing to kissing. That wasn't Ted. The guy wasn't as tall. Besides, who snuck out of her house to make out with her own husband? So much for Deena's marital counseling.

I decided to wait them out. The wind picked up and a few snowflakes fell. When I heard voices, I ducked behind one of the large oak trees by the sidewalk. They came around the corner. Deena started back toward housing. The guy headed over toward the gym. After they were both out of sight, I cut over to Travis Street. I didn't like being on the main road, but I hoped to spot the guy again. He might be heading up toward the dorms, and I could find out who he was.

A car engine started somewhere behind the shoppette. I picked up my pace. A car pulled onto Travis. It turned up the hill toward the Offutt gate. I didn't have to try to follow. I recognized the car. It was Tyler's.

Getting off base is normally a lot easier than getting on. Occasionally they'd do random ID checks as people left. Sometimes worried parents called the security desk if their child took off when he or she wasn't supposed to. Then the gate guards checked every vehicle and person as they left. If an alarm sounded in one of the high-security buildings, the gates would shut. Everyone would be let out, one by one, after the cars had been searched.

I jogged off, waving a quick hand at the guard shack. With the wind and snow, the guard wasn't very curious about who I was or where I was going. His job was way more about keeping people off than keeping people on.

Tyler and Deena made an odd couple. I didn't care what they did or how they met. The only reason I'd gone on base was to find a connection between Deena, Ted, Tiffany, and Jessica. The purple notes proved Ted and Tiffany knew each other. I patted the notes in my pocket and declared the night a success.

The wind picked up as I started the four-mile walk back to Bedford High School. It was too late to call Carol for a ride. She always claimed that when her kids could drive, she'd pick them up wherever they were—no questions asked. That philosophy wouldn't extend to me, especially if I wanted her to pick me up this close to base. I didn't want to hear what she'd have to say about this latest adventure. James would grill me if I called him. Even calling a taxi would leave a trail if things somehow went south.

No sidewalks were on this section of Hartwell. Dark office buildings and trees lined the street. I stayed as close to the edge of the shoulder as possible, although no cars had gone by. Even the cleaning crews had left by this time of night. Snowflakes coated the front of my hoodie. I bent my head against the increasing wind. I couldn't make it all the way back to Bedford on my own. As I decided a taxi was my only option, I saw lights glowing on the right-hand side of the road.

I'd forgotten about the restaurant up ahead. It changed hands often and was closed as much as it was open. I'd heard it had once been an upscale Italian restaurant. When we moved here, it did a brief stint as a sports bar. I'd call a cab from there. Calling a cab from a restaurant wasn't nearly as suspicious as calling a cab from the side of the street in the middle of office complexes.

The sign said, GILLGANINS AUTHENTIC IRISH PUB. The parking lot was full for midnight. Heat rolled over me as I opened the door.

"Sarah." Stella sat at the bar, waving me over. She looked at my bedraggled state and turned to the bartender. "We're going to need an Irish coffee."

"Thanks, Stella. I'll be right back." I went to the bathroom and cleaned up as best I could. I smiled at my bedraggled self in the mirror. I'd gotten on and off base without getting caught. Evidence pointing to Ted sat in my pocket. It might even get CJ released. Now that I was warm and safe, I was ready to celebrate. Stella was the perfect person with whom to celebrate.

The Irish coffee waited for me when I slid onto the stool next to Stella. I clasped my hands around the warm mug before taking a drink.

"Who's the girl I hear singing 'The Star-Spangled Banner'? She has a beautiful voice."

"Is it driving you nuts? I'm sorry."

"Not at all. I enjoy listening to her."

"It's Chelsea Pellner, Scott's daughter. She's going to sing it at the Celtics game next week."

"She must be the one dating my friend Deena's son. His name is Kyle." Calling Deena a friend at this point went way beyond white lie.

"Chelsea talks about him all the time. I've been giving Chelsea voice lessons since she was in third grade. She thinks of me as an aunt and tells me her woes. She likes to picture them as star-crossed lovers."

"Their families don't want them to date?"

"No. He lives on base, and she lives in town. Neither of them drives. Seeing each other is complicated."

"Deena's worried Kyle's involved with drugs. Do you think Chelsea is?"

"No way. She's a serious student. Wants to go to Juilliard. She wouldn't do anything that would damage her voice or her chances. Scott would kill them if he thought either one was doing drugs."

"They always say cops' kids and ministers' kids flip out during their teen years."

"Not Chelsea. She'd drop Kyle in a heartbeat if she thought he was. The girl is focused. Between voice lessons, choir, and family duties, she doesn't have time to get in trouble. Her mom's a bit of a flake. Chelsea has a lot of responsibility at home."

"Her mom's a flake?"

"I shouldn't say that. She's from the South and runs on a different timetable than Yankees do. It causes some talk around town."

"What doesn't?" I asked.

"Amen to that, sister," Stella said, and we clinked our glasses.

Stella wowed the audience with her karaoke skills. After a couple of Irish coffees, I jumped up on the little stage with her. I rode on Stella's coattails and enjoyed the applause. We stayed until the place closed. She dropped me at my car without questioning why I'd shown up at the bar looking bedraggled, or why my car was at the high school.

"Thanks, Stella," I said as I got out.

"If you ever need to talk."

"Thanks."

On Friday morning, I chugged water to relieve my dry mouth. During the night, I'd tried to figure out who should get the notes I'd found in the Browns' garage. Agent Bristow might throw me in jail if he knew I was on base. James was another possibility. He wouldn't be happy, but I didn't think he'd be so angry that I'd end up locked up and having to call Angelo to get the number of his cousin, the Mob lawyer.

CJ was my last resort. I hated reminding him of the disastrous night when I'd brought up the first round of notes. Depending on how the day went, I might have to show them to him.

I mulled over Tyler and Deena's relationship. According to Stella, Tyler took classes at Middlesex Community College. Deena had to be five years older than I was. Between the gym and the late-night runs, she kept in great shape. I wondered how she explained the runs to Ted. If he slept as soundly as CJ, he might not notice she was gone. Tyler might be the elusive drug connection, and the drug connection went from him to Deena.

After my shower and makeup routine, I decided to head to West Concord Seafoods for a lobster roll. I could try to pry some information out of Tyler, get some food, and put off worrying about the notes until later. Maybe with a full stomach, the best course of action would come to me.

The sun warmed my back as I walked into the eatery. Tyler stood behind the counter. His eyes drooped, but he smiled when I ordered.

Tyler brought out my lobster roll and fries. "Why don't you sit with me, Tyler? I hate eating alone." I'd come before the noon rush on purpose.

Tyler glanced around the empty store before nodding and sitting down.

"Want some of my fries?" I asked him. I wasn't about to share my lobster roll.

"Naw, I'm good." He yawned and stretched.

I smiled to myself, knowing why he was tired. "Rough night?"

Tyler shrugged. He wasn't much of a conversationalist. The few times we had talked, I'd pulled answers out of him.

"Have you lived in Ellington long?" I asked.

"Naw. You?"

"I used to live on base. Have you ever lived on base?"

He shook his head no.

"Ever think about working on base? You can find some good jobs."

"Naw. I checked into the security guard jobs. I've done it before back home. It didn't work out."

If I could have yelled an "aha," I would have. "It's a good way to meet girls."

He ducked his head and started to blush.

"Why don't you live on base anymore?" he asked.

Yeesh, I was supposed to be the one asking the questions. He might open up if I did. "Divorced. It's brutal. My husband had an affair. It still stings." If I couldn't get any information from him, I might be able to wake him up to what he was doing with Deena.

"Suppose it does." He glanced over at the door, like he was hoping someone would come in and end this conversation.

"Where's back home?" I asked.

"Here and there. You?"

"I grew up in California. Have you ever lived out there?"

"No. You gonna go back? I've heard it's nice."

"It is, but I like it here."

"Tryin' to stay around for your husband?"

"No. Something about New England just feels right to me. What about you?" Might as well try again.

"Don't know. It's cold and expensive."

"But it's charming, too. That part reminds me of Monterey."

The door opened and a group of people came in.

"Gotta get back at it." Tyler went back around the counter. Darn, just when he'd finally started talking. I ate as slowly as possible, to the point that it was becoming awkward. A steady stream of people came in. I couldn't sit here all day, hoping to chat with Tyler. He'd wonder what I was doing.

CHAPTER 26

I spent the rest of the afternoon getting ready for Betty's preview party and garage sale. It was a great distraction from thinking about CJ being charged with the murders of Jessica and Tiffany. I put flyers up in Lexington, Concord, and Bedford, farther afield than usual. I put ads online. With all the tourists in town for the Patriots' Day events, I hoped Betty would have a huge turnout.

At four-thirty, I drove over to Betty's house. Since the hard work was done, I dressed in a flowered, spring-looking skirt, with a sweater that picked up the pink of the flowers. Then I moved a few things from one place to the other and dusted some of the furniture. By the time I was done, it was fifteen minutes to showtime. A few of her friends had shown up early. I shook my head—early birds at a preview party. Betty had ushered them into the house and out of my way. She'd set up a table with wine and cheese. A little wine always helped loosen the purse strings.

Betty had so many beautiful things; I was certain she was set to make a killing tonight and tomorrow. She'd enlisted her sisters and cousins to come help run the sale tomorrow. It kept me from having to hire anyone and her costs down.

"It's almost five," Betty said. "Okay, if I bring my friends out?"

"I'm ready."

A crowd swarmed in—Betty had a lot of friends. If this kept up, she wasn't going to have any worries about selling stuff.

Betty handed me a large cardboard box. "I decided to get rid of this box, too."

The box was filled with photographs, some tintypes, some just old. I looked up at her.

"My husband thinks the pictures are creepy. I never did anything with them."

I quickly sorted the tintypes from the old pictures. I held up a bunch. "Are these relatives? Are you sure you won't regret selling them?"

"I have three more boxes inside, just like this one. My husband's threatening to use them as kindling in the fireplace. Better someone else enjoy them."

As the evening progressed, several of Betty's friends asked for my number. They wanted me to organize garage sales for them. I jotted my phone number down for them. No one wanted to leave. Betty kept telling them she had an early start as she edged them toward the door.

We shooed the last of them out at five minutes after seven. Betty counted money as I reorganized the room. It would be a shambles after the first hour tomorrow. At least it would look nice for the first people at the sale.

One of her friends had bought most of the tintypes. I rifled through what was left to see if I wanted any of them. The people sat in stiff, formal positions, wearing elaborate clothes. Probably the best things they owned. Smiles were rare. The pictures Tiffany had of her with CJ were almost as formal as these.

Betty interrupted my thought process by handing me a large bundle of cash. "Here's your part of the take. I added in a bonus. You did a great job. I'm glad some of my friends wanted your number."

"Me too."

Was it possible that this could turn into a real job? Could there really be enough call for someone to make a career out of organizing garage sales? Lots of places offered to haul off your junk. People paid a hefty price to get it out of their house. I could give those people an alternative. Get rid of your junk—and instead of spending money, make some.

After parking my car at home, I decided to eat at DiNapoli's again. Tomorrow I'd go grocery shopping. With my alimony, portion of CJ's retirement, and savings, I survived easily enough. I'm not sure my waistline would agree if I kept eating out this much. On a whim, I knocked on Stella's door. I heard her singing "I'm Gonna Wash That Man Right Outa My Hair" from Rodgers and Hammerstein's musical *South Pacific*. As she opened the door, she sang, "And send him on his way."

"Man troubles?" I asked.

"Not this week," Stella said with a grin. "I sent him on his way."

I hadn't ever seen Stella on a date, but she was young and single—so, why wouldn't she?

"I'm heading over to DiNapoli's for something to eat. Want to come?"

"Absolutely. I'll grab my pocketbook from my rum." Stella pronounced the word "room" as "rum," a peculiarity of speech in this area. "Come on in." She hummed Beyoncé's "Single Ladies" as she headed for her purse. I leaned against the doorjamb.

"I'm going to run up and change out of this skirt," I said.

"You look nice," Stella said.

"For once. I'd rather drip pizza sauce on jeans than this outfit. It's cold outside. I'll be right back."

We strolled across the common. Ellington's drum-and-bugle corps played lively music. Lots of tourists posed for pictures with members of the Ellington Minuteman Company who milled about. Several kids wrestled on the lawn.

"This is my aunt's doing."

"The cage fighter?"

Stella laughed. "The town manager. She's trying to promote tourism. Ellington, Massachusetts, as a tourist destination."

"Concord and Lexington sure are. It's not like the Ellington Minuteman Company didn't do their part on the first day of the Revolution." We dodged a kid playing with a hoop and stick.

"She stole the hoop-and-stick game idea from Hartwell Tavern. The woman doesn't have any original ideas."

"She should throw New England's largest garage sale."

"That's a phenomenal idea. I'll tell her. At least that would be something new and different in Ellington."

I pointed to Carol's shop. "Have you been to Paint and Wine? My friend Carol owns it."

Stella shook her head. "I've never been."

"I'll have to introduce you to each other."

Rosalie greeted us at the counter. "Do you have a half-off coupon?"

Angelo yelled from the back. "We don't do coupons."

Rosalie tossed him a look, suggesting he was wrong. She grabbed a pen and wrote on a napkin, *Coupon 50 percent off.* She handed it to me and then snatched it out of my hand. "She has a coupon, Angelo. What do you want, honey?"

"We'll have a medium bianco."

Rosalie yelled, "A medium bianco, Angelo."

"No, you don't want the bianco. Have the sausage and Kalamata olive. It's excellent tonight," Angelo said. He put his fingers to his lips and made a kissing motion.

I looked at Stella. "I think if we stick with the bianco, we'll get the sausage and Kalamata, anyway." She shrugged. "Okay, Angelo. We'll go with your recommendation."

He nodded approvingly. "Good choice."

We found a table. As we sat, the guy who'd been in line behind me said he forgot his coupon. Rosalie looked over at Angelo. He raised his shoulders and put his hands out as if to say, *Now, what are you going to do?*

Rosalie turned to the guy. "Here take this one." It was the same one she had used for us. Angelo muttered and tossed the pizza crust with a vengeance.

Rosalie brought over a tray with a pitcher of water, two red plastic glasses, and a couple of kiddie sippy cups, complete with lids and straws.

"We ordered iced tea," Stella told her.

"I'm almost out of glasses. I thought you wouldn't mind." She winked and walked away.

I took a cautious sip. *Sangria!* "It's sangria," I said, keeping my voice low. Stella and I toasted silently.

After polishing off an exceptional pizza, we stood to go. Rosalie shooed us back. "Angelo made a cheesecake that is to die for. Cannoli. He used cannoli shells for the crust, instead of graham crackers, and piped cannoli cream on top of the cheesecake, sprinkled with some chocolate shavings."

We told her we'd share a piece. The cheesecake was wonderful. Stella left, but I decided to have an espresso before leaving.

Angelo came over and sat down with me.

"How's Stella doing?" he asked.

The question surprised me, but Stella had told me she'd been in trouble with the police. "She's good, as far as I know. We're just getting to know each other. I like her. Stella said she'd had trouble with the law once. Do you know what it was?"

Angelo took a minute. He realigned the napkin dispenser, jars of Parmesan cheese, and hot red-pepper flakes. It looked like he was making a decision. I understood. Stella was a native. Her family had lived in Ellington for generations. I was the newcomer. Angelo was fond of me and believed I'd been wronged; but in New England, being from here meant more.

I patted his hand. "Never mind. I shouldn't have asked."

He grabbed mine, holding it in his calloused one, which surprised me.

"Stella had a drug problem."

CHAPTER 27

"Stella?" I asked. "She's the last person I'd expect you to say that about."

"It started when she went to Europe. The pressure to succeed, to always be the best, was tremendous. The town made much of her going, like her success made us all better. It just added to the pressure." He released my hand. "She left Europe and moved to Los Angeles. She didn't leave the drugs behind. She was arrested in Los Angeles. Nothing much came of it—some community service or something like that. She moved from city to city, each one smaller than the last. Seattle, Indianapolis, Salt Lake City." He ticked them off on his fingers.

"Stella told me she lived in Europe. I thought she moved right back here."

"She wants the past in the past," Angelo said.

"That's understandable."

"Somewhere along the line, she straightened herself out and came back home, where she belongs." Angelo stood and headed back to the kitchen, muttering about why anyone would ever want to leave Ellington.

Stella had overcome a drug problem. It didn't fit

with the Stella I knew. She'd told me so casually something about "who didn't have trouble with the police?" Then a little thought snuck in from the back of my mind. One I wanted to push aside. She had kids, teenagers, in and out of her house all the time for music lessons. What if she hadn't left her old life behind? The music lessons would be the perfect cover. I hoped I was wrong, way off the mark.

I studied the pictures hanging on the wall: a young Angelo and Rosalie cutting a blue ribbon in front of DiNapoli's thirty years ago; former mayor of Boston Tom Menino biting into a piece of pizza, with cheese dripping off the sides; Ted Kennedy, with an arm slung around Angelo's shoulders, back in the day when Angelo had hair; Guy Fieri cooking with Angelo for an episode of *Diners, Drive-Ins and Dives*. Angelo made it clear to everyone that DiNapoli's wasn't a drive-in (obviously) or a dive (not as obvious, but no one was willing to contradict that statement), so it fell into the diner category. Angelo, however, preferred to think of DiNapoli's as a restaurant.

I realized how different these pictures were from the ones Betty had sold at the garage sale. And from the pictures in Tiffany's room. She'd had a couple of her horsing around with kids from home. It struck me again that the pictures of her and CJ were more similar to Betty's formal pictures than the ones hanging in here. I'd like to see those pictures again. Someone would know where her stuff was. I just had to figure out who.

I settled on trying to get a hold of James. I could trust him to either help or tell me that he wouldn't, without reservation. James might have information for me about Deena and her affair. Maybe I could tell him about the purple notes. The clock to Saturday ticked faster than I wanted it to. I had to do whatever I could to help CJ. Otherwise, he'd end up in jail at Billerica tomorrow.

"I'm playing baseball up in Lowell," James said when he answered his phone. "Why don't you come up?"

I had just enough sangria in me to think it was a good idea even if it was pretty late. James gave me directions to the park. Thirty minutes later, I sat on a cool metal bleacher watching James pitch under the lights. I looked around nervously for Seth. He wasn't sitting in the stands, but why would he be? I couldn't see the faces of all the players. Seth really didn't look like the baseball-playing type, even though his body was certainly athletic enough. My face warmed at that thought. Lowell was a big city by Massachusetts standards. I was being paranoid to think I'd run into him.

I didn't recognize any of the people watching the game, either. This wasn't one of the base teams trying out some new competition. I didn't want to make nice or answer awkward questions. Anonymity could be a good thing. James had a strong arm and struck people out right and left. After the game ended, and a brief celebration of the win, James snagged two beers from a cooler over by the dugout and joined me on the now-empty bleachers.

"I didn't recognize any of the players or spectators."

"It's a police league. Pellner got me into it."

"Scott Pellner? How do you know him?"

"I've been thinking about getting out after my enlistment's up. I've been talking to Chief Hooker about a job in Ellington. I got to know Pellner through him."

"What's Pellner's tie to Lowell?"

"He's from here. Most of his family lives here."

That might be why Pellner knew about my night in Lowell. "You have quite the arm," I said, accepting the beer he handed me.

He shrugged. "I used to dream about playing professionally. What kid doesn't have some kind of unattainable goal when they're little?" He took a swig of his beer.

"Like Tiffany dreamed of being a colonel's wife."

The corners of James's mouth turned down. He stared over the now-empty field. "It probably wasn't her first dream. It sounds like she was always looking for a way out."

"First, out of a coal town," I said.

"Then a fast way out of being enlisted. She didn't want to take the time to go to college."

I sipped my beer. I had to stay sharp. CJ would be moved tomorrow. Someone turned out the lights on the playing field.

James hadn't brought up Deena, but I had to, especially given what I'd seen last night. It would be easier to ask about Deena in the dark. "Did you find anything out about Deena?"

James shifted away from me. "That's one screwed-up family. But, no, I haven't heard any of the guys talking about her."

"I saw her with someone last night on base."

"You were on base?"

Oh, rats. I shouldn't have said anything about base. "Yes, but that isn't what's important here."

"Did someone escort you?"

"No."

"So you weren't supposed to be on base, but you went, anyway?"

"Yes. Please don't lecture me. I had to. CJ is going to end up in the Billerica jail tomorrow if Tiffany and Jessica's murders aren't resolved."

"How did you get on?"

I shook my head. "I just did."

"Promise me that you won't do it again. If there's a hole in base security, you should report it."

"Until CJ is out of this mess, I can't promise you anything. I will tell someone how I got on when the time comes."

James didn't look happy, but he nodded. "What was Deena doing?"

"I saw her making out with someone. My next-door neighbor. I questioned him today."

"*You questioned him?* You can't go running around doing things like that."

"'Questioned' was too strong. We just had a conversation. Like neighbors do. He said he'd never worked on base. Can you find out how he's getting on? His first name is Tyler."

"I can't help you if you are going on base when you aren't supposed to be."

I guess James wasn't the one to tell about sneaking into Deena's garage and taking the notes. "Please," I said again. Dear God, I hoped he didn't ask me why I cared. If he did, I might run down the bleachers, screaming in my best imitation of a raving lunatic.

"I'll see what I can find out. Colonel Hooker was always decent to me. Do you know Tyler's last name?"

Embarrassed that I didn't, I made a quick call to Stella. "It's Shimkus," I said after hanging up. "I thought about the pictures in Tiffany's room," I continued. "The ones of her and CJ. She didn't have any casual shots of them. Just official ones or ones clipped from the paper. What do you think that means?"

James took my empty beer bottle, trotted down the bleachers, and tossed them into a recycling bin. I followed him.

He slung an arm around my shoulders and headed me in the direction of the Suburban. "I think it means CJ was careful enough to make sure none were taken."

I sucked in a breath. James was probably right. "Do you know where her personal stuff is?" I leaned against my car.

"CJ might know. I have no idea. You want to go through it? Looking for what? Pictures that will only hurt you more? Let it go."

"I can't let it go. Bristow told me the DNA results came back and that they prove it's Tiffany."

James looked stunned. "When did he tell you this?"

"I met him yesterday morning."

James shook his head. "He lied to you. I worked all day. I would have heard if they came back. Did he ask you anything?"

Bristow lied to me? I didn't answer for a minute. "He told me if I knew anything, now was the time to tell him."

"Bristow used a classic interrogation method on you. He tried to shake you up by making up a story about the DNA, to see if you were holding something back."

"That jerk." I hoped that meant CJ wasn't going to be charged in Jessica's murder and the baby's—that Bristow had lied about that, too.

"You didn't hold anything back, did you?"

"No." I hated to lie to James, of all people. "I have to go."

"Sarah, wait." James tilted my chin up. "You've been hurt. You are worth more than that."

I didn't say anything for a minute. "Thank you, James." I jumped in the Suburban and took off. I had to talk to CJ.

CHAPTER 28

I headed back to Ellington. For a minute, back in Lowell, I'd thought James was going to kiss me. I hoped I'd misunderstood James's actions—that he didn't think of me romantically, when I thought of him as a friend. He was right about my being worth something. It's why I'd left CJ. It's also why I didn't plan a repeat of a night with Seth or with anyone else.

I parked across the street from the Ellington Police Station. My access to CJ would be limited when they moved him tomorrow. After talking to him, I'd decide if I needed to fess up about the bloody shirts.

More than the normal number of people worked this late on a Friday night. They moved slower, heads down, as if they'd given up. The energy was different in the station.

For once, I didn't have to sit out in the lobby, hoping I'd get to see CJ. After surrendering my purse, an officer escorted me to the same room CJ had been staying in and locked me in. There was a time in my life when I would have been thrilled to be locked in a room with CJ.

The cot still didn't have a pillow. An old, bulky TV

sat in a corner. A stack of thrillers stuck out from under the cot: David Baldacci, Robert Crais, and Michael Connelly, CJ's favorite authors. A camera still hung from the ceiling, pointing down at CJ.

He looked a heck of a lot more cheerful than everyone else did when I walked in. A game of solitaire sprawled across the cot.

"Not quite poker night," he said, gesturing to the cards. He moved to me like he was going to hug me, but he stopped when I took a step back. "What are you doing here?"

"I have to tell someone I had the shirts first. I can't let you go to the Billerica jail over this."

"It's not just the shirts. It's my ID card, my fingerprints, last-known person to have the statue."

"That's not true. James's partner at the crime scene, the day I found Jessica's body. She said it was Tiffany's. Other people had access to it, too."

"I explained to you before that I trust in the process. The charges will be dropped. If you tell, once the charges are dropped, no one will trust me."

"Agent Bristow told me they're transferring you to Billerica tomorrow."

"A few days in Billerica won't hurt me. I might learn something."

"Come on. I've always known you were an optimist, but you can drop the act. This is serious."

"Billerica is hardly Souza-Baranowski. It's not a maximum-security prison. I'll be fine."

"I've heard what happens to cops in jail."

"They'll probably keep me separated from the general population."

"*Probably?* Or they will?"

"They will." The lack of conviction in CJ's voice and his unwillingness to look at me told me otherwise.

"I have something to show you." I took the notes out of my coat pocket, glad I'd remembered to take them out of my purse before I went into the police station. I turned my back to the camera and handed them over to CJ.

He read through each one, his face stoic. "You said Ted threw these away."

"These are different ones." I told CJ about what I'd done last night. CJ shook his head while I talked, but at least he listened.

"What the hell, Sarah? You have no proof where you found these."

"I do." I showed him the pictures on my phone.

"That's not proof. Even if it was, it was obtained illegally. Sneaking on base, breaking into the Browns' garage, stealing from them. You, of all people, should understand the chain of evidence."

I grabbed the notes and stuffed them back into my pocket.

"You don't realize how close you came to getting caught. How much trouble you would have been in."

"What are you talking about?"

"Deena was picked up a couple of hours ago for drug trafficking. A lot of the evidence was in their garage."

Holy crap. "Who told you?" Why hadn't James told me? "Was Ted involved?" I asked.

"Pellner told me. Ted's denying it. Deena's saying someone planted it."

"Was anyone else arrested? Anyone in Ellington?" I thought about Tyler and Stella.

CJ shook his head.

"Do they think anyone else is involved?"

"They think she's the only link between a supplier in LA and the base."

It was a relief to know Stella or Tyler wasn't involved. At least I wasn't living in the middle of a bunch of drug lords.

"If you'd left the notes, they'd have been found and investigated."

I filled in what CJ left unsaid, "You might have been released." I paused. "Agent Bristow told me the DNA results were in. That it was a match to Tiffany."

"What? No one told me."

"That's because it isn't true. He lied to me. I talked to James and he told me the results weren't back yet."

CJ looked thoughtful. "James always really liked you."

"He's been a good friend. I can always count on him." I hadn't meant it as a slam to CJ; but from the expression on his face, that's how it came off.

"Are you sure you can trust him?" CJ asked.

"Of course. I can't believe you'd even ask me that." We sat for a minute, watching each other.

"Anything else you want to tell me?" CJ asked.

"Bristow's trying to get me to tell him something—anything that will convict you."

"Keep our secret about the shirts. Promise me you'll keep it."

"For as long as I can." I stood to go.

"I'm starting to wonder if you are trying to help me or get me locked up for good."

CJ's last comment did nothing to improve my mood. As I picked up my purse, I smacked my hand down on a desk. Heads jerked up. "Do something, damn it," I said.

I looked at them with disgust and headed to the front door. Someone muttered, "I'd like to arrest you."

I decided to drive the route I'd taken the day Carol and I went to garage sales one more time. I might have missed something when I tried it last week. I had no idea what I'd find, but it beat going home and sitting around wondering what I might have been doing. I headed down Bedford Road. As I passed Sleepy Hollow Cemetery, clouds moved over the moon, blanking out the light. It was dark enough to imagine the Headless Horseman could be here, too.

The moon came back out as I hit the rotary in Concord. Light reflected off some of the dark windows at the Colonial Inn. It was rumored to be haunted. I'd heard a story about an air force officer who had stayed there. In the morning, he came out looking pale and asked where the library was. The librarian later called the hotel to tell them an air force officer had been in, and he was researching ghost stories about the inn. On a night like this one, I could believe in ghosts. If a ghost could give me answers, I'd be happy to encounter one.

I crept by the house where we'd gone to one of the garage sales. Despite the late hour, cars crowded the street on either side. Tiny white lights draped all over the trees in the backyard. People danced on the front porch and the front door was wide open. It looked fun.

I wound my way around, past the Paul Revere Capture Site and the Minute Man National Historical Park Visitor Center. I kept going until I arrived in Lexington. Some of the houses were set back farther from the street. It was difficult to see much at this time of night. I thought about CJ's comment about trusting James.

I'd just seen what a strong arm James had—one

that could easily strike a blow—but lots of people were strong. Jessica said Tiffany wouldn't give the enlisted guys the time of day, but she never mentioned James by name. James had no reason to kill Jessica. He told me he barely knew her or Tiffany. He'd brought Jessica over to my apartment because she needed a ride.

As I drove around Lexington, I realized I'd had the same set of headlights in my rearview, on and off, for almost the entire drive. It wasn't like they were always there, but they were distinctive. Halogen bulbs set in a line, the kind that came on high-end SUVs. I made a couple of turns I didn't need to and the lights disappeared.

I decided to drive by the few remaining houses Carol and I had gone to, just in case. The Victorian was dark; a Cape the same. I took it as a sign. *Go home. There's nothing to learn out here.* I drove down a side street heading toward Lexington Town Center. Headlights flashed into my rearview. The same ones. Again.

I sped up, slammed on my brakes, and angled my car across the street, blocking it. An easy feat, given the narrowness of the side streets and cars parked on either side. The SUV started to reverse. I rolled down my window and snapped a photo of the license plate. I wouldn't have taken the risk if I'd been out in the boonies, but I was a stone's throw from the Lexington Police Department.

I maneuvered my car around and headed up the street. I turned into the Lexington Police Department lot, parking in the first open space. The SUV pulled in behind me, trapping me.

CHAPTER 29

I couldn't run into the station. I dialed 911. A car door slammed, or, in this case, an SUV door. As I waited for dispatch, I looked in my rearview mirror. Scott Pellner stood behind my car.

"Where's your emergency?" the dispatcher asked.

I looked back at Pellner and sighed. "Never mind. It's a case of mistaken identity."

"Where's your emergency?" the dispatcher asked again.

"I'm in the parking lot of the Lexington Police Department. Really, it's okay. Someone I know accidentally scared me."

"Stay on the line."

I knew they'd send someone out to check. For a moment, I savored a thought of telling the LPD officer that Pellner had been stalking me or tried to run me off the road. Picturing him in handcuffs made me smile.

I rolled down my window and stuck my head out. "Pellner, I called 911. You scared me. I tried to tell the dispatcher to forget it, but someone's probably going to come out."

A cop ran out of the building. Pellner already had his badge out and open.

"Hey, Scott. What's going on?"

Great, they know each other.

I climbed out of the Suburban and walked over to where the two of them stood.

"You the lady who called in?" the burly cop asked me.

"Yes."

"Can I see some ID? License and registration."

"It's okay. I'm sure Officer Pellner didn't mean to scare me."

"I meant your license and registration."

"But—"

"You can be charged for making nuisance calls to 911."

Pellner stood stoically, eyes on the officer. He was probably savoring the thought of me being taken away in handcuffs.

I grabbed my license and registration out of the glove box. "I thought someone was following me. I felt threatened."

The officer looked over everything and handed it back. "We good here?"

I started to answer, but I realized he was looking at Pellner.

Pellner stood silently; then he gave a slight nod. "Yeah, Carl. Let her go."

Let me go?

"How's Junior doing at Fitchburg?" Pellner asked him.

"Loves it. He'll be playing tight end for them next fall," the cop called over his shoulder as he reentered the building. He stopped in the doorway and pointed at me. "Watch the calls. Leave the lines open for people with real emergencies."

When he'd gone back inside, I turned on Pellner. "What the hell? You've been following me since I left Ellington. You made it look like I did something wrong."

"Sounds like you were a little hotheaded down at the station. I wanted to make sure you didn't cause any trouble."

"More like you wanted to be there if I did." I headed toward my car, but I turned back to him. "How did you know about Lowell?"

"Lowell may be bigger than Ellington, but it's still a small town."

"That's not an answer."

"My cousin owns the restaurant across the street from the bar. I saw you hanging on the sidewalk and Seth giving you the eye."

"You know Seth?"

"Of course I do. He's the DA."

"What? You followed me that night, too? Into the bar? You watched me?"

Scott shook his head. "I have better things to do. One of the bathrooms at my cousin's restaurant was having some problems when I left the night before. I brought up some parts and tools the next morning so my cousin could open for the day. Doesn't take a genius to figure things out. I saw you hopping out of Seth's car and back into yours in the same clothes you had on the night before."

"Why do you even care?" The same question everyone had been asking me lately.

"I like the chief."

I wondered about that, but I wasn't going to bring

it up now, while we were out here alone. He could whack me over the head, stuff me in his trunk, and dump my body somewhere. I'm sure that as a cop he knew all the best places for hiding bodies.

"You keep running around acting like you're worried about Chuck. And yet you're seeing the DA. It looks to me like you're helping Seth build the case against Chuck. Letting Chuck think you're trying to help him. You have a lot of reason to be mad at Chuck. Could be this is your way of getting back."

"I'm not dating Seth. And I am trying to help CJ." Pellner was as suspicious of me as I was of him.

Pellner held up his hands. "Call it what you want. I figured if you knew I had something on you, you might leave Chuck alone. He's a good man who made a mistake. Let him move on with his life."

Like I believed anything coming out of Pellner's mouth. "Whatever."

"Hey! I'm not going to tell the chief, if that's what you're worried about."

"Go ahead and tell him, instead of threatening me." I really hoped he wouldn't.

"He's got enough on his mind. You shouldn't be out adding to his worries."

"Leave me alone." I climbed back into the Suburban. I only had a few hours left before CJ would be transferred.

It was almost four in the morning when I arrived home. I tossed my keys on the trunk in front of my couch. Sleep would have to wait until I found something out that would help CJ.

I grabbed my laptop and set it up on the kitchen

table. After reactivating my Facebook account, I looked at Jessica's page. It had a big *RIP* across the top. Hundreds of condolence comments were posted, along with a link to her obituary. Services were pending.

Tiffany's Facebook page had been taken down. I Googled her. I found local articles about her being missing, her presumed death. One article about CJ's arrest popped up in conjunction with Tiffany. Not what I was interested in or cared about. It was a topic I was all too familiar with.

I tried a search for "Tiffany" and "West Virginia." Several older "hometown girl makes good in the Air Force" articles appeared. One included a picture of CJ giving her the Airman of the Quarter Award. Instead of facing the camera, Tiffany stared up at CJ— one might describe it as "adoringly." I resisted the temptation to plant my fist in the middle of her tiny, smug face.

I clicked on another link. Pictures of a homecoming parade the year Tiffany graduated popped up. As homecoming queen, she rode on a float with the king, surrounded by the court. They sat stiffly in crepe-paper-draped chairs in the back of a pickup truck. No convertible corvettes for this town.

I zoomed in on the picture of the kids in the pickup. I studied each face and realized why the pictures at the garage sale today had set me searching. The homecoming king, quarterback hero who was Tiffany's boyfriend, the one she'd left behind, was my next-door neighbor.

It was Tyler.

CHAPTER 30

Pieces of information clicked through my brain. Tyler could have moved here when Tiffany did or sometime after. Stella would know when he'd moved in. He was already living here when I arrived in January. Who knew how learning about the news of Tiffany's pregnancy and her affair had affected him? Maybe it was enough for him to kill her and frame CJ. He could easily have put the shirts in my Suburban during the night.

I drummed my fingers on the kitchen table. What was he doing with Deena? If Tiffany slept with Ted and CJ, both Tyler and Deena had reason to be furious. One could have killed her and the other covered it up. Then in some twisted way, they'd turned to each other for solace. I didn't have any proof and no clue how to get any. I had to tell CJ.

I rushed out of my apartment. Tyler stood by his door in his standard outfit of jeans and hoodie.

"Hiiii, Tyler. I'm heading out. . . ." My voice trailed off as I tried to figure out what to say. I didn't owe him any explanations. "What are you up to?" As if I didn't know. I edged toward the stairs.

He looked at my outfit: jeans, V-necked sweater, and silver ballet flats. I had my keys in my hand and purse slung over my shoulder. Our eyes met and I knew he knew that I knew. I lunged for the stairs. He took two strides and grabbed me. He yanked me back against him. I stabbed at him with my keys. Tyler knocked them out of my hand. I opened my mouth, letting out an ear-piercing scream before he cut it off with a hand over my mouth.

"Scream all you want. Stella drove Mrs. Callahan to the hospital an hour ago. Chest pains. No one is home to hear you."

Tyler looped his arm around my neck, applying just enough pressure for me to see dots, but not enough for me to pass out. I tried to stamp my foot on his insole. He deftly moved it out of the way.

He dragged me back toward my door and opened it. In my rush to leave, I hadn't even locked it. I kicked and pounded the floor as much as I could. I hoped he was lying about Stella. Since he didn't seem to mind, I stopped. I was wearing myself out. I didn't know when I'd have a chance to escape. I had to be ready for it.

Tyler released me. I turned in time to see his fisted hand heading at me. I threw my arms up to protect my head. The blow landed right above my belly button. It flung me back on the couch. My head cracked against the plaster wall.

My eyes blurred with tears. My nose and mouth filled with mucus. I gasped in little pants of breath. No one had ever hit me before. I didn't realize one punch could create so much pain. I blinked, trying to clear my eyes. I could hear Tyler rummaging around in my kitchen.

I stood, but I doubled over. I wrapped one arm

around my waist. I reached a hand out, searching for something to balance on. My hand landed on the trunk I used as a coffee table. If only I kept a knife on it or a heavy vase. I didn't think the latest issue of *Flea Market Finds* would let me beat Tyler senseless, which was what I really wanted to do right now.

I hobbled forward a step before I realized he stood there, watching me. He cracked me across my jaw with his open hand. Pushed me back on the couch. I tried to curl away from him. Tyler sat on my issue of *Flea Market Finds* and cut a length of duct tape. He must have found it under my kitchen sink with my kitchen shears. I screamed, even though my throat was raw, hoping someone out on the common would hear me.

I kicked out at him. He pinioned my legs between his. He wrapped duct tape around my arms until I couldn't move them. Tyler cursed once, but he mostly ignored me. I was about as threatening as Lexi. He seemed so calm, even though his breathing sounded jagged like mine.

He looped layers of duct tape around my ankles until I wouldn't be able to walk. Tyler headed into my bedroom. He came back with one of my white gym socks and stuffed it in my mouth. I almost retched. After a quick nod, he left.

I started working my mouth, sore jaw, and tongue, trying to get the sock out. My jaw already ached from having my mouth braced open. I inched the sock forward enough to give my gag reflex a break. I managed to get a bit of the sock out, but part of it dangled on my chin.

The door swung open. Tyler stepped back in and yanked a girl in behind him: Tiffany.

CHAPTER 31

She wasn't dead. A thousand questions ran through my mind and not one answer. Her mouth was duct-taped shut. Her greasy hair looked tangled. Her eyes were red and swollen, like she'd been crying. A lot. Maybe for days. She wore leggings and a loose sweater. Tyler had duct-taped her hands behind her back. He pushed her down on the couch next to me. She didn't even try to fight when he pulled my roll of duct tape out of the pocket of his hoodie and taped her legs together.

He stood over us, looking back and forth. Then he pinched the bridge of his nose like he had a terrible headache. It looked like he wondered how his life had come to this point. I knew I did. He snatched the sock out of my mouth and tossed it across the room. I gulped in air.

"Don't do this," I said between breaths. "Just go. We won't tell anyone. We'll come up with a story between us somehow."

Tiffany nodded frantically.

"I may be from coal country," Tyler said with an exaggerated Southern drawl, "but as my mama always tol' me, I didn't fall off no turnip truck." He unrolled a four-inch piece of duct tape, slapping it over my mouth. He rubbed across it until it was good and stuck. He stepped back and put his hands on his hips, like he hadn't planned his next move. I just hoped maybe he hadn't.

He scanned my living room and spotted my box of curtains. I'd never taken the time to put it away. Tyler picked up one of the blue silk ones I'd decided not to hang. After jerking me up off the couch, he wrapped me in the curtain. It wasn't tight, but it covered me head to toe. He tossed me over his shoulder in a fireman's carry. The top of the curtain flapped over my head. I couldn't see anything, but I could tell he was trotting down the steps.

Cold air seeped through the curtain. We must be outside. Tyler tossed me back down. My head hit something hard. A door slammed. I thrashed around, trying to wiggle out of the curtain. I wanted to see where he'd dumped me. Then I smelled cinnamon. It stopped me. I must be in the back of my Suburban. *"Don't ever go to a second location."* I'd learned that watching *Oprah*. Nothing good ever happened at a second location. I struggled against the curtain and duct tape.

I listened, waiting for the engine to start. Footsteps headed toward me. I rolled from side to side, trying to make the Suburban move. Maybe whoever it was would see it and come investigate. The back door popped open and cold air rushed in. Something thumped and the Suburban shifted. Tyler must have put Tiffany beside me.

I expected to hear the doors slam shut again. Instead, stuff was tossed on top of me. A crinkle of plastic made me think it was bags of clothes. Even if we did somehow manage to free ourselves or even sit up, if someone glanced in the back of the Suburban, all they would see would be junk.

The engine fired up and the Suburban began to move. We backed out onto the street. We turned right onto Great Road toward Bedford. I tried to keep track of where we were. Tyler went straight for a bit. He started a series of turns. I couldn't keep up with them. He stayed at a steady pace, not too fast or too slow— nothing that would attract attention.

Maybe an Ellington police officer, one of the many who liked to stop me, would spot my car and pull us over.

Pellner, please be out on patrol. Notice I'm not driving and pull us over.

Tiffany was near me; because on sharp turns, we'd roll into each other. After driving about ten minutes, we made another turn. The Suburban bumped along. We were on a dirt road. That couldn't be good.

Tyler drove a few more minutes before rolling to a stop. The driver's door creaked open and then slammed, rocking the Suburban. I waited, listening, worked to loosen my arms from the duct tape. The back of the Suburban opened. Tyler grabbed my ankles and dragged me out before tossing me over his shoulder again. He huffed as he carried me and muttered something about someone could stand to lose a few pounds.

He dropped me, jarring my bones, on a cold, possibly dirt floor. I smelled hay and earth. I rolled onto my back, tossing my head until I freed myself from the curtain around my face. Light filtered in from somewhere. I saw beams, unfinished wooden walls, and tall stacks of hay bales. I was in a barn. They dotted this area. I could be anyplace. Tyler had left me in a space between the hay and the wall; my head was near the wall, my feet by the bales.

The bales on the bottom sagged a little. The twine holding them together looked old. An odd musty smell emanated from them.

I listened for a moo or a snort, something that would give me hope we weren't in an abandoned barn. I heard some scratchy, rustling sounds and figured it was mice, hoped it wasn't rats. Prayed they wouldn't come over to investigate. A few minutes later, Tyler tossed Tiffany beside me. Then he left. I wondered if he was coming back or someone would just find our rotting bodies someday. Tyler returned a few minutes later and set a smoothbore musket, just like the ones that were in Betty's husband's gun cabinet, in the corner.

"Damn town's so quiet, no way I can shoot you two without everyone knowing. Too many people at the shooting range to take you out there. I'll be back later. When someone does find you, it will be too late to figure out why you're here. Maybe even who you are."

Tyler left. The Suburban fired up and drove away. I pictured the bits of metal at the bottom of the glass at Betty's house. No wonder Tyler said no one would recognize us. A blank would blow our faces into thousands of smidgens of flesh and bone.

I worked on my arms until I was so tired, I couldn't move anymore. Tiffany was either knocked out or asleep. I couldn't tell which. Eventually I fell asleep, too. I was too tired to struggle, too tired to fight.

* * *

The sound of a gunshot woke me. Another phone call. The ache in my back and cold reminded me where I was. Right now, a phone call with a gunshot didn't sound so bad. Bright light filtered through cracks in the barn. It must be midmorning. I was supposed to be at Betty's house running her garage sale. She must be furious with me.

The single shot was followed by a far-off volley. Shouts rang through the crisp air. We were in Lincoln. I knew what Tyler had planned. Today was the Bloody Angle Battle Demonstration at the Minute Man National Historical Park. The event commemorated the first time the colonials fired on the British soldiers. I could hear the words ringing in my head: *"Fire, men. For God's sake, fire."* They did, and a war was born. Later, Emerson had coined the famous phrase "the shot heard round the world" in his poem "Concord Hymn."

During the demonstration, minutemen chased the British Regulars from the Bloody Angle to the Sam Hartwell House in Lincoln. The battle passed by the Hartwell Tavern. This old barn was by the Hartwell Tavern. I'd watched the reenactment enough times to know the troops would run by the barn, but not come in. The barn was all but abandoned.

Tyler would be back anytime. He'd said it was too quiet around here to get away with shooting someone. The fire from the reenactors would cover the sound of Tyler's gunshots. Tyler could easily shoot us and no one would think anything was out of the ordinary. If we were found shot by the musket, everyone would assume we were in the wrong place, that something had gone horribly wrong. Tyler would disappear.

I wriggled around until I was completely free of the curtain Tyler had draped over me. I kicked at Tiffany with my feet. She stirred and the curtain fell from her face. Her eyes grew large as she registered the gunshots; what was about to happen to us dawned on her, too. She started struggling against her ties. At least CJ wouldn't be blamed for our murders because he was still in jail. I was filled with a thousand regrets of what I should have done and said, but it was too late.

I stared up at the tall bales of hay. I worked on my binds again. Nothing gave. The duct tape was as tight as when Tyler had wrapped it around me. I closed my eyes, wondering when he'd come back. The shots were getting closer as the minutemen chased the Regulars back toward the Sam Hartwell House. I pictured all the people lined up and down the trail, watching the reenactors, not knowing that only feet away two women were hog-tied and helpless.

Tiffany sniffled. God, she was young. Whatever she'd done, she didn't deserve this. Adrenaline surged through me. I kicked my bound feet at the bottom bale of hay. I wasn't sure what it would do, but it was better than doing nothing. I hoped the stack would fall over and draw someone's attention. Maybe it would topple over and kill us before Tyler got a chance. The duct tape around my ankles loosened, just a bit, as I kicked. Tiffany stopped sniffling. Using a wormlike motion, she inched her way over and started kicking, too.

At first, nothing happened, but we kept at it. Some of the hay broke away around our feet. The bales didn't budge. We panted as much as we could with duct-taped mouths. We both stopped for a moment. A new volley of shots got us going again. Too close. Time almost had to be up. I kicked and kicked, pretending I was kicking Tyler's face.

"What the hell?" Tiffany and I turned our heads toward Tyler. He was dressed in red, the uniform of the British Regulars. He blended right in with the crowd outside.

Tiffany and I looked at each other and started kicking again. Tyler cursed. He grabbed the musket he left last night. I remembered Betty telling me it took an expert about fifteen to twenty seconds to load and fire one. Not much time to save ourselves. Fortunately for us, Tyler was no expert. He cocked the hammer of the musket back halfway and took a paper tube out of his pocket. He ripped off the end with his mouth, poured some black powder into the musket, dropped in the paper and a musket ball. Tyler tamped it all in with a ramrod. He poured more gunpowder in the top of the musket near the hammer and closed it by flipping a part on the top.

We kicked at the hay the whole time he loaded the gun. Sweat poured off our faces. With my mouth taped shut, breathing flared my nostrils. I wasn't sure if my light-headedness was from fear or a lack of oxygen. Tyler pointed the musket at Tiffany's head.

"After what Tiffany did to you, you ought to get to watch her die."

I gave the hay bale another kick. The hay teetered, but it settled back into place. Tyler inched the hammer back. I kicked again. The string holding the bottom bale sprang loose. The bales rocked. The top ones tumbled loose. The first knocked the musket out of Tyler's hands. It went off with a deafening blast. He screamed and put his hands up, trying to ward off the heavy bales. One hit him square in the chest. It knocked him to the ground.

Others fell, slamming around us, shaking the ground. The air filled with hay and dust. One after the other rained down around us until they landed on us with crushing blows.

All was dark and quiet. I could barely draw a breath with the weight of a bale on my chest. I hoped Tyler couldn't, either. If this was it, at least I'd gone out with a fight.

CHAPTER 32

"What the heck happened in here?" a man asked.

"Looks like the hay fell over."

"I'm not stupid, George. I can see that."

"Let's go. They're getting to the good part. I love watching the British hightail it back toward Boston. We can worry about this after the crowds leave."

No, no, no! Don't leave.

I sucked in a small breath of air. My upper body was pinned, but my legs weren't trapped. I thrashed around, hoping it wasn't too late or that I was too far under to be seen. I kicked some more, feeling light-headed and beyond any sort of weariness I'd ever experienced.

"What's that, Gus?"

"Don't know. Might be a dang snake. Let's get out of here."

"No. Looks like a foot. We'd better call someone."

I heard shouts; minutes later, the weight was lifted off my chest. Someone brushed the straw off my face. A grizzled face peered into mine. Sirens wailed from somewhere.

"You okay?"

I nodded. I moved my hand as much as I could, making a V with two fingers. The guy staring at me looked puzzled. He eyed the duct tape across my mouth. I wiggled the two fingers at him, then jerked my head at the straw.

"There's two more in here?"

I nodded again.

"We need some help in here!" the guy yelled out the door.

Sirens wailed, sounding closer and closer. The barn filled with British and colonial reenactors. Men heaved bales of hay out of the way. They found Tiffany first. She had a painful looking knot on her forehead, but her eyes were alert.

"Someone's over here."

EMTs ran in.

"This guy looks half dead, but he has a pulse," one of them said.

Two of the EMTs lifted me onto a board and snapped a brace around my neck. They carried me to an ambulance. One cut the duct tape, freeing my arms and legs. The other hustled back to the barn. I saw Tyler being rolled out of the barn on a gurney and loaded into an ambulance. Part of me wished one of the hay bales had killed him. The doors slammed and the ambulance took off. Two other EMTs rolled Tiffany toward the back of another ambulance. She gave me a long look before she disappeared inside.

My EMT looked at the duct tape on my mouth. "I'll be as gentle as I can. It's probably going to hurt."

I guessed that was an understatement of huge proportions. He started at one corner, tugging gently on the tape toward my mouth. He did the same at each corner, prying up as much as he could.

Scott Pellner stuck his head in the ambulance. The EMT held a hand up for him to stop.

"I'll count to three, then rip."

I lifted my chin.

"One, two—" He ripped; it stung; my eyes filled. I sucked in deep breaths of air. The EMT applied some kind of salve on my lips that took some of the sting away.

"Thank you." I looked over at Pellner. He probably enjoyed watching that. His face looked a little pale and he shuddered.

The EMT put a blood pressure cuff around my arm.

"Feel like talking?" Pellner asked.

I stretched my mouth around. Touched my tender lips. "Yes, of course. The man in the ambulance was my next-door neighbor Tyler Shimkus. He was going to kill us. I think he probably killed Jessica."

Pellner used his mike to notify someone to put a guard on Tyler. When he finished, I managed to give Pellner a fairly calm version of the rest of the events. I had to take a couple of deep breaths when I got to the part with the musket pointing first at my head and then at Tiffany's.

"I'm sorry," Pellner said.

That's not what I expected to hear. "Why?"

"I knew something was wrong. I tried to stop it. That night I pulled you over and hauled you to the station, I was sure someone was after you. They disappeared before I got them."

"Why didn't you tell me?"

"Would you have believed me? You've been darn sure I was a bad cop. Out to get you."

I stared at him. "You messed up my license plate on purpose."

"I figured the only way to keep you safe that night was to make sure you were at the station. I cleaned it before I left the station."

All this time, I thought CJ had cleaned it for me.

"On the drive to the station, you made sure I was tossed around the back of your car."

He shook his head. "One of the guys thought he saw the gray sedan you'd spotted that night over near the Bedford border. I was hauling ass trying to catch up. Wanted to see if you could confirm that was the car."

I remembered blasts of codes coming out of his radio. "You went to my apartment and destroyed it."

"I went to your apartment to make sure it was safe before you got home. Tyler must be the one that tossed it. I've always wondered what he was looking for."

He studied me. I looked down. No need to mention the bloody shirts now. Thoughts tumbled through my head. What I thought I knew to be true was so far off base that it was in another game completely. "Your wife told me you wanted to be chief. Maybe you're making all this up to keep your job."

Pellner shook his head. "My wife wanted me to be chief. I like being out on the streets. I'd go nuts sitting behind a desk, handling personnel issues and dealing with the town manager. Representing the city at events. The chief has a gift for that kind of thing." He looked thoughtful and then gave a short laugh. "Just because my wife wanted me to have the job didn't mean I did."

I hadn't met one military wife who wasn't mad as heck when her husband didn't get the promotion she thought he deserved. You made the sacrifices, moves, deployments, missed anniversaries, birthdays, even births—and then your husband was passed over. It stung. Pellner's wife could feel the same way.

"The town manager told me you applied for the chief position. Well, she said Stella's high-school boyfriend."

"You think I'm the only guy Stella dated in high school who's on the force? Ellington's a small town." Pellner looked out of the ambulance and sighed. "I did apply."

I started to speak, but Pellner plowed on. "I promised my wife I would." He looked at me. "I'll tell you a secret. I withdrew my application without telling her. I didn't make any promises about that."

He knew my secret and now I knew one of his. "You told me not to mess with your family."

"Damn right. I'd do that again in a heartbeat. To you or anyone. My family's off-limits."

I thought about the time he'd stepped in front of me at CJ's house. He'd done it without hesitation. He wasn't the guy I thought he was. Maybe none of the guys in the police department were. "I'm sorry. I thought . . ." What could I say?

Scott got a little twinkle in his eye—one I hadn't seen before, or at least had refused to see. Now his dimple looked cute, not threatening. "Well, I can't deny the guys at the station had a little fun messing with you. Chief's a great guy. You should give him another chance."

I opened my mouth, but I didn't have any response.

"I know he's been hiding something—something that probably kept your butt out of jail. I'll keep it between us. Unless you say something, he'll never know."

CJ's words rang in my ears. I wasn't about to confirm or deny what Pellner had just said. I'd promised CJ I wouldn't.

"Fact is, I need to go free him." Pellner climbed out of the ambulance. "You kept him out of Billerica. Good job."

"Wait," I called after him. "What about the police corruption in Ellington? The links with the drug ring on base."

"Every police department has someone mad at them for something. Citizens think they shouldn't have been arrested or Uncle Joe didn't deserve a ticket. All of a sudden, it goes from that to corruption. Rumors about drug abuse." Pellner shook his head. "The chief runs a clean station. He wouldn't put up with anything."

That sounded like CJ.

The EMT fiddled with the blood pressure cuff. "Your blood pressure was all over the map. Understandable, given what I just heard. Let's leave it on a few more minutes. Then you should be good to go."

The EMT finally took the blood pressure cuff off. I climbed out of the ambulance. The reenactment was winding down. Soldiers, women, and children all in colonial dress milled around, but they weren't allowed to get close to the barn or ambulances. Some of the tourists watching pointed toward the scene and snapped pictures.

Tiffany called out to me from her ambulance. "Sarah, can we talk?"

CHAPTER 33

Talking to Tiffany appealed to me about as much as having duct tape reapplied to my lips and ripped off again. But she looked pitiful stretched out on a gurney with an IV stuck in her arm.

"Okay."

"Climb in," she said. She turned to the EMT. "Can you give us a minute?"

The woman eyed me, but she jumped out.

"I'm sorry," Tiffany said.

"For?"

"Dragging you into this mess. For the gunshot calls."

"It was you." I wasn't surprised. After nearly losing our lives, it seemed kind of insignificant.

"I'd go down to the range, call you, and fire a round," Tiffany said. "I thought if I scared you, you'd leave town."

"So CJ would be available. How'd you pull the gunshots off after you supposedly died?"

"Tyler took over. He'd go to the gun range in Billerica. He worked hard to make me think he was on my side—an old friend who just wanted me to be happy."

"I saw him with Deena Brown."

"He hooked up with her a couple of times. Part of his attempt to convince me we were just friends."

I'd seen them together just the other night. No reason to point that out. "How'd they meet?"

"At West Concord Seafoods."

"What changed?"

"When I miscarried, Tyler lost it."

"You grabbed the nearest thing to stanch the flow? Your old fatigues and CJ's shirt."

"I swiped the shirt from your house. The night I slept with CJ. I called Tyler when I was miscarrying. I wanted him to take me to the hospital, but he came up with a crazy plan to get back at CJ. I was stupid enough to go along with it."

"Did Tyler kill Jessica?"

Tiffany started crying. "He got her number off my phone. He'd heard from a friend she'd been calling people back home." Tiffany wiped her free hand across her eyes.

"Why'd he kill her?"

"She was nosing around some of Tyler's friends. Asking where he was. Where I was."

"She died because of a few phone calls?"

"Jessica found out one branch of Tyler's family owned a mortuary. She started calling there, wondering if the bones were planted. His cousin blew up. Told Tyler he had to fix it."

"He thought killing her was the solution?"

"It wasn't only that. Tyler freaked when CJ wasn't arrested right away. He'd left CJ's ID by the bones. Gave you the bloody shirts. Tyler thought if CJ was in jail, I'd abandon him and turn to Tyler. Instead, CJ was free. He fixated on Jessica. Saw her as the solution to two problems."

Waves of cold, like I'd been plunged into an icy river, passed through me. I couldn't understand how anyone could view Jessica as a solution to a problem. "Jessica wanted to meet me the day she was killed. She said she had information. Did Tyler set that up?" I asked.

"He made up some story about you two being in danger. He didn't want to talk about it over the phone. Just in case."

That kind of intrigue probably appealed to Jessica. If only she'd told me. Tyler killed her and stuffed her under the lift. He left the statue so it would look like CJ killed Jessica.

"Why didn't he kill me, too?"

"Because you were nice to him. Friendly. He never wanted to hurt you until he realized you weren't going to butt out."

"You went along with Tyler's plan to make it look like you were dead."

"Willingly, at first. I fought with CJ. He refused to marry me. I wanted to hurt him. The cousin at the funeral home back home helped him get the bones of a Jane Doe about my size. Tyler wanted everyone to think I was dead and for CJ to be blamed."

"What about when the DNA results came back?"

"Tyler thought we'd be long gone by then."

"How could you do that to CJ?"

"I was mad."

"When did things change?"

"I stayed in a motel until most of my cash ran out. Tyler snuck me up to his apartment one night. He isolated me more and more. Took my phone and computer. He started handcuffing and gagging me when he left. After he killed Jessica . . ." Tiffany took a deep, shuddery breath. "I didn't find out Jessica was dead until Sunday. I tried to leave."

Sunday was the night the music had blared from his apartment. I'd thought he was having a party. Tiffany had been fighting for her freedom.

"After that, he kept me handcuffed all the time."

I shook my head. "Why did Tyler break into CJ's house? Tyler said he was going to kill me."

"He thought it was empty."

Part of me wanted to throttle her for all her excuses and "I didn't know" answers. "Why go? All he took was a couple of pictures of CJ and me from CJ's nightstand."

"He thought if I saw the pictures, if I knew CJ didn't care about anyone but you, I'd leave with Tyler. He wanted us to head to Mexico. I have no idea what he thought we'd live on. Neither of us has any money."

I didn't know what to say to all of this. It was almost too much for my tired brain and body to take in.

"I realized I was wrong. *About everything.* I decided to fess up to the whole mess. Tyler went nuts." She sighed. "All along, he had planned for us to start a new life—as if I'd go to Mexico."

Tiffany was so young. I leaned over and took her hand. She'd tried to do the right thing. "I'm sorry," I said.

She snatched her hand away. "Don't be nice to me." Tiffany's voice cracked. "There's more. I didn't sleep with CJ."

I stared at her. "Sure you did." What mischief was she up to now? One of the bales must have whacked her a little harder than anyone thought. "CJ told me.

Apologized a thousand times. I was in your dorm room. Saw the ultrasounds."

"Okay, I might have slept with him. But he didn't, we didn't, ever have . . . sex."

I started to get up. I really didn't need this, whatever this new game was.

She grasped my hand. "Listen to me. I might not have the courage to do this later. You and CJ always joked about how soundly he slept. That he could sleep through anything. Especially after a few beers."

My stomach started to churn.

"I was already pregnant. It was Tyler's. It's why he went crazy after the miscarriage. I didn't want to go back to West Virginia and be a coal miner's wife. You were out of town. CJ left the bowling alley. I went to your house. I stuck my arm through the mail slot. Unlocked the door. I undressed and climbed in bed with him. A few hours later, we woke up. I convinced him we'd had a night of wild passion. It wasn't hard. We were both naked in your bed."

I leaped out of the ambulance, ran to the side of the barn, and vomited.

My EMT ran over to me. "What's going on? Maybe you're concussed. Let's get you to the hospital."

"No. It's not that. It's . . . Can you find me a ride home?"

CHAPTER 34

Carol picked me up. My Suburban had been found parked behind an office building within walking distance of Hartwell Tavern. I couldn't get it back, since it was being processed as part of the crime scene.

"Come home with me," Carol said as soon as I got in the car. "I'll fix you something to eat. You must be starved."

"Not as hungry as you might think. I have a favor to ask."

"Anything. Name it."

"Can I borrow your car?"

Carol turned from the road to look at me. I pointed at the road. She swerved missing a tree by inches.

"I really don't want to face my apartment yet. Or have to talk to anyone."

"That's why you should come to my place."

"I just need some time to think." I told her what Tiffany had told me about CJ.

Carol gasped at the news. She drove along in stunned silence. Usually, Carol knew what to say and when. "Okay. We'll stop at my house. I'll make you a sandwich at the very least. Brad can take me to the store in the morning. I'll get the car back then."

When we got back to Carol's house, I ended up going in. Brad and the kids were at the boys' soccer game. I scarfed down the toasted ham and cheese on focaccia, plus chips. I didn't decline a big wedge of chocolate cake.

Carol handed me the keys. "Are you okay?"

"'Okay' would be a stretch."

"Why don't you just take a quick nap?"

I shook my head. "I'm not ready to close my eyes."

"You don't want to talk about what Tiffany told you?" Tears formed in her eyes. "I can't believe someone could be that horrible to another person."

"Not now." I gave Carol a hug. "I have a lot to think about."

I drove to Great Road and took a right on Bedford Road. I followed it to Sleepy Hollow Cemetery. I parked and grabbed a sweatshirt I'd found on the backseat of Carol's SUV. I pulled on the sweatshirt. My chest now blazed with a Texas longhorn bull. All it needed was Angelo's quote: "Be the bull."

I followed a paved path up the hill to Authors Ridge. Oaks and pines shaded the area. Scattered among the graves were the family plots of Concord's famed authors: Thoreau, Hawthorne, Emerson, and Alcott. Small stone markers engraved only with their names marked the resting places of Thoreau, Hawthorne, and Alcott. People had placed small stones, pinecones, and flowers on or near the stones. I wished I had brought something with me to leave.

Nathaniel and Sophia's great love for one another

was well-known. Hawthorne's wife and daughter, Una, had died and were buried in England. In 2006, a hawthorn tree planted next to their graves fell and damaged Una's headstone. Hawthorne's relatives decided to move them back to Concord to reunite the three. A horse-drawn carriage had carried their remains, retracing the path of Nathaniel's funeral procession 142 years earlier.

Emerson had a large marble boulder for his marker. A quote engraved on a bronze plaque came from Emerson's poem "The Problem": *The passive master lent his hand to the vast soul which o'er him planned.*

I wandered a bit more before sitting on the ground with my back against an oak tree. It wasn't the first time I'd come here to think.

Scott Pellner wasn't the jerk I'd made him out to be. Tyler had shared a wall with me, killed Jessica, kidnapped Tiffany, and was happily going to kill us both. How could evil be so close without me even guessing?

I tried to process what Tiffany had told me. Tiffany's lies had driven a life-changing wedge between CJ and me. I didn't know what would happen to us now. I'd thought our love was a great one, like Nathaniel and Sophia's. We'd been happily married for the most part, hadn't we? I looked up at the gently swaying branches of the oak. A few buds had started to form, the sky above them a bright blue.

I remembered CJ saying, "I can't believe I did this to you. Forgive me." He'd cried when he told me, but I hadn't. Just a few days later, I'd moved to the apartment. So easily. So quickly. Maybe things weren't good in our marriage if I could do that. We might have been too busy to notice. Then I'd gone to Lowell. Now who had betrayed whom?

Would I tell CJ about Lowell when we talked? We would have to talk and soon. Being here was my way of avoiding him. A robin landed on the branch above me, the first one I'd seen this spring. Nope, I wouldn't tell him. I'd never tell him. There was no reason.

A car door slammed at the bottom of the hill. I'd been lucky to be here alone this long on a weekend when lots of tourists were in town. I stood and headed back to the car, undecided if I should be grateful or angry someone had intruded on my peace. At the top of the hill, I looked down. CJ smiled up at me. He ran up the hill and swept me into a kiss.

"You're safe," he said when we broke apart.

He had figured out where to find me. He knew me so well.

I put my head against his chest. "I'm safe."

Garage Sale Tips

Tips for Sellers:

- Make sure to have lots of one-dollar bills and assorted coins available for making change.

- If possible, keep the money on you. You don't want to get distracted and have a box of money walk off.

- Price your items so it is easy to total a sale. Dollar and fifty cent increments are much easier to add.

- Organize your sale by grouping like items together, clothes in one area, kitchen items in another, and so on.

- Be sure to have someone on hand to help you with the sale. Sadly, people will even steal from a garage sale.

- Be prepared to bargain. It is half the fun for people attending the sale.

Tips for buyers:

- When you see something you've longed for at a tag or garage sale, don't act too excited. It ruins your chances to negotiate a great lower price.

- Look at everything first and then bargain for what you want most.

• When deciding where to go, closest isn't always the best. Find the sale that sounds the most interesting and head there first. You might use more gas, but you also might find exactly what you are looking for.

• Smell whatever it is you are considering buying. You may look ridiculous with your nose stuck in a dresser drawer or a handbag, but better that than taking home something that reeks.

• Take a backpack. It leaves your hands free to rummage through things.